G R JORDAN

A Giant Killing

Siobhan Duffy Mysteries #1

Retired is being twice tired, I've thought, first tired of working, then tired of not.

RICHARD ARMOUR

Contents

Foreword

The events of this book, while based around real locations in Northern Ireland, are entirely fictional and all characters do not represent any living or deceased person. All companies are fictitious representations. Basically, it's a bit of a yarn!

Acknowledgement

To Ken, Jean, Colin, Evelyn, John and Rosemary for your work in bringing this novel to completion, your time and effort is deeply appreciated.

Novels by G R Jordan

Siobhan Duffy Mysteries

1. A Giant Killing
2. Death of the Witch
3. The Bloodied Hands

The Highlands and Islands Detective series (Crime)

1. Water's Edge
2. The Bothy
3. The Horror Weekend
4. The Small Ferry
5. Dead at Third Man
6. The Pirate Club
7. A Personal Agenda
8. A Just Punishment
9. The Numerous Deaths of Santa Claus
10. Our Gated Community
11. The Satchel
12. Culhwch Alpha
13. Fair Market Value
14. The Coach Bomber
15. The Culling at Singing Sands

Kirsten Stewart Thrillers (Thriller)

12. Traitor

Jac Moonshine Thrillers

1. Jac's Revenge
2. Jac for the People
3. Jac the Pariah

The Contessa Munroe Mysteries (Cozy Mystery)

1. Corpse Reviver
2. Frostbite
3. Cobra's Fang

The Patrick Smythe Series (Crime)

1. The Disappearance of Russell Hadleigh
2. The Graves of Calgary Bay
3. The Fairy Pools Gathering

Austerley & Kirkgordon Series (Fantasy)

1. Crescendo!
2. The Darkness at Dillingham
3. Dagon's Revenge
4. Ship of Doom

Chapter 01

It was a damp morning, grey in the extreme, with a faint drizzle falling down. James Mulholland was recovering from a rough night. He knew it would be a mistake, but he'd agreed to go along to the pub at the late hour of ten o'clock, sure it would shut by eleven. He'd be back home, having had a pint or two, none the worse for wear, and possibly even off to sleep in a quicker fashion than normal.

Then the pub had locked the doors, and James was still on the inside. It had been all right while the pints had come out. He'd had three or four, and yes, he probably would've had to stumble home in not the most expeditious fashion. Maybe he'd have ordered some ridiculous takeout if they still were open. Yet he'd have got back to the house, rolled out of bed the next morning feeling rough, but he would've been functional.

James did not feel functional right now, wrapped up with his waterproof jacket over his top and his waterproof trousers. He was dry, except that he was sweating on the inside. He was just glad that he hadn't driven to work that morning. His neighbour had given him a lift. Emma had been going that way, anyway. Yes, it was a slight detour; she was driving into Portrush, so a couple of minutes at most. She had offered the previous day.

Emma's a nice girl—woman, he thought. *She's a woman. How did I get to that age when I started calling women, girls? I'm not that old,* he thought. His divorce had been a nasty one several years ago, but James had picked himself up and at least his view of women wasn't one where he didn't want to go near them again.

Yes, Emma was nice, but clearly, she hadn't been that nice, for he'd stayed in the pub and rolled out at about half-three in the morning. He had gone to bed for a while, then suddenly woken up and realised that she was downstairs banging on the flat door. He'd opened it up, standing in his boxers. She'd looked a little sheepish, but he'd been quick. He'd even scrubbed his face briefly before sitting in the car looking like death warmed up. Emma thought it funny. At least he hoped she thought it funny. The last thing he needed was her thinking he was a pisshead.

The good thing about being a warden along the Causeway Coast was that early starts meant that no one else was about. He had his radio and the early workers would be at the centre at the top of the Causeway Coast, but he would be out on his own.

He remembered the causeway back in the day before the centre. There had always been the hotel at the top, but then you'd wander along the path with nothing else about. Now, they had the bus that ran from the centre down. They also had the centre at the top, up to date and expansive, with modern-looking, well-controlled car parking facilities. It was good; you had to agree with that. Parking and information were always one of the difficult things around any attraction. It was so old, been there for thousands of years, and hopefully for many more.

He popped in via the centre that morning, but only briefly to use the facilities. It looked different when it wasn't lit up fully. All the tales of the giant, Fionn mac Cumhaill, or Finn MacCool as it had been anglicised to, including his battle with the Scottish giant in which he dressed up as a baby. The tales were funny, good for the tourists as well, but the actual star was the causeway itself.

James never tired of the hexagonal rocks, placed one beside each other, almost as if crafted rather than formed. Then there were other features that hugged the coast; the Giant's Boot, the Wishing Chair, the Camel, and the plateau.

But he liked it at this time of the morning. There was rarely anyone around, only occasional dog walkers, but they were like him. All looking for a bit of solitude, or on the move, making sure that pet of theirs got some proper exercise.

James started the walk down from the visitor's centre towards the causeway. It descended rapidly before swinging around the coast. One thing that always struck him was how everyone talked about the causeway, the rock formation at the end. Everyone wanted to run out along with it. Stand by the water until it came up and over to such a point that the trust volunteers had to keep telling people to get back.

The wilder the weather, the more they wanted to stand where the waves could hit them. More like where the waves could wash them away, but they didn't realise the danger around here. They also didn't realise the beauty of the other bays; it was the entire coast that meant something. The fauna, the wildlife, not just the rock. Sure, the rock was what everyone marvelled at, the story of the giant, the object that made the place into a legend. Yet, anyone looking at this glorious tableau would be startled, blown away by the sheer wonder of nature.

James was still feeling a touch of that this morning, but he was also feeling very sick. He dandered down and stopped a couple of hundred metres into his walk, hands on his knees. Breathing in deeply, he tried to suck in the sea air, hoping that it would make things better. It didn't appear to be doing the trick.

He reached inside his bag and pulled out a bottle of water, gulping it. Then stopping, as he felt it lurch back to the top of his throat. He stood upright, swallowed hard, and kept it down. Things were bad when you wanted to throw the water back up.

He continued down on his path and then stopped for a second. *What had Emma said before he got out of the car?* Emma was at least ten years younger than he, possibly fifteen. James hadn't had the courage yet to ask her what age she was. You didn't do that to a woman, did you? Anyway, what did it matter? He was in his early forties, she was probably thirty, maybe twenty-seven, twenty-five? Younger than that?

When had he not been able to identify ages? It all seemed so easy. He pulled down the hood over his head and let the drizzle assault his face. It felt good, for he was sweating now inside his waterproof gear. That was the booze, last night's alcohol causing that. Maybe he would sweat away the headache, for it was pounding, pounding hard.

What had Emma said? Something about a Chinese? Was that it? Indian? No. Had she been talking about a person? Had she been talking about food?

He couldn't remember. In fact, come to think of it, he was struggling to remember what she was wearing. It must have been that skirt with the suit top. She was off to work, after all. She worked in an estate agents in Portrush. Emma had arrived at the door, pristine, neat makeup on, smiling, and then in shock at this barbaric excuse for a man in boxer shorts. But she'd stepped inside.

James became suddenly aware that he'd arrived at the stones. There was a little turning area where the bus would get round. He always marvelled at the drivers, especially in the summer. The tourists crammed there, desperate to get a bus back up the hill that anyone in any sort of shape could get back up easily. But no, they were all crammed there, and this bus driver would turn it around, desperate not to hit anyone. They all wanted to be there to get on, even though, clearly, they needed another four buses before they would've all been getting on one from that queue.

He took a walk up onto the causeway. As he got up, the stones seemed to get blacker as they went closer to the sea. Some of that was because of the tide crashing onto them, but the stones were also darker. He looked down at the little pools on each rock. The rocks were just a little bigger than your foot, which made it look like hundreds of stepping stones out to the sea. They went up, down, some of them smoothed over at the edges, but most with a little indent in the middle where little pools of water sat down from last night's rain.

That's right, the rain at half-three in the morning, and with a belly full of various liquids, he wasn't sure what he was drinking. And he'd wandered out, stumbled about for a bit. In fact, he'd stumbled about for a while, hadn't he? He wasn't sure how long, but it had been long. Then he got a taxi, but the taxi ride hadn't been that long. He thought about where he lived. *That taxi rank's around the corner,* he thought, *that's why they hadn't charged him much.* They'd taken £2 off him. He must have got a taxi for all of three hundred metres.

James plonked himself down, looking out at the water. *My goodness*, he thought, *was I really that bad?* He looked around and saw a dog walker coming towards where the buses turned. The person had obviously followed him down from the centre, and they now joined him out on the causeway stones. The dog was on a lead, for you had to be careful with animals here. They didn't see the danger, a bit like kids. Actually, a bit like tourists.

'It's not a bad morning, is it?' said the man. He was older, maybe sixties or seventies, a brisk moustache, but he was friendly enough. James just wasn't in the mood to talk. 'It's not bad,' said James. 'Sorry, if you'll excuse me, I need to get on. Enjoy your day.'

He wasn't sure if the man gave him a grump, annoyed that there wasn't more conversation. People expected that, didn't they? Not just a good day, not just a hello. You had to have a few other words, usually about the weather.

James came down off the causeway, passed where the buses turned, and went through the small gap that led round to the rest of the coast. He followed the path along, looking up at the high cliff to his right. *Stunning*, he thought, *quite stunning*. Yet all he wanted to do was vomit. It wasn't really a great advertisement for the causeway today, but he was here, and he was doing his job. He couldn't complain.

He sat down on the little bench beside the path, looking at the stony path in front of him. Then slowly he raised his head, looking at where the tide was. The giant's boot was in front of him. Smooth slabs shaped in the image of a massive shoe and now with somebody lying on top of it. James gave a shake of his head, looked again. There was a figure there.

He looked around. There was no one—no one here. He walked down a small path towards the shoe and stepped off across more rocky terrain to reach it. As he got closer, he could see a pair of knees looking back at him, feet below them. The person had been in a pair of heavy black trousers.

'Come on, sunshine. Hey, fella,' he said, 'get up.' They were men's legs. At least he presumed they were because most women's legs were a lot slimmer than that. Looked like the guy could be well-set. The last thing he wanted was any confrontation. After all, the fella was probably only pissed. That could have been James, except his taxi ride was a better option. James followed the knees up to the torso and then he looked at a head that was hanging backwards.

It wasn't just hanging backwards; the head was remaining attached by a small flap of skin at the neck. The neck had been severed such that the top half of it had gone one way, the bottom half the other. Where the cut had stopped halfway through, the two parts were desperately remaining attached. James turned in an instant, and vomited onto the rocks beside him. His knees went weak. He fell down to the ground and continued his eruptions. There was nothing in his stomach except water, but whatever was in there was coming out.

He hauled himself to his knees, fighting for any energy he could find. James didn't want to turn and look, but there was something inside of him that made him, something that drove him on to check he'd seen what he'd seen. He turned his head, saw the neck that looked like a large piece of cut ham, and turned back to vomit again. This time, when he stopped, he pressed the radio.

'Centre, it's James. Anyone in the centre? It's James.' There was silence. 'Centre, this is James. Bloody hell. Somebody, talk to me. Where the hell are you? Please?'

Again, he forced himself to his knees, turned, and looked at the body. It was sprawled backwards over the boot, lying there like kids would sometimes do, but they were animated. This one almost seemed precariously balanced. The arms were resting inside the pockets of the trousers.

James tried to stumble back to the path. He put his foot in his own sick, but it didn't matter. There was somebody coming. It was a woman jogging along. On another day, James would've been pleased by the sight because she was one of those who obviously took jogging seriously. Either that or she had the most pristine gym membership ever. He wasn't sure how she was jogging, but she had one of those outfits that showed she was a serious runner in every way that meant you weren't. Tight, figure-hugging, and yet completely impractical for a long-distance runner, James knew, he'd been one twenty years ago.

He stumbled towards her, lurching this way and that, the woman trying to avoid him, but he clapped his hands on her shoulders.

'He's dead. Bloody dead. We need to get someone.' He fell forward onto her top and she pushed him back. *Had he just been sick again?* She ran screaming.

He pressed his radio button. 'Centre, it's James. Where the hell? Dead. He's dead. He's dead.'

'James, this is Sonya. What's up? You all right?'

'I'm not bloody all right. He's fucking dead.'

Chapter 02

*W*ell, this is it, she thought, *finally, on the Gold Coast. Here I am on the Costa del Donaghadee.*

Siobhan smiled to herself. In truth, she wouldn't be anywhere else; this was her dream home. After many years abroad, she'd finally come home properly. This was retirement. This was where she was going to be.

She looked around her. The garden was wonderful. It was going to take a bit to get it into shape but that was okay because that's what retired people did. They did their garden; they went bowling; kept themselves busy. The good folk now without jobs would be down at one of those little coffee shops or garden centres.

Garden centres, she thought. *They were ingenious, weren't they?* She couldn't remember garden centres existing thirty years ago. Well, not like this. Now they did, and they existed in a very special way. They weren't there simply for people to buy plants. Indeed, most now had a range of products that went well beyond plants. They had plenty for the interior of the house as well. But the revelation, the bastion on which the garden centre had been built, was that they all had somewhere to have a spot of lunch. Somewhere for a coffee with a wee bun or a scone. Somewhere to go for the elevenses, or at mid-afternoon. That was the thing about retirement. What did you do?

Siobhan's life had been different. Although they'd always had a house here in Northern Ireland, they hadn't always been here. Certainly, she hadn't. After all, she had been a travelling saleswoman for so long. Her husband had never understood that. Why did she want to do that job when he had so much money?

Andrew had made his money during the Troubles. And he'd been working so hard she wasn't sure he'd missed her. She had been part of a small firm, as he saw it, that supplied machined parts to other regions of the world. She had travelled everywhere with it, always accompanying her boss. The one thing that had always surprised her was that Andrew had never accused her of having an affair with him. She hadn't been. She'd done nothing like that. Well, not often. And not with her boss. That was because her boss travelled the world selling parts while Siobhan went to those places to work for the British Secret Service.

She was a field agent originally. Then she developed into more of an analyst. That was part of the reason she was getting out. That and the fact that Andrew was now dead.

He had died of a massive heart attack brought on by too much drink and too many cigarettes. She didn't hate her husband, but there had been little love either. At the start, they were infatuated with each other, but he'd got his business and she'd gone elsewhere. He'd had plenty of lovers, she knew that. She didn't begrudge him, as she wasn't there. Siobhan was out doing what she wanted to do, changing the course of history in places, or at least that's what she told herself.

He'd bought himself some ridiculous house on the Belfast to Bangor Road. She didn't want to live on a road like that. He hadn't even got the decency to go down to the seafront at Helen's Bay. Besides, that road was always busy. He would sit in the traffic, getting to Belfast every morning. There were four lanes and yet it was the most congested bit of traffic she'd ever seen.

You had to get up through Holywood. Then there were the lights before you got onto the main section of road, the dual carriageway, where it truly opened up. Then there was the chaos of the Sydenham Bypass. Things were better now, better since they put in the M3, the bypass road for the city centre, taking you out to the motorway. That comprised the M2 and the M5, two motorways together that most people truly didn't know how to drive. They never got there were two motorways side by side. People jumped back and forward like they were just the one.

Siobhan smiled. It was good to be home, or at least where she was going to make home. Her new house was on the sea side of the Donaghadee Road out of Bangor. It was before the golf club, and from her back garden, you could step out down across a few rocks and into the actual sea. It was no longer the Belfast Lough, but out towards the Irish Sea, Scotland far beyond, and on most days, you saw the Copelands in all their glory.

The garden was gorgeous, but fairly simple. There were a few bushes here and there to provide some shelter and a bit of privacy. There was also a small house in front of hers just as you came into the driveway. That was where her housekeeper lived—Kylie, a young girl who had a rough start in life.

She'd been taken advantage of by a man and then she'd lost

her kid. Lost her kid after she'd made the brave decision to look after him, to bring him up, even though the father had cleared off. A few years of her life chucked away. Thrown away because of love. She missed out on schooling, too.

Kylie had wanted a job, but she also wanted away from a community that was pointing fingers at her. Some church communities were like that. Siobhan had heard of her plight and offered her the job. One, because she was a sucker for sob stories like that, but two, because she wanted a bit of company. She didn't want older company because Siobhan didn't feel she was old.

Kylie was currently hanging up the washing and was the attention of one Declan Smith, Siobhan's groundsman, as she rather gallantly called him. He would do the odd jobs, anything about the house. The joy of Andrew's death had been that he'd left her all his money and her bank account was overflowing. The house had cost a pretty penny, but nothing like the one she'd sold on the Holywood Road.

But this was the one that she wanted. This was the one that reminded her of childhood, walking along the Donaghadee Road. Days out when you went to Millisle to get an ice cream wafer at that old ice cream parlour. It was old when she was there and wasn't really open in its full glory. But the ice cream was special.

There had been the pools at Donaghadee as well, and she had splashed around in them as a kid. You'd maybe have a picnic lunch with you, and when the sun beat down, there was no better spot.

Down was a great wee place. Out on the arm of Northern Ireland, Bangor, Donaghadee, Millisle, right down to the tip and then back up the other side. She remembered going out on car runs that way, back when Sundays were a day of rest, funnily enough. It made her laugh now. There wasn't football. Well, not on her side of the divide.

She had been a child of the Troubles too. The Troubles had driven her out of the province and Siobhan regretted having been away so much. She was coming back home despite who she'd been. She'd never worked in Northern Ireland in her official capacity. Never worked for the Service in that way. It was always far overseas.

She always thought she was like a lot of the people in the province, just wishing the troubles would go away. What was it they said back in the day? If they'd all just take themselves off to a wee field somewhere and blow the hell out of each other, then the rest of us could get on with it. Things didn't work like that, not in Northern Ireland, not anywhere else.

Siobhan stepped back inside the house briefly and looked around at the various security cameras she had. She checked the secret door in the alcove beside her front door. Kylie hadn't understood what it was. There was a section of wall at the front door that could open up, allowing Siobhan to step out to the front door without the front door having to open. It looked like a normal piece of wall, but it could move quickly when you wanted it to. Of course, normally it was locked up and from the outside, you wouldn't see it. It was enough to squeeze easily through. More importantly, it was enough to put a hand through, put a gun through.

Siobhan kept a weapon or two. It was important. She kept a few that weren't on her own grounds, too. She never knew when the past would come back.

But enough of that, she thought as she walked through the house. Kylie had helped her, and they'd got the place looking just as Siobhan wanted it. There was the quiet study. The kitchen table. A pair of chairs where she'd sat and talked with Kylie the previous night. *The shower, it's so important,* she thought, *to have a good shower.* There was a separate bath as well. Yes, she'd prepared the house. Now she had to get her life going. That would be more difficult, but she would get there; she was sure of it.

Siobhan stepped back outside into a momentary blaze of sunshine before a cloud passed over. Kylie was attaching a peg to the top of a sheet, then reaching across for another one. She sported a good figure. Not one of those models, not long and thin. Siobhan was longer and thinner than Kylie. Well, not that long. She'd always kept in good shape, and she would still go running.

When she was a field agent, she had to be in shape. When she became an analyst, she just did it out of habit. The same now. If she didn't run during the day, she would walk. Not that she ran fast anymore. Kylie had gone out running with her. The girl clearly had run little, for the style was all wrong. All arms and legs going instead of being compact, trim.

But she was that age when the shape just came to you and you didn't have to work at it. Siobhan watched as Declan appreciated that shape. In front of him was a trowel, which was currently dumping soil onto a plant beside the one he was putting into the ground.

'Declan, would you come here a minute?' asked Siobhan. The boy looked up. *He was a boy, after all, wasn't he? Twenty-one,* she thought. And he certainly knew his gardening. He told her he had been brought up to it by his uncle, and he'd worked many a summer with him, transforming people's gardens, but now he was out on his own. Siobhan was happy to pay him a bit to keep the house in order, to do the odd jobs. But what she wasn't happy with was paying him to look at Kylie's bum.

'Yes, Mrs D?' said Declan, arriving. He wasn't as tall as Siobhan. Around five foot eight. Siobhan was five-eleven, tall for a woman, certainly from Northern Ireland. She did like Declan's grin.

'I'm paying you to put plants in the ground, not to pour soil from one over the other.'

'I wasn't aware I was.'

'No, you wouldn't be, Declan, because, frankly, you were staring at Kylie's bum.'

He did this thing where he put his tongue into his cheek as if considering his response. There was no sign that he was going to cover up what he was doing. He was just simply trying to come up with a reason.

'Just a little worried about her.'

'What?' said Siobhan. 'How?'

'I thought she was looking frail this morning,' said Declan. 'You two weren't having a few last night, were you? I noticed one of those bottles of wine was . . .'

'Catch yourself on, Declan,' said Siobhan, putting on a rather harsh tone. 'You like her? That's fine. But you like her on your own time. Okay? Now get back out there and get those plants in. Next time I see you looking at her backside, I'm just going to give you a kick up yours.'

'That's employee abuse, Mrs D.'

'You're right, Declan, and it will be proper abuse. Let's not discuss what you leering at her backside is. But more than that, I'll announce it loudly next time to make sure she hears.'

'You're a one, Mrs D,' said Declan, but he turned and hurried back and started on his plants.

Siobhan walked over to where Kylie was finishing up hanging the washing.

'You don't have to do that, Siobhan,' Kylie said. 'I know. It's all right. He's not a bad one.'

'No, he's not. That's why he's here. If you're done with the washing, you wouldn't mind making a cup of tea, would you?' asked Siobhan.

'Surely,' Kylie said. 'I'll just get one now. It is your usual? The smelly stuff?'

'Lapsang souchong, yes,' said Siobhan, and watched Kylie disappearing in through the front door. A casual glance saw Declan was looking again and caused Siobhan to laugh. Kylie was probably out of his league. Probably. She heard the garden gate, though, and saw the postman walking down the small path to her front door.

'Ah, just over here,' she said. 'How are you? Don't think I've caught you yet.' The man looked over in his shorts and red post office top.

'No, I'm Alan, and I take it you're Mrs Duffy?'

'Siobhan, nice to meet you. Have you got much there?'

'No, not really. Just one or two for you. I think they're bills, by the looks of it. Oh, and here's your paper. The boy was just passing by, said I should drop it into you. That is right, isn't it? You do get one? He hasn't cocked it up, has he?'

'No, that's lovely. Thank you. I'll just have a wee read this afternoon.'

The paper, thought Siobhan, *the mainstay of the retired community. People waiting for when the paper would arrive, when the paper would get in. You couldn't go out to the shop until the paper would be there.*

She laughed and opened up the front page. There was a large picture on the front and she recognised it as the Giant's Causeway. She'd heard something about that a day or two before in passing on the radio. She looked at the photograph and saw the shoe, the Giant's Boot, as they called it. They'd found somebody lying over the top of it, throat slashed. It sounded pretty gory.

Siobhan knew that there were plenty of gory murders in Northern Ireland, especially associated with the Troubles. But this seemed strange, a very peculiar place to be dragged out to. She looked at the photograph for a moment and then she tore off into the house, running into her study. Siobhan threw the newspaper on the table, taking out a magnifying glass.

She looked at an area just to the right of the Giant's Boot. It was another rock. There was nothing about the shape of it. It was just a rock unlike the strangely formed boot, which took on a unique characteristic, but Siobhan saw something on the rock, a mark she recognised. A mark that came from the past. She left the paper in the study, marched out to the living room to flick on the TV.

'Where do you want the tea?' asked Kylie. There was no response from Siobhan. 'Tea?' repeated Kylie.

Siobhan didn't respond, instead flicking the channels until she got to the news. She stood there for a couple of minutes before it came up. The news was talking about the murder. For murder was what they were calling it, slashed across the neck, an unknown man abandoned there.

Siobhan's heart thumped. The mark was running through her head. That mark. It had been a while, a long time actually, but that mark. Siobhan watched as they talked about the murder. Nothing of detail, just about the shock and horror. Then there was a photofit picture put up. It was like an artist's impression, except it would be the man's dead face reanimated to life. They'd use techniques to bring the dead face to life rather than show the public a corpse's face. Especially if it was attached to a cut off neck.

As the picture came up on the screen, Siobhan felt a chill run down her spine. She knew that face.

Chapter 03

Siobhan locked the door of her study, rolled back the carpet, and pulled up a floorboard. She reached down, all the way up to her shoulder, fumbling around in the darkness underneath. It wasn't the one on the left, and she moved across two other small file boxes before pulling one out from the hidden space. She replaced the floorboard, rolled the carpet back, and then unlocked the door.

Her study was small, with a desk and laptop in front of her. On the right-hand side, she could slide her chair over so she could write by hand or spread out many documents to look at. She told Kylie that part was there for when she had to look at bills, but it wasn't.

It was a force of habit. She always laid her desk out like this, laptop at one side and an open space to spread things out. There was a blank wall behind her. Kylie had said it would suit pictures to be put up, but Siobhan had said no. That was where she would stick the photographs. That's where you drew your lines in. That's where you made everything connect—on a wall like that. There came a knock on the door.

'Come in,' said Siobhan.

The door opened and Kylie placed a cup down at the desk. Siobhan could smell the pungent, choking, burnt smell of the tea. She'd grown a fascination for Lapsang Souchong, just one of those things that you did in life. Was it the best tea ever? No, but it was what she liked and what a lot of other people hated. It was hers. When she'd grown up, they'd all drunk Tetley, but she'd always wanted something different.

'Did you find something interesting?' asked Kylie.

'Maybe,' said Siobhan. 'I could do with a bit of peace and quiet, though. I need to look at something.'

She hadn't opened the box file yet, and she wouldn't do until Kylie had stepped out of the room.

'All right,' said Kylie. 'I'll take Declan his cup. Anything you want me to be getting on with while you do this?'

'Will you pop down to the shops for me? I was going to have some salmon for tea, but we have got nothing in.'

'Anything else while I'm out?'

'A bit of veg with it, whatever.'

'Are you making or am I?'

The word to Kylie was that sometimes Siobhan would like to cook, and sometimes she wouldn't, so Kylie was to ask her. At the moment, the constant questions were frustrating Siobhan.

'You cook, please. Now, I need some time.'

'Okay,' said Kylie. 'Just asking. I'm gone. I won't disturb you.'

'Thank you.'

Kylie closed the door and Siobhan moved to sit in front of the open desk space. She took a sip of the tea, sniffing in that burning smell. Maybe she should have been a pyromaniac. The tea seemed to be made for people of that ilk. She flipped open the file and looked at a large photograph, one that matched the photograph on the television, except the face was younger.

Eamon McNeil, spy for the British, but a spy who had never worked Northern Ireland. Well, at least as far as she knew. You didn't get to find out everything about everybody. You didn't get their entire work history. Even when you were higher in the Service, a lot of things were on a need-to-know basis, and Siobhan hadn't needed to know about a lot of that.

When she'd worked with Eamon, it had been in Russia. He had taught her street craft. He had taught her how to look after herself. She was young then. 'Up and coming,' they'd put it. She'd realised that the marriage had gone south, and she was happier being away. Realised that Andrew was happier with her being away, and Eamon had been charming. He'd also been very competent.

Siobhan took out other bits and pieces from the box, including an old photo of a riverbank. She thought back to the river. They'd walked along the banks of it in Russia, like two ordinary people. In some ways, places had been bleaker back then. The two of them were operating out of the British Embassy. They were probably being watched, but it didn't matter because they weren't out on business. Just out on a walk, Eamon showing a young girl the place.

They'd stopped by the river, and he'd taken her hand. That had been the start of it. Eamon had been a stocky man, capable of handling himself, but he had an astute mind, a mind that Andrew never had. He was cultured, but he was also quick-witted.

Over the next year, they would get involved in many scrapes together, life and death situations and other routine drops to keep the engine running. They would also share a bed. He had been an excellent lover, attentive and fascinated by her.

Siobhan thought many men didn't get that. They didn't clock that a woman wanted you to be fascinated, wanted to be the mystery the man wanted.

He was her mystery. Andrew was so dumb by comparison. She felt bad thinking that after Andrew was gone and she was sitting in the proceeds of his endeavours, but all he did was clean up broken glass. Eamon had walked on the wild side and taken her there. He'd given her a love of classical music, one she still harboured to this day.

That was the thing about Siobhan. She took on her experiences. That's why she was eclectic in her musical taste, but classical always held a spot for her. It always reminded her of him. She hadn't thought about him for a long time now, not since she believed he was dead. 'Well, he hasn't come back,' they said. 'Hasn't come back from a mission amongst the cartels out in Colombia.'

There was a knock on the door. Siobhan put the photograph of Eamon back in the file box and closed the lid.

'Come in.'

'Sorry, Mrs D,' said Declan, marching in. Siobhan looked down and saw the mud on his boots.

'We talked about this, Declan. Your boots off when you come in the house.'

'Oh, boy,' he said, looking down. 'Sorry, Mrs D, I'll get a brush and pan and sort that out.'

'No, just tell me what you want.'

'Where did you want the begonias?'

'Which ones are the begonias?' asked Siobhan. Just because they said that you had to get a garden didn't mean she understood all the plants that went in it.

'What do you mean, which are the begonias? They're the

begonias,' said Declan.

'Imagine I don't know what begonias look like, Declan. What would I be looking at? What am I looking for? Colour? What colour are they?'

'Oh, they're different colours.'

'Declan, for pity's sake, just put them in somewhere.'

'I thought you'd want to know. I want you . . .'

'Declan, I'm busy, okay? I'm busy.' She watched Declan look at the desk. All he saw was the box file and nothing else, because Siobhan had put it all away when he'd knocked. Except for the cup of tea.

'I like a cup of tea on my own sometimes, too,' said Declan. 'A bit where you can shut out the world. That bit where you can just relax all on your own. It's terrific, isn't it, Mrs D?'

'Yes, it is, Declan,' she said, sighing, hoping the message was getting across.

'Of course, my uncle, we would always have had the tea together because we were working together. He always said a good cup of tea on the job has you thinking. It stirs the imagination for the next day. It...'

'Declan, the joy about a cup of tea alone is that it's alone.'

'You're right there, Mrs D,' he said.

The man had a childlike view of people. He just wanted to talk. He just wanted to share. It was like a five-year-old coming up to you and showing you their new book and expecting you to instantly read it with them and to enjoy it the way they did. Declan thought everybody was like himself. While that was incredibly charming, right now. it was taking Siobhan to the limit.

'Declan, when God was handing out the awareness radar, were you just not there? Were you at the back of the queue when he ran out?'

'I don't know what you're talking about.'

'You really don't, do you?' said Siobhan. 'You really, really don't. Declan, just get out. All right? I'm in the middle of something. I don't want to be disturbed. Get out.'

'With you right there, Mrs D. I get like that sometimes. I need . . .'

'Declan, . . .' Siobhan stopped herself. She wouldn't say it. When it came to Declan and to Kylie, they could be coarse at times. They could say words that really shouldn't be in Siobhan's vocabulary. She needed to set them a higher example as the older person. Language was there to be used to better society. We should talk to each other with civility and with kindness, and that meant using words that weren't abrasive. Words that didn't hurt.

At the moment, she wanted to give two words to Declan. The second was off, and the other one was the language that she never would use, unless under extreme pressure. It was in her vocabulary, but she wouldn't use it. Declan was testing her bounds.

'I find when I want to be alone,' said Declan, 'that people come in and you have to be quite subtle with them. You find that, Mrs D? You must let them know you want to be alone. You have to . . .'

'Declan, piss off!'

He stopped and looked at her. 'That's quite forward, Mrs D,' he said. 'I've used that before myself.'

I'm going to turn round and say the word I don't want to say, she thought. Instead, Siobhan stood up, walked straight up to Declan, put a hand on his chest, and pushed him backwards, so that he stumbled out into the hall beyond.

'Declan, this is my door. It's about to be shut. When it's shut, you will remain on this side of it. I will be on that side of it. If you have a question, you will wait until I come out. Do I make myself clear?'

'I think so. I find making myself clear to people . . .'

Siobhan stepped inside and shut the door. There were times the boy was charming, but sometimes, he just . . . well, she wouldn't say it.

Siobhan pulled out the photograph again of Eamon, stared at it. Then she took a blank piece of paper. Over the next five minutes, she drew down eight different symbols, all unique. One was a circle with lines inside of it. Another was a cross. Another was a star. All distinct marks. All unique. She looked at the third one. It was one that only she and Eamon had used out in Russia. Maybe he had used it with someone since. But was it a call to her?

She pushed away from the desk for a moment, her wheeled chair sliding out into the middle of her small office. She stood up, reached over, took a drink of her tea, then she took another. She placed the cup down, picked up the photograph, turned, pinned it to the wall behind her. Then she took the symbols and pinned them beside it. With a red pen, she ringed the symbol she'd seen in the paper.

Siobhan opened the door, marched out, and found the paper where she'd left it by the television. She walked back in with it, cut up the photograph of the Giant's Boot, and placed it on the wall beside the other pictures. Taking a pen, she wrote the word 'me' with a question mark.

Had Eamon been looking to communicate with her? It had been so long since she'd been at the causeway. They'd gone there as a family when she was young. She'd gone once or twice with Andrew when they'd had visitors. Doing the tour, so to speak. But that was a long time ago.

Siobhan needed to go. She had to see the mark in person. She needed to see where he had been. Calculate everything around it. Why would he have put it there? How did he end up dead beside it? Obviously, he did it prior to his death, but he must have done it without being seen. Otherwise, it made no sense. They'd have removed it. Who had done it? Why had they done it? What was he doing here? The man was meant to be dead. And now he was.

Siobhan was retired. *I'm out of it. It's time to settle down and join different clubs. Go for my lunch at the garden centres. Time to take it easier. Time to wind down.*

She turned and stared at the photograph of Eamon. He had been beautiful, inside and out. Something inside her would not let this go. *Bollocks*, she thought, and opened the door. She walked through the house, looking for Kylie and Declan. Then she opened the front door and saw Declan among the plants, but he was standing up, running across to Kylie with the shopping.

'You two,' said Siobhan. 'We need to go to the Giant's Causeway.'

'What?' asked Kylie. 'Why?'

'You don't need to know why. I need to go to the Giant's Causeway.'

'When?' asked Declan.

'Soon as. We could go now.'

'It'll be dark in about three or four hours. What's the point in that?' asked a bemused Kylie.

She's right, thought Siobhan. 'Tomorrow. We're going to the Giant's Causeway tomorrow.'

'Why?' asked Kylie.

'It's quite nice up there,' said Declan.

'We're going because I want to go,' said Siobhan. 'I pay the bills here. It's my rodeo. The two of you will get your backsides in the car tomorrow and we'll go to the Giant's Causeway. Get us some sandwiches and that,' said Siobhan.

'I've just done the shopping,' said Kylie.

'Fine. We'll eat out,' said Siobhan, 'but we're going to the Causeway.'

Siobhan walked back inside the house, and could feel the bemusement behind her. It didn't matter. She wasn't going up on her own. She would go with company. That way, she wouldn't look so suspicious.

She stepped back inside her office and looked at Eamon. Is that what this was? Suspicious? She'd find out. She owed him that. The least she could do was find out what had happened to him.

Chapter 04

'Are we seriously going to the Causeway on a day like this?'

Siobhan stared out the window, ignoring the comment from the backseat. Kylie had been on about this all day. From the moment they set off in the morning, she'd been in a bad mood because Siobhan had insisted on them getting away at seven o'clock in the morning. Declan, on the other hand, had pitched up bright and breezy, excited about driving the car. Siobhan couldn't face that length of a drive, much more suited to the younger person. Besides, she had too much to mull over on the way up.

Kylie was annoyed because she'd had to get up even earlier and make some sandwiches, flasks of tea, and still be ready to go by the time seven o'clock came. Siobhan had made sure that everyone had good waterproofs and stout shoes with them, but the day did not look like a fun trip.

After they cleared the motorway and drove out past Ballymena on the way out to the Causeway, Siobhan realised she had missed this country. She'd been in places with deserts, places with snow most of the year-round, others with quite glorious mountain ranges. Yet nothing was as compact as

Northern Ireland. Nothing was so near to itself.

You could be in the mountains and within half an hour, you were in the city, or you were down at the beach, or you were in a forest. You could get across the province in an hour and a half maybe, and everywhere was green. Lush and green! Sure, it had rain, but the rain only made the place more beautiful. Siobhan wasn't sure if she was just happy to be home or whether she truly had missed the place that much.

'So, we're heading to a crime scene,' said Declan.

'We're heading to the Causeway, Declan,' said Siobhan. 'They will not have a body lying there. In fact, if it's opened again to the public, it'll mean they've come in and done all their scenes of crime work. I doubt there's going to be anything much to notice.'

'You noticed something in that paper,' said Kylie, 'because you disappeared off with it, then you wouldn't come out of your office. Don't play us for fools.'

'That's right,' said Declan, 'you saw something; otherwise, why would we be going?'

'I'm just interested. I had a busy life before I came back here.'

'Well, why didn't you stay there? Keep busy?' asked Declan.

'Declan,' said Kylie from the backseat. 'She lost her husband.'

Kylie was correct, Siobhan had lost her husband, and that's where the money came to get the property just outside Donaghadee. In reality, he had lost her a long time ago and she, him. She'd got out because things had got heated in some of her previous jobs. She couldn't look after herself the way she used to.

Besides, she'd been an analyst for too long. It wasn't like she could go back out into the field. They wouldn't let a fifty-year-old go out that way. Instead, they'd keep her in an office. She'd see reports, dwell over satellite images, this and that, brought in to give her advice when possible. Everything except the action.

'It's all right. I'm over Andrew. I'm getting on, starting afresh.'

'But Declan shouldn't be so insensitive, honestly.'

Siobhan saw that Declan's cheeky smile had faded, rebuked by Kylie. He wouldn't like that, not when he was trying to make an impression on her. He looked quite smart today as well. Yes, he had his waterproofs, but he had a jumper on, walking boots. His long straggly hair looked as if it had been brushed.

Kylie looked neat as ever, but then she always did. Even more so than Siobhan. Siobhan had on what she considered her trademark jumper. It had a rolled neck, but one of the long ones that exposed the flesh around your neck. With her figure, it was reasonably snug, and yet you could pull the arms up and it gave the idea of a neat rug pulled over you.

Siobhan had jeans on underneath. She wasn't someone out looking for a man, but Siobhan did like to look good. She'd worked hard for her shape over the years. There was nothing wrong with letting it show, although whether anybody looked these days was another matter. Kylie would take all the looks, for she had the long brown hair, not the dirty blonde and definitely aged look of Siobhan. You could do whatever you wanted with makeup except keep those lines away from the face. She'd had times of real turmoil in the job, and they showed, but hey, she was far from dead yet.

As they neared the Causeway, Siobhan looked out and saw that the clouds were not going anywhere. The rain was still coming down, only now it was bouncing.

'Well, at least there won't be many people there,' said Declan. 'Don't see tourists piling along in this weather.'

'Won't be anyone sensible out there,' said Kylie.

'That's okay.'

'Are you a member, by the way?' said Declan.

'A member? Yes,' said Siobhan. Andrew had bought them lifetime memberships of the National Trust at some point. She never really used hers, but it'd been one of the cards she'd found when going through her stuff. Siobhan had tucked it away. She wasn't someone for grand houses and that, but she guessed that maybe, now she was retired, she'd have to be. Took you out for the day, didn't it?

'You reckon they'd think we were your kids?' said Declan.

'Declan!' said Kylie. 'You don't want to say that to a woman.'

'Well, just saying, we wouldn't have to pay to get in then, would we?'

'You don't have to pay to get onto the Causeway, anyway. You have to pay into the centre,' said Kylie. 'Some of my friends were up in the summer.'

'I'll pay whatever needs to be paid,' said Siobhan. 'I'm the one dragging you out here.'

The car turned silent. She stared out the window at the rain as Declan went down the country lanes that led up to the causeway. It was well signposted, but you got the feeling you were going rural. So much of Northern Ireland was rural. That was the beauty of it. Once you got out of Belfast, got out of Derry, everywhere else was a smaller place, a smaller town with the countryside right on the edge. *Compactness, that was the word*, thought Siobhan. She loved the compactness of it all.

The car park wasn't busy, and they got a space. Rather than go to the centre, Siobhan insisted on them making their way straight down to the Causeway. This annoyed Declan because he thought that the rain would clear soon. Siobhan doubted that, and together, the three of them started down the road that ran by the front of the cliffs.

There was a bus going down, but Siobhan ignored it. She wasn't sure why. If she'd still been a spy, there might've been a camera on the bus and she could've been traced, but what was the problem with that? She was here just at the Causeway. Nothing unusual about that.

She strode down and then eventually stopped, turning around to see that Kylie was going slowly. Declan was with her, coming up behind her as if encouraging some child down the road.

'Would you two get a move on? I'm the oldie,' said Siobhan. She was ratty because she wanted to get going. She knew where she had to go, and what to be doing.

They walked down along the road, following the footpath until they came to the stones of the Giant's Causeway, the hexagonal shapes clear even from the side before you were on top of them.

'Do we go straight round to the Boot?' asked Declan.

'No,' said Siobhan, 'let's go up onto the stones. Might as well while we're here. They are special. That water's going to be rough at the end of them today.'

Together, the three of them stepped up onto the rather large stones. Siobhan placed her hand on her knees at one point to drive herself up and onto the top layer. She looked out towards the sea which was crashing ashore further down the Causeway. Declan made off as quick as he could to get there and got a shout from one of the wardens to take it easy.

Siobhan turned. From her standing point, she could see the Giant's Boot. She scanned around it. It had been general practice, surveying the land before you entered. She may no longer be a spy, but procedures didn't leave her.

'Are you coming down to the end?' asked Kylie.

'No,' said Siobhan.

'I'll go rescue idiot then.'

'He's quite sweet though, isn't he?' Siobhan said to her.

'Sweet, in what way?'

'Well, I'm his boss and I'm paying him to be here. It was you he was looking out for on the way down because you were getting behind. He didn't leave you. He was like some sort of puppy, making sure you were okay.'

'Please,' said Kylie. Looking at her, as Kylie strode off, Siobhan watched the girl walk down towards the stones and then watched Declan turn to see her. Oh, his face was like a puppy. For a moment, Siobhan remembered Eamon.

His face hadn't been like a puppy, but it had been pleased to see her. Delighted, in fact. His face took on something over that year when the two of them had been intimate, but he had gone. He had gone off to another part of the world. He never wrote, but then again, she never wrote to him. They were spies. It would've been difficult. You could have been dead within a year or two, or you could have been having to lead a double life somewhere else. Baggage just got awkward.

Baggage, thought Siobhan. *How is it ever baggage? We were good together. Not just in the bedroom—we were good everywhere.*

Being a spy had taken a lot from her, but that was one of the most important things. The chance to have developed a long-term relationship. She stood in the rain, the wind blowing across her face, until Declan and Kylie came back. Declan was still hovering like a puppy.

'Come on,' said Siobhan, 'let's go have a look at this.'

Together, the three of them descended from the Causeway and walked round and approached the Giant's Boot. There were a few people about who had been up on the Causeway, but not many. Siobhan scanned them, taking in who they were, but she didn't notice anybody out of place. Everyone looked like a tourist and that kind of idiot tourist who would've been out on a day like this.

Oh, maybe that was harsh. Maybe they didn't have time. Maybe this was part of the schedule. Siobhan didn't like schedules on holidays. You needed to go where you wanted. You needed to have that wandering, that ability to just dander about. Dander, that was a proper word from home, wasn't it? The ability to walk with no actual intent, just plod about here and there, happy in the world. She hadn't dandered enough in life. Maybe that's what she needed to do in retirement, dander! But she wasn't dandering now.

Siobhan walked the short path down towards the Boot to have Declan standing beside her.

'Not much here, is there? I mean, there really isn't. You're right, they took the body away.'

Siobhan looked at him. Did he really just say that? Was it really essential? Sometimes she couldn't decide if Declan was a lovable idiot or just an idiot, or did he just have difficulty in talking to people? He said stuff that wouldn't offend. Well, not unless your husband had just died. That was the thing about people. They came at things from their own perspective. You never knew what people have been through.

'You two, focus on this. Get a camera out, take some photos.'

'Okay,' said Declan, grabbing his phone.

'Of me?' said Kylie. 'He's not taking me.'

'Yes, he is. Take your hood down as well. Make it look like you're enjoying it. I need to look at something over here.'

'What are you looking at?' asked Declan.

'None of your business, now would you just do it!'

Siobhan watched until Kylie stood there smiling, as if she didn't know it had previously existed. Declan was in his element, genuinely having time to photograph Kylie. Not that there was anything sexual or sinister about it. Siobhan knelt down a little way off the Boot at the large rock that she'd seen in the paper's photograph. The marking was no longer there except it was; she reached out with her hand and she felt where grooves had been dug in. Previously, the stone had been marked and the new surfaces could be seen. Not so now. However, he had dug into it. Eamon had made a proper mark.

She needed her hands to be traced over it, but it was there. Siobhan looked at the rock; it was heavy, but two, three people could move it. But Eamon hadn't been two or three people; he had been just one. She looked at the surrounding land. It was beach, sandy and rocky. The tide had been over and back several times, but there were a lot of stones here; things wouldn't have moved the same. The ground had some sort of stability to it.

That was the trouble. If you put things on a beach, the actual sand moved. Could you be sure it would be in the same place? Especially when the tide came so far up towards it. Of course, you couldn't, but you could here, where the rocks were. She would need to dig down to see if she could find what he'd left. She looked around her. Not now.

'Come on,' said Siobhan, 'let's head back up. We'll get a

coffee or a tea or something, a wee bun back up at the centre.'

'Now, you're talking,' said Kylie. 'Oh, and Declan, you give me those photographs.'

'Why? What's wrong with them?'

'Nothing, but I want you to get rid of them.'

'Why?' asked Declan again.

'Well, why do you want them?'

'Can't I have photographs of a friend?'

'Declan, we work for the same employer. When did we become friends?'

That was harsh, thought Siobhan. *It's one thing to let him down and tell him you're not happy or you're not interested, but my goodness.*

'Quit quibbling,' said Siobhan.

Twenty minutes later they were sitting, dripping, in the coffee shop at the centre. Siobhan had a scone with butter and jam and some ordinary tea in a cup. She'd wanted something fancier, but they didn't have it. She watched Kylie with her hot chocolate and Declan having exactly the same.

'Was it worth the trip up then?' said Kylie.

Siobhan looked round at the centre. There weren't many people in it just now and certainly no one was close by.

'So far,' said Siobhan, 'I need to ask a favour of the two of you.'

'Well, you can ask,' said Kylie.

'We need to go into town and buy a spade. We need to come back here in the middle of the night, and we need to dig up by the Boot.'

'What?' asked Kylie.

'Tonight then?' said Declan.

'Yes, tonight,' said Siobhan.

'Good job Kylie made those sandwiches then,' said Declan cheerily.

Chapter 05

'Now, just a moment,' said Kylie as they left the Giant's Causeway centre. 'What are we going to do from here?'

'Well, we're going to into Portrush or Portstewart and I think we'll get a spade and trowel. Maybe some other items,' said Siobhan.

'And then do what?'

'Find a hotel, get you one with a swimming pool, if you want,' said Siobhan.

'I don't have a swimming costume with me,' retorted Kylie.

'I'll find you one. We'll have dinner. We'll have a bit of fun and then we'll pop out tonight. I can get done what I want to do at the Causeway and then back to the hotel, make our way home tomorrow.'

'And then what? Just go on? That's not going to happen, is it?'

Kylie's too clever by half, thought Siobhan.

'What else are we going to do?' asked Declan. 'We can't hang around here the whole time.'

'Are you not even a bit curious why Siobhan wants to be here? Why we're going back with a spade?'

'Mrs D wants to dig. Mrs D gets to dig. Not the point, is it?'

Declan is just happy, thought Siobhan, *that he is going to be out here with Kylie. The idea of possibly going for a swim, having dinner, being in the woman's company. He couldn't even care less about the impending digging, either why or what that would mean. He isn't even thinking about that.*

'You want to dig at the Giant's Causeway in the middle of the night beside a large rock that had a dead body on it not so long ago. Why?' asked Kylie.

'Just indulge me.'

'Indulge you? You're going digging in a murder scene.'

'It's not a murder scene. They've cleaned it. Forensics will have been all over it. That's not what I'm about.'

'Well, what are you about? You're not telling us,' spat Kylie.

'Easy, Kylie,' said Declan suddenly. 'Mrs D pays us the money.'

Siobhan wasn't sure if Declan was worried that Kylie would lose her job, or whether they both would. Yet Siobhan could understand why the girl was laying it on strong. After all, this was unusual activity.

'You said you worked in exports.'

'I did,' said Siobhan, 'travelled most of the world.'

'I don't get why you want to do this and what did you see, anyway? You were looking at that rock. There was nothing on it.'

'Nothing on it you could see,' said Declan. 'Mrs D may have better eyes. After all, that's what happens when you get old, isn't it? Your eyesight gets better.'

'Your close-in eyesight gets worse, Declan,' said Kylie, almost shaking her head.

'She's absolutely right,' said Siobhan. 'Your eyesight gets

worse, but what I found you could feel by touch.'

'And what did you find?' asked Kylie.

'Enough,' said Siobhan. 'Let's go get our stuff. Let's go see if we can have some fun until tonight and then back we come.'

Declan drove the car into Portrush where, in the hardware store, they picked up a spade and a couple of trowels. After that, they checked into a hotel, finding one with a small swimming pool. Siobhan was true to her word and went to a sports store where they could pick up costumes. Declan bought a pair of Speedos and was suggestive, not lewd, but certainly more figure-enhancing swimwear than what Kylie had in mind.

Siobhan didn't care. She bought herself a swimsuit, but when they got to the hotel, she came and lay in the white towel robe that came with her room. She had picked out three rooms, an expensive one for herself and two standard ones for the other two. It was only money after all, wasn't it?

Siobhan was taking her time to understand just how much she had. She had no children, no siblings, no one to spend this on. She might as well spend it on herself, and her gardener and housekeeper.

Siobhan lay with her book while the other two played in the swimming pool. *Kylie was warming on him*, she thought. Declan had been insistent, a rascal, but one you couldn't fail to notice. A genuinely nice rascal. She thought Declan had a heart, certainly a better one than Andrew had possessed.

They ate dinner that night inside the hotel, and Siobhan asked if they wanted to get some sleep beforehand. After all, they could be out into the small hours. They disappeared to their rooms and Siobhan woke them up by phone when it was just turning midnight.

'Make sure you're wearing something dark,' she had said, and they had done. They had little choice because they were wearing what they brought with them, but it seemed to be dark, anyway. Together, the three set out, retracing their steps back to the Causeway. The night was overcast, but it wasn't raining, Siobhan wasn't sure if she was glad of that or not.

Rain was a brilliant cover. If it was dark enough, you could stay hidden from eyes. The wind meant you could stay hidden from ears. It was difficult to pick out the noises when the sheet rain was piling down, and Siobhan wished it had been like the daytime.

They parked just off the road, towards the hotel at the causeway before walking through the sizeable gap at the centre. It let those who didn't want to use the centre make their way down the Causeway path. There was no bus running now. There was nobody about, and they walked down in silence until Siobhan saw Kylie about to switch on her phone.

'Don't. Make sure they're all on silent as well.'

'Why?' asked Kylie.

'In case someone knows we're here,' said Declan. 'Pretty obvious.'

'I got that bit,' said Kylie. 'Thanks. What I want to know is why. What are we doing that you're worried about people seeing?'

'We're at an old crime scene. I don't want people to get the wrong impression.'

'And what's the impression is that?'

'That we're doing something illegal,' said Siobhan.

'Are we?' asked Kylie.

'Not that I'm aware of.'

The conversation died and together the three trudged along in silence until they reached where the Giant's Boot was. The coast looked different at night, especially with no clouds overhead. You lost some of the grandeur and the magnificence. Although it still loomed over you, it still threatened. Declan was carrying the spade and the trowels, but he was still shepherding Kylie as they continued to walk out towards the Boot. Once at it, Siobhan found the rock with a scratched-in sign on it.

'Start digging just behind here,' she said to Declan. 'You too, Kylie.'

'But he's got the big spade,' she said.

'Yes, and you'll do the fine work. They'll be something here, trust me.' Just as they put the spades down, Siobhan stopped them. 'Hang on a minute,' she said. 'You two get together like you're making out, like you're getting it on.'

'What?' blurted Kylie.

'Like this,' said Declan and grabbed her, pulling her in.

It wasn't the most convivial coming together of a pair, but at least she didn't shout out, 'Get off me, Declan.' Siobhan disappeared into the shadows of the night. Somebody was up on that path.

Slowly she crept round off the path, putting her feet down on unsteady ground. The wind was blowing, masking some of her sounds. The person seemed so intensely interested in what was going on at the Boot that she was never in any danger of being seen. Carefully, Siobhan crept forward.

On active service, she'd have grabbed them, taking them down, maybe knocked them out with an injection before getting them back to the base. There, they'd have been interrogated.

Here and now, she wasn't kidnapping people. This was retirement, a new life. The rules were different. She slowly took out her phone. Holding it close in, she switched it on and then she pressed for the phone camera to come on. It did so, and Siobhan stole in closer. When she was a mere six or seven feet away, she ran forward and tried to take a photograph of the man's face.

He was quick. She had to give him that, although she thought she was slow. He hit her smack on the chin and she fell back onto her bottom. He turned and ran.

Siobhan was too dazed to get back up and go after him. Slowly she got back to her feet, shaking her head, groggy from the effects of the punch. She stayed off the path and tried to walk round and see if anyone else was about. After twenty minutes of no sign of anyone, she returned to the other two, where Declan still had Kylie held tight.

'Is it over? Would you tell him it's over?'

'Very convincing,' said Siobhan. 'Somebody was watching us.'

'What?' said Kylie. 'What do you mean somebody was watching us? Who's watching us? Who's tailed us out here in the middle of the night?'

'We weren't tailed,' said Siobhan.

'How do you know?' said Kylie. Siobhan bit her lip.

'What you need to understand is we weren't followed. They were here watching the site, here to see if anyone would turn up. They must have known something was up.'

Carefully, Kylie withdrew herself from Declan. 'Is there anybody else about?' she asked.

'I've looked and I can't see anyone.'

'But how would you know?' asked Kylie.

'Because she's had a look,' said Declan. 'She just told you that.'

'That's all right, Declan,' said Siobhan. 'Yes, I just said.'

'You told me what you did for a living. You didn't tell me how you did it, what goes on in your head.'

'No, I didn't,' said Siobhan, 'and I may never but here,' she said, handing the spade to Declan and a trowel over to Kylie. 'We don't want to be too long about this. Dig down quick as you can.'

Declan nodded, but Siobhan noted Kylie kept looking back at her. How long would she just accept what was being told of her, asked of her to do? How long would she keep that natural curiosity in check? Siobhan believed not long, not long at all.

As Declan sunk the spade into the sand, Siobhan rubbed her chin. It was quite a punch. Back in the day, would she have come back from that? Maybe, but at her current age, she was doing well to have kept her head straight. What was in the sand? It was time to find out.

Chapter 06

'We need to move the rock and then dig underneath it,' said Siobhan to the other two standing in the darkness of the Causeway Coast. She could hear the tide coming in, not paying a blind bit of attention to what time of day it was. That was the thing about the tides. They were relentless, either slipping away or flooding in. Siobhan reckoned they had maybe a couple of hours before the water would be back towards where they stood. Would it quite reach? She wasn't sure. It would be another few hours before she would know. Even then, maybe the tide would come up from underneath the sand, not just over the top.

'Let's move the rock then,' said Declan.

'You want me to put my shoulder into that?' said Kylie. She looked at Siobhan.

I'm the one who's fifty-plus, Siobhan thought. *I'm the one who should sit and complain about moving stuff.*

'Shoulders to it,' said Siobhan. Together, the three of them pushed the rock. It rolled slowly, leaving the space underneath it. 'Start there,' said Siobhan to Declan.

Despite the strangeness of the situation, Declan was enthusiastic, shifting sand like there was no tomorrow. There was the occasional clatter as the spade hit rock and Siobhan told him to slow down and be quieter. She set Kylie to dig with the trowel around where Declan was working. An hour and a half later, they had dug holes, but there was nothing there.

'Who was that out there?' asked Kylie.

'Not now,' said Siobhan. 'We need to find this before the tide comes back.'

'Find what?' asked Declan.

'Whatever he's left me. He's left me something here. It's my mark,' said Siobhan under her breath. But of course, it would have taken three of them to move it. It wouldn't be under the rock, it would be around, maybe under a small one.

'We need to dig out and around,' said Siobhan. 'Anywhere where there's a smaller rock, lift it up, and dig.'

'You've got to be joking,' said Kylie. 'You've got to be absolutely kidding me. Are you off your head?'

'Come on, let's get at it,' said Declan.

'Declan, listen, look where we are. What are we doing?' asked Kylie.

'We're searching for something,' said Siobhan. 'Now get on to it, move some of them rocks. Declan, get the spade into it.'

'Are you wise?' raged Kylie. 'Seriously, are you wise? Has somebody broke in during the night and nicked your brain? Look at this. There's nothing on the front of that rock.'

'Yes, there was,' said Siobhan. 'There was a distinct mark. I know what I'm doing.'

'Absolute madness,' said Kylie. 'You're away with it. You're away with the fairies, woman.'

'Shut up,' said Siobhan. 'Shut up. Really, just get on with it like Declan's doing. You'll see.'

Kylie glowered at her, but she got down on her knees and

dug with the trowel, making any of the holes that Declan had started bigger. Siobhan went down with the second trowel and began pushing rocks away. As she dug, she felt her shoulders getting tired. It had been a long day and that punch to the jaw was still ringing. Nobody had been about, but that was over a couple of hours ago. Maybe they'd come back. Maybe they were watching now. Somebody had been watching, but why? They'd known. This wasn't just some random spot where Eamon had been killed. Eamon had been up to something.

She could reach out to the Service community, she thought, but not until she knew what was going on. Don't make a fuss. Don't look like you're involved until you have to. Play it cool. Though somebody was already on her tail.

'Do you get crabs here at night?' asked Kylie.

'What?' said Siobhan.

'Do you get crabs? I don't want to be digging down if crabs are going to nip me.'

'Kylie, just get on with it.'

'But crabs; crabs can get a real hold of you. Have you ever been held on to by a crab? The bit where they get their claws together and it's like really hard to prise apart. Say if your finger's in that or your toe . . .'

'Seriously?' said Declan. 'When did you get nipped by a crab like that?'

'Well, I haven't, obviously,' said Kylie, 'because I wouldn't put my hands anywhere near where crabs are. But . . .'

'Quiet,' said Siobhan, 'people will hear us up and down this coast.'

'And why shouldn't they?' said Kylie. 'Are we doing something wrong? Are we doing something . . .'

'Shush,' said Siobhan. There was a light wind blowing now. Combined with the surf coming in, it made it difficult to ascertain if anyone was around. Siobhan scanned into the gloom but could see no one moving.

'I want my bed,' said Kylie. 'When we get back to this hotel, I'm having a shower and then I am going to bed. You better not be waking us up early in the morning. The thing is . . .'

'The thing is, you're talking,' said Siobhan. 'Talking, talking, talking. Get digging! The sooner we find this, the sooner we get out of here.'

'What is it we're looking for?' asked Kylie, raising her voice.

'Shush. Just work.'

'Are we getting extra for this?'

'Are you what?' asked Siobhan.

'Are we getting extra for this? I don't work this long normally.'

'Kylie, you get a house. You get a house at the end of my drive.'

'I don't,' said Declan. 'I just come and do your garden. I mean, I am going above the call of duty here, Mrs D.'

'That you are, Declan, and I thank you for it, but we'll talk about things like that back at the hotel, not now. Now we dig. We get on with it.'

'Right you are, Mrs D,' said Declan. And sure enough, the man went back to work, but Kylie was faffing. She was an excellent housekeeper, but covert digging was not her speciality.

'What are you doing?' asked Siobhan of Declan. 'It's bad enough she doesn't get on at that pace but . . .'

'Something here,' said Declan. 'I hit something with that last shovel. There's something down here.'

Siobhan stood up and looked around her. She couldn't see anyone. Now was as good a time as any to lift it out. She knelt down beside Declan and attacked the sand with the trowel. Carefully, though, trying to make sure that she didn't stick it inadvertently into something she shouldn't. She saw the strap of the bag. More of a satchel than anything else. Slowly, she moved the sand away until she found the main strap of the satchel, and pulled at it.

Slowly, it was freed away from the sand and she lifted it clear.

'Should you really be opening that? You don't know what that is. There could be a bomb or something inside.'

'Kylie, quiet. There's not a bomb inside. Stop getting overexcited. You're letting things run away with you.'

'Letting things run away with me!' said Kylie indignantly. She stood up with her hand on her hip. 'I'm being dragged out here in the middle of the night, digging where there's been a murder, and now we're pulling bags out of the sand. I suggest it's a bomb and I'm the one with a fantastical mind. How does that work? How do you know there's not a bomb in here?'

'I know the man that put the bag here. And I told you, it's been marked for me.'

'Kylie's got a point, though, Mrs D.'

'No, she doesn't, Declan. I know what I'm doing. Now shush while I see what's in here.'

Siobhan pulled at the clasp on the satchel, opening it up. Inside were the remains of a lunch. There were also several pens, but everything was wet through. The only thing that was possibly dry was inside a zippy bag. The thing you would put your lunch in. Except in here was a small notebook.

'No bomb, then,' said Declan.

'No, Declan, no bomb,' said Siobhan.

She unzipped the plastic bag and found the notebook inside to be damp, but not sodden like everything else in the bag. Siobhan took out the notebook and went to open the pages. But they were stuck together, damp. It hadn't dried, and the pages were literally stuck together, hard to separate because of the dampness.

Siobhan slowly lifted the top off the first page and found a blank page beneath. One by one she kept pulling the page away until somewhere in the middle of the notebook she found one page with words on it. The ink had smudged a bit, and it was hard to see in the lack of light.

'Get round here. The two of you crowd round me. I'm going to get a small penlight on here, but I don't want it to be seen.'

'Why do you not want to be . . .'

'Shut up, Kylie,' said Siobhan, trying not to raise her voice. 'Just do as I ask, okay? I'll explain another time. Right now, I need to do this.'

'Okay, Mrs D. No need for the two of you to get out of sorts with each other,' said Declan. 'We're all on the same side here.'

'What side?' asked Kylie.

'My side,' said Siobhan. 'My side, that gets you a house. My side that pays the bills. Okay, now shush.'

Reaching into her jacket, Siobhan pulled out a tiny pen torch. Making sure the others were crouched over the top of her, she switched it on, holding it tight to the paper. She pulled it away just enough so that she could read what was there, or at least she tried.

I need my bloody glasses, she thought. It wasn't like this when she was a spy. Back in the day of the information drops, when she worked in the field, you didn't have time to stop, pull out your glasses and check what was being written. You had a quick look at it, and by quick, it was a couple of seconds. You memorised it. It went to your head like a photographic memory. Then, having torn it up, you would get back to the flat or wherever and you would jot it down. You'd go over and over and commit it to memory. And then you'd tear up any written evidence of it. Right now, Siobhan couldn't even see the evidence.

'I can't read this. Kylie,' she said, 'read it for me. Declan, stay crouched over the top of us.'

'It's a poem,' said Kylie. 'Why is he writing you a poem . . .'

'Shush. Don't ask about what's going on. Just do as I tell you. Now, would you read that poem?'

'No need to get your knickers in a twist. I just want to point out that this is the crappiest night adventure I've had.'

Siobhan put her hand up to her chin, feeling where the punch had clocked her. She'd had more fun ones as well.

'Just read the darn thing.'

'Okay,' said Kylie. 'By the waterfall in the sun's pale light, you fell for me in a trilby and suit. But the wind is cold and howls at night where we used to listen to whispers abroad. He's not very good, is he?' said Kylie. 'That doesn't even rhyme.'

'I don't understand poetry,' said Declan. 'I never have. My Uncle John was a talented poet. Of course, he wasn't actually my Uncle John—he was just a neighbour, but they all called him Uncle John. Well, Mum called him Uncle John whenever he was round. But . . .'

'Quiet,' said Siobhan, wanting to keep Declan's voice down. She also wasn't wanting to follow the line of attack that realised that Uncle John was a bit more to Declan's mum than maybe Declan realised. 'Read it again, Kylie.'

'By the waterfall in the sun's pale light, you fell for me in a trilby and suit. The wind is cold and howls at night where we used to listen to whispers abroad.'

'Do you know what that means?' asked Declan.

'No,' said Siobhan, 'I don't, but we need to clear up. We've found it, that's what matters. Let's get the sand back, all the holes, and we need to roll that rock back as well.'

'What do we do with the satchel?'

'We put it back. Not the paper,' said Siobhan. She stuffed the little notebook into her pocket, replaced the satchel back in the sand and buried it. Quickly, everything else was replaced back. Within half an hour, they were walking back along the coast road up to the centre and then down one of the minor roads where they had parked the car.

Dawn was still far off and Siobhan felt chilled. It was because she'd stopped digging and the cool of the night had finally hit her. They saw no one on the climb back up towards the visitor centre. But she realised that Declan and Kylie made such a noise that anyone with half a bit of training would have heard them.

Everything was quiet as they got back in the car and Declan drove to the hotel without a word. He had the radio on and Siobhan just let the music play. 'By the waterfall,' churned over in her head. 'Sun's pale light,' where could that be?

When they got to the hotel, Declan went to his room, but Kylie stopped Siobhan.

'I don't get what we're at here,' said Kylie.

'Don't worry about it,' said Siobhan. 'And I'll give you something for what you did tonight. I'm not asking you to come out here for nothing.'

Siobhan noticed Kylie was staring at her. 'You've got a bruise on your chin,' she said.

'I fell when I was walking around.'

'You told me to get into Declan's arms. You went off and chased someone away. Who's out there at that time of night? Who, seriously?'

'You get pervs sometimes wanting to watch young people who have nipped out for a bit of nookie.'

'Nookie?' asked Kylie. 'What's nookie? What sort of word is that?'

Siobhan realised she was talking to the younger generation. 'Sex,' she said.

'No,' said Kylie. 'Why would you go down there for a start, to have sex? And second, when would you be watching? You would go to somewhere where cars are parked up. Who in their right mind goes out and does stuff like that?'

'Your generation's just not got the same adventurous spirit,' said Siobhan. She turned to her room, opening the door, and bid Kylie a goodnight. She hoped that would suffice. Kylie was asking too many questions, and she couldn't really blame the girl. After all, it was all odd.

Siobhan thought about going straight to bed, but she stripped down and sat in the bath, letting the hot water soak through. Occasionally she put her chin into it, trying to take away the sting that was there.

Back in the day, she'd have dealt with a sucker punch like that. She'd been an analyst too long. She'd have to be careful, and she'd have to be careful of the other two. If Eamon got killed for this, if that's what really happened, then it wasn't a simple feud. She could tread into places that she would have been wary of while she was with the Service. Nowadays, there was no backup. She truly would have to be careful.

Chapter 07

Siobhan had to knock on the doors of the other two to make sure they were up for breakfast in the hotel. Kylie looked like the world had collapsed, large bags underneath her eyes, whereas Declan was fairly bright. Siobhan was tired. She'd gone through enough of these nights in her life to have a second wind. It didn't matter though, because Kylie and she could sleep on the way back.

'You had any more thoughts on what that poem means?' asked Declan at breakfast. 'You're quite clever, Mrs D, aren't you?'

'I wouldn't go that far, Declan,' said Siobhan. In front of her was a cup of ordinary tea that she'd been avoiding drinking. She should have brought some of her own tea bags with her. She wanted that smoky feeling from her Lapsang Souchong, but instead, she was having to deal with the dull monotony of hotel tea. 'What time do we have to be out at?' she asked.

'Midday,' said Kylie. It was only ten o'clock. Breakfast was just finishing, but Kylie's head didn't lift.

'You're going to need to brush that hair,' said Siobhan. 'Did you have a wash last night?'

'No,' said Kylie. 'I know my hair's a mess. I know, but

frankly, I don't feel like doing anything at the moment.'

'Did you want to take a run out, Mrs D? Did you want to have another look at the scene?' Declan raised his eyes as he said the word.

'No, Declan, I don't want to. We're going home.'

'And then what are we doing?'

'You, Declan, will do a little gardening this afternoon. Kylie will have her other work to do. I've got a bit of thinking to get on with. Some things I'm going to have to look into.'

'We could give you a hand with that,' said Declan.

'Look, I've brought you both out here and it's been a bit of an adventure. That's it, okay? We go back. I'm not here to stir up a hornet's nest.'

'Why would there be a hornet's nest?' asked Kylie.

Shouldn't have said that, Siobhan told herself. *Why did I mention that?* 'Let's just get home, okay?'

Siobhan stood up, and walked over to the reception desk outside the restaurant. There she paid the bill before turning around and looking inside the restaurant. She stared at the faces. No, she thought, they're not watching us, are they? If they are, they're doing a superb job.

It had been a long time since the field, but the instincts were there. She felt that some people at breakfast just didn't feel right, but there was no evidence, of course, and what was she going to do? Grab them in the corridor and threaten them? She couldn't do that either. Back home, she'd make sure the cameras were on. She had planned to send Declan home and tell Kylie to go to sleep when she got back to the house. However, having people about made it easier for anyone spying to be spotted.

Everything she'd ever done in terms of the spy world had

been away from Northern Ireland. She'd never had to be in her own house thinking there were people watching her. When they lived back on the Belfast Road, the house had all the modern security gadgets, but that's because Andrew had wanted them. That was okay, because Siobhan would have put other things in place.

Her spy life was abroad, and she'd come back to pick up her life in Northern Ireland. She was going to live down there on the so-called Gold Coast, out on the Donaghadee Road and while away her time, enjoying herself. And then Eamon had showed up, in possibly the worst fashion. He'd left her the biggest compliment, though. He'd trusted her. Somebody killed him, and prior to that, he had trusted Siobhan with something.

'By the waterfall? By the waterfall?' It wasn't talking to her at the moment, but it would. It was one of those things. Maybe she was sharper back then. Maybe she'd have got it by now, but she would. She would sit down, and she would get on top of this.

When the trio left the hotel, Siobhan sat up front with Declan driving and Kylie collapsed in the back seat. She may have had her seatbelt attached to her, but her legs had moved up. The drive home was uneventful, and as soon as they made the driveway, Siobhan was giving out instructions.

'Kylie, get some lunch on. Get Declan something to eat and he's out in the garden. I want you to sort out that bedroom of mine. It needs a clean. Do the sheets as well.'

The sheets don't need a clean, thought Siobhan. *They are only on a couple of days ago, but it will keep Kylie busy. Keep her about the house and out of her hair.*

'I want to go to bed,' said Kylie.

'You can sleep tonight.'

'I can always do the sheets and stuff, Mrs D,' said Declan, 'if Kylie wants to sleep.'

He really is trying too hard, thought Siobhan. 'No, Declan, you're not going into my bedroom. I think that's highly inappropriate, don't you? Next, you'll be asking to wash my underwear.'

Declan looked over, wondering how Siobhan had come up with that idea. 'Mrs D, I mean you're a good-looking lady and that, for your age, but really, I'm not interested in that way. I hope you don't think of me in those terms.'

'One has to be careful, Declan. My time of life.'

He didn't get the joke at all, but simply nodded, happy that she wasn't accusing him of anything. Looking into the back seat, she saw Kylie shaking her head. He was like a lovable puppy, wasn't he?

The day wasn't particularly bright, and the heating in the house was on. *Just as well*, thought Siobhan, as she stared into the mirror in the hall. Her hand rubbed her chin. There was definitely bruising coming up. She took a moment to stare at herself. Yes, there were lines. *But I look okay, don't I?* she thought. *I mean, I still—still what? What am I looking for?*

Maybe it was thinking about Eamon again. Maybe Eamon was the thing. She was in her prime with Eamon. She was about to think about Eamon a lot more.

Siobhan made herself a cup of proper tea and took the smoky-smelling mixture into her little office, closing the door behind her. She brought up the maps function on her laptop and honed in on Russia.

Siobhan saw Moscow and its rivers. She always liked the rivers, so did Eamon. Zooming in on one, she remembered the cool air. She thought of how he'd held her hand. Then she'd leaned into him. That was the first time they'd kissed. They were being watched, she remembered. Watched from the other side of the bank by a man in a rather dodgy coat, but he wasn't some pervert. He was simply one of the local KGB monitoring them.

They had been embassy staff. That's all they ever were out there to the KGB. But they'd run many agents together. Siobhan remembered the adrenaline kicking in. She remembered what it was like. Various nights they'd nearly got caught. She remembered one, hunched down in a room for forty-eight hours. Eamon and she had listened to their stomachs rumbling before in the small hours of the morning, making it back to the embassy.

They had sat in the embassy kitchen stuffing themselves. Then going up to his bedroom. You'd have thought after being awake for that long, from fighting off hunger, you'd have just wanted to go to bed. That would be the case nowadays, not back then. What always got her, was there was never a question of it becoming a permanent thing. She had Andrew. He was already sleeping with other women then, and she knew it. She didn't care because she was out living her own life.

Andrew and she had a strange relationship. He would suggest things to do when she was home. They'd go out to the theatre together because they both enjoyed it. Andrew was like a friend, not a close one, but one you would see occasionally. Was there love? She didn't know. There was something there. He'd left her everything, after all.

Siobhan looked out of the window to the water beyond her office. It was good to be back by the sea. *It calms you*, she thought. By the waterfall?

Something struck Siobhan. They'd been talking about Northern Ireland, she and Eamon. And on that Moscow riverbank, he'd been asking about the different places that Siobhan liked. Places she would return to. Back then, she had talked about where her family had taken them. Time and time again, her mother would want to go back to the same place.

Falls? It wasn't really a waterfall, was it? Eamon hadn't understood. Siobhan's mother liked Dunseverick Falls and Eamon talked about how waterfalls were great. But at Dunseverick, it was not really a waterfall in the classic case, a very slow descent. More running over rocks and down a gradual slope. No high drop. You could walk down to it from the road.

Dunseverick. She thought back. That was the only time she'd mentioned Dunseverick to him. About her mother. About what her mother had done. Every year, going back two, three, four times. How her mother loved to see the running water. Preferred it more than the large drop. But it was the falls, the sea beyond them, the calm, the tranquillity.

Siobhan clicked on the computer and brought up a picture of the falls. Using the function on the screen, she turned the image this way and that. Somebody's photograph, one that went all the way around, one of those panoramic ones that were now being used by the mapping company.

She could see it all now but realised it was also a rather strange place. There weren't many places to hide things. Maybe she wasn't seeing it right. Can you leave something in the falls, bound by the river? That was dodgy. When he was at the Causeway and he'd left something, he was then found dead shortly afterwards. Maybe he was up against it time-wise, but Dunseverick Falls wasn't a place to hide anything, was it? Was she not seeing this correctly?

She'd have to go. Siobhan went to stand up to tell the others what she was planning, but found herself sitting back down again. She was charging off. *Was she ready for this? What did the rest mean?*

The sun's pale light. Trilby and suit. Whispers abroad.

Siobhan took a moment and sipped her tea. A chill ran through her. The spy game had been deadly, truly deadly. She thought about the colleagues she had lost along the way. Northern Ireland had been a safe haven. Every time she'd come back here, although she took her precautions and made sure that nobody was watching her, here was a safe haven. As crazy as it seemed, in a time of the Troubles, and her being a British spy, she found Northern Ireland to be her haven. Home.

Maybe that was why there was still a fondness for Andrew, because he represented that, too. Coming back to him was back to security. Eamon was all passion, fire, and excitement. But the passion, fire, and excitement were coming here now. This home was meant to be her . . . not fortress, but her pad. Her luxurious home to wind down in.

She knew she would find winding down difficult, but now there was an opportunity for adventure. Something else that would stop that from happening, delay it. And she realised that part of her was running for that retirement, jumping on board quickly. She'd have to be careful. The people that were coming along with her were not trained agents. Even if her field craft was old, at least she had the training. She had the eyes for it; she had the sixth sense.

She would leave Declan at home this time. He was excitable. Kylie would just look like a bitter daughter, out for the day with mother. She would go to Dunseverick Falls and see what she could find. They would not do any digging, though, not yet. She'd do that on her own if she had to. First, she'd see if anyone was there watching her. If this all got too much, she'd make sure the others were out of the way.

She thought about bringing somebody else in. About talking to somebody from the old days, but who? She didn't know enough yet. And, at the end of the day, Eamon was dead. That put up a red flag. She would want to know what was happening first, before she trusted anyone from her days in the Service.

Chapter 08

Siobhan called Kylie and Declan into the kitchen late that afternoon.

'You best be getting home soon, Declan,' she said. 'Tomorrow, I want you to come and keep working in the garden.'

'What bit do you want me to do?' he asked.

'You decide. You know what needs done in it. Just make it look good.'

'I thought I might need to talk with you about some plants I was thinking of putting in.'

'Declan, I trust you with it, okay? You will not turn me into a full-on gardener. I just want a garden that looks nice, one I can sit in and one that you can maintain. If you want to put some rather special-looking flowers and plants in them, that's fine. I've got the money to do it.'

'Okay, Mrs D, are we not going hunting tomorrow though? You made any headway with that note or the poem?'

'I'm taking Kylie with me tomorrow to Dunseverick Falls. So, we're driving back up, Kylie. Make sure you get some sleep tonight.'

'What?'

'You heard me, Kylie. I said we're going to Dunseverick Falls.'

'Why am I not going?' asked Declan. 'You don't want two ladies going on their own. There was somebody about that other night, wasn't there?'

'Declan, I valued your physical strength so much that I actually left you with Kylie and went off on my own to see if there was anyone there. I then chased them off on my own. I don't need your protection. Your muscles for digging were very handy. The fact you drove me was very helpful too because I don't like to drive for too long. But one thing I don't need is protection.'

'You're getting older, Mrs D. I really think you might think twice about that.'

Siobhan went to shake her head, but saw Kylie still staring at her.

'You're taking me though,' she said. 'Why?'

'Well, you can drive, and Declan here needs to get on with the garden. I think you're up to date with what needs done inside.'

Kylie shrugged her shoulders, and Declan went to complain again, but Siobhan silenced him. 'Mrs D has made her mind up,' she said to him. 'Mrs D has said, and Mrs D is paying the bills, as you reminded Kylie when we were up at the Causeway. I think it's an okay day tomorrow as well. You enjoy the garden, Declan.'

The next day, Kylie and Siobhan left at eight o'clock in the morning. Declan had already been there for an hour and the amount of times he checked Kylie was okay was becoming ridiculous. Siobhan settled down in the front seat while Kylie drove her car all the way back to the Causeway coast.

Dunseverick wasn't far from the Causeway and the day was turning into a bright one.

Siobhan wasn't sure how she would react arriving there, a place of many childhood memories. She wondered if she'd maintain her cool to look at the place with a dispassionate eye. As she stared off at the passing fields of green on the journey, Kylie turned the radio down and asked questions.

'Siobhan, why are you retired? I mean, you're just past fifty. Why? Most people work until they're sixty, sixty-five.'

'I don't want to work like that,' said Siobhan. 'I want to enjoy my retirement. I want to be free to do things. Andrew earned a lot of money. I earned some decent money too.'

'You earned money being away, working abroad,' said Kylie. 'What sort of things did you do?'

'It was quite boring really, business and that. I negotiated contracts. Back in those days, getting into Russia and other places was difficult as a firm.'

'It's just I've been thinking,' said Kylie. Siobhan noticed Kylie looked at her nails on the steering wheel as she did this. And that's where the catch came with Kylie. By her own admission, Kylie would be someone who would sit and watch programmes about who was dating who. How to look glamorous on the scene somewhere in America. All these rather boring lives of celebrities. But Kylie was not stupid. She was sharp.

'Why are you on this investigation?' asked Kylie. 'I don't understand. If all you did was deal with company issues out there, why are you looking into a dead man? A man who was murdered. Also, you have us digging up things in the middle of the night? Declan might think it's good fun, but I'm thinking it might be dangerous.'

'You're a sharp enough girl, aren't you?' said Siobhan. When she turned to look at Kylie, the young girl smiled, but the eyes were still penetrating, looking for answers.

'Eamon was a colleague of mine.'

'Working for the same company?'

'He was. And like anyone, when your colleague is murdered, you want to look into it.'

'Most people don't look into it,' retorted Kylie. 'Well, not in the way you're looking into it. Most people might want to find out from the police what had happened. They might phone up the old company and ask if there was anything they could do to help. But you don't. You take a housekeeper and a gardener and go digging up underneath rocks. You get messages left to you by the dead person. Did your company do a lot of that?'

The question was left hanging, and Siobhan gave a smile. 'My company did a lot of that. I don't talk about what my company did a lot. And if I tell you, you can't talk about it either.'

'Why?' asked Kylie.

'Because, Kylie, we live in the province of Ulster and the province has had its bad times. And there are certain people who would like to know what I did for a living. Although I did none of it in Northern Ireland, they wouldn't take too kindly to it if they knew. So, everything I'm about to tell you is off-limits to anyone else.'

'Why are you telling me, then?' asked Kylie.

'Because you need to be aware. You're asking questions, you're digging deep, and I don't want you to dig too deep. I'll be honest with you. At the moment, I'm getting slightly concerned that I may take you into a place that you shouldn't go. You're okay today. We're out in the open. Not much is happening. Highly unlikely that anyone watching us will look for answers from us. If there's anyone watching, they'll be keeping tabs on us.'

'You went off the other night and you came back with a bruised chin.'

'Yes, I'm a little slow. I found someone, and I chased him off, but he clocked me on the chin before I had the time to deal with him.'

'Are you serious?' asked Kylie. 'That's wild. That's wild talk.'

'I can see why you'd think that.'

'You had us out in a bay digging up things and yet you disappeared off and left us there. I mean, Declan's not going to be much help for me, is he?'

'You weren't in danger, and besides, you'd cuddled up together.'

'I didn't appreciate that either,' said Kylie.

'Eamon was a close colleague and I need to find out why he's dead, so I need you to come with me. But I won't bring you into anything that's dangerous.'

'Were you some sort of spy?' asked Kylie suddenly.

'Operative is the word,' said Siobhan. Although, in her head, spy was probably more accurate. For she had been a spy. 'I worked in many places around the world, Russia being the main one, but also many others.'

'Can you speak Russian?'

'Fluently, and a few other languages. I used to be out in the field, but for the last ten or fifteen years, I've been what they call an analyst. Looking at situations, making plans, not actually being out there. I used to run like the wind. I used to handle myself in a fight and I used to not get caught with a sucker punch like that.

'You get older and when Andrew died, I thought I would come back and try to leave it all behind. But this came up. There was a mark there that Eamon would have left for me back in the day. To show he'd left something. And there is something. And now he's left me a cryptic note. I'll find out what Eamon was doing. And if need be, I'll do something about it.

'And then I will settle down into looking out at that sea every morning that separates Northern Ireland and Scotland. Enjoying the occasional days of sunshine. Enjoying the days of rain. Pottering around the house. I'll maybe take up boules. I'll maybe take up some other sport. Maybe golf. Who knows? I may go dancing. Basket-making, I don't know. I will settle down and be happy. And you won't have to worry about people coming after you. You won't have to worry about being hauled here, there, and everywhere in the middle of the night.'

'That makes a lot more sense,' said Kylie, and started concentrating simply on the road ahead. Her questions were done.

I've just told her I was a spy. I've just told her I'm currently chasing down the killers of my murdered colleague, and she just seems satisfied. Siobhan laughed inside. Then she felt slightly mischievous.

'What do you think of Declan?'

'He's a talented gardener. Knows what he's doing with those plants because you clearly don't. You and plants are about as far apart as the Loyalist and Republican paramilitaries. I can see why you brought him in. You want a pleasant garden, but you don't want to spend time doing it. You're not that sort of hands-on person, taking the time with the plants. I'm in the house because you don't want to be bothered with the housework. Did you have a housekeeper elsewhere?'

'I had one when I was home. When we were away, we could get that sort of thing paid for. Seemed to have more time as well. And I never enjoyed washing. I never enjoyed doing all the chores of the house. Guess I got used to not doing most of them.'

'And that's why you got me,' said Kylie. 'I mean, it's your money. Fair do's if that's what you want to do with it. But you strike me as someone that needs the excitement. You had a husband and yet you were off round the world being an operative. That's what you said, wasn't it?'

'But back to my original point. What do you think of Declan?' countered Siobhan.

'I think he's trustworthy. He's a bit loud at times.'

'No. I mean, what do you think of him?'

Kylie looked away, out the other window, before flicking her head back several times to watch the road. 'I don't know what you mean.'

'I didn't come up the Lagan in a bubble,' said Siobhan. 'I can see it. The guy is desperate for you. "Oh, Kylie, let me walk you here. Oh, Kylie, let me get that for you. Is Kylie all right?" Stuff the fifty-year-old woman who's paying his wages. As long as Kylie's all right. More than happy to protect you the other night.'

'He was not protecting me. You told us to do an embrace, we did it. It was just cover for whatever.'

'Maybe for you.'

'Don't!' said Kylie. 'Don't.'

'He is nice, though. He's got a splendid physique on him.'

'Yes, he does,' said Kylie. And then she went quiet, her cheeks going slightly red.

'You don't have to tell me,' said Siobhan. 'It's up to the two of you what you have.'

'We have nothing! Now enough. Did you ever think about aerobics?' The sudden change of conversation gave Siobhan a start.

'Not really. Why?'

'I was doing some the other day. Slightly different from what I normally do.'

Siobhan sat back in her seat as Kylie talked away about the new workout routine she'd been doing. Siobhan wasn't even vaguely interested. Instead, in her mind, the poem was going through her head.

'By the waterfall, in the sun's pale light, you fell for me in a trilby and suit. But the wind was cold and howls at night, where we used to listen to whispers abroad.'

Whispers abroad? Where were they listening to whispers abroad? So many places, she thought. *We eavesdropped on people so often it was a routine part of the game. 'The wind was cold and howling at night,' that could be most of blooming Russia. What was he at? What were you thinking, Eamon?*

Siobhan tugged at the turtleneck of her jumper that left her neck bare and she put her hand up, rubbing it across the base. As she did so, she realised that was what Eamon used to do. She would sit cross-legged in front of him, he sitting with his bum on the ground behind her, an arm around and a hand rubbing her neck. Always gentle. And then he would lean in and whisper in her ear.

They were good times. He was a good friend and an

excellent lover. She needed to do this. And then maybe she'd take up Kylie's blasted aerobic workouts. After all, she had to do something in her retirement, something other than this.

Chapter 09

Dunseverick Falls was located just off the Causeway road. There were several sheep grazing in the fields nearby as Siobhan and Kylie wandered across to the main part of the falls. It was stunning, absolutely stunning, considering you were looking at water that had little height to it. And yet, it was almost as if the falls were insignificant.

You could drive past on the road easily without seeing them. But when you walked over, the simple runs dropping to the shoreline just seemed to ease away everything, leaving you in awe. Siobhan looked around in what was fairly grey light at the beauty before her. There were several other people milling about, but unlike some places along the Causeway road, this wasn't the busiest.

Siobhan gazed out across the falls and wondered just where Eamon would have buried something. 'By the waterfall, in the sun's pale light.' It wasn't sunny today, which was a problem. Siobhan tried to work out where the light would come from. Just where would it fall?

It wasn't unusual for an operative in a foreign land, or indeed at home, to leave details of what they were doing secretly. Somewhere that only an ally could pick them up.

Detail them in a cryptic notion in case someone found the message. Eamon had been caught out and paid for it with his life. But he clearly had stashed somewhere detail about what he was looking into, and now that detail would need to be found by Siobhan.

Meanwhile, Kylie was traipsing her way across the falls, trying to skip past here and there, across the loose rocks. She was gradually descending to the sea. Siobhan thought the items would be buried under the ground, higher up. Less chance of them going missing. She scanned to see if there was anywhere that showed recent digging, but she could find nothing.

'So,' said Kylie, approaching her, 'where would you be looking for said items?'

'Said items? I don't know if he's dug into the ground. I don't know if he's hidden them in plain sight, or if there's some other clue.'

'You don't know a lot,' said Kylie.

Kylie was getting on Siobhan's nerves. If you'd said that to Declan, Declan would have begun a search. Kylie was much more questioning about what you were doing. Siobhan was also feeling cold, for she'd left her jacket inside the car, currently standing in her jeans and baggy rollneck jumper. She could feel the chill across her face, and it was seeping in through her meagre protection.

Siobhan stumbled down the falls to the beach and stood looking back up. She wore her hiking shoes, or at least the modern equivalent that weren't used for hiking, but walking around town, a fashion-savvy version. The water was running round them, but she wasn't worried, for they were waterproof. She crouched down, and Kylie crouched beside her.

'What are we doing?'

'I'm scanning. I'm looking for anything unusual.'

'Like what?' asked Kylie.

'Anything unusual.'

'How do you know if something is unusual?' asked Kylie.

'I know it when I see it.'

Kylie stood up and walked away again. Siobhan spotted a family making their way across the top of the falls and down to the other side. She ignored them. There was a man further up. He kept glancing over at her, so she deliberately walked up towards him and got close. He smiled, said hello, and then turned away.

This happened a lot, or at least on a reasonably regular basis, when you're out in the field. It was that daily occurrence when people would look at each other. Those little moments in life when they see a pleasant face they like, or maybe a figure, and they just acknowledge it. The brief nod, the little hello. It said a lot. It said enough to be part of songs that were written. And it made Siobhan feel good about herself. It wasn't necessary, of course. She had confidence. She'd been a spy for long enough. One thing the job required was confidence, touched with a good deal of self-awareness. Knowing your faults and knowing how to protect against them.

'Siobhan, come here a minute,' shouted Kylie from the other side of the falls. Siobhan hobbled down, watching her footing as she rounded across the beach over to the far side where Kylie stood looking up the hill.

'What is it?' asked Siobhan.

'Under my foot,' Kylie stepped back. 'Do you think that could be something?'

That's a farmer's installation. That runs up to the water tap at the end,' said Siobhan. 'So no, it's not unusual. It's just part of what would be out here.'

'Only trying to help,' said Kylie. 'I tell you what, though. That man at the top's watched you the whole way across here.'

'I know,' said Siobhan. 'I think he's taken a liking to me.'

Kylie nearly burst out laughing. 'Why would he look at you?' she said.

'I'm fifty. I'm not dead,' Siobhan spat back.

'Well, he's not looking at me,' said Kylie.

'He probably wants a woman, not a girl.'

Siobhan stormed off up the hill. If Kylie was going to speak like that to her, she'd soon be out of employment. Siobhan stood at the top, looking down again before she walked back to the car. Five minutes later, Kylie plodded in beside her.

'Is that us,' she said.

'No, drive for ten minutes somewhere, then come back.'

'Why?'

'I need to reset. I need to come at things from a different angle.'

'You're not for real, are you?' said Kylie. 'What's going to be different? It's falls, it's got water. It's not big, and there's a beach. Yes, I'm sure some people find it really nice. But at the end of the day, he has left nothing here.'

'He has left something.'

'Why are you assuming it's here? What did it say in it? It said, "by the waterfall where the sun shines."'

'No, it didn't. It said, "by the waterfall in the sun's pale light. You fell for me in a trilby and suit. But the wind is cold and howls at night where we used to listen to whispers abroad."'

'Whispers abroad, "we" used to listen. That's you and him, isn't it?'

'Could be figurative,' said Siobhan. 'He would have liked it here, Eamon. But drive, please.'

Kylie sighed. She switched on the radio, started the car and took off down the road. There was some sort of pop music on and Siobhan switched it off.

'Hey.'

'Hey, nothing—I'm working.'

There was tension in the air. Siobhan couldn't be bothered with it. She was thinking. She was trying to get to what was being said by Eamon. Kylie took the car about four miles down the road before turning and coming back to the falls. She parked up in just about the same spot, but facing the other direction.

Siobhan didn't wait and got out straight away, this time taking her jacket, zipping it up and going to the top of the falls again. She sat down. There were dribbles of rain in the air, and she saw Kylie arrive beside her a couple of minutes later. The girl was in a large jacket. She had gloves on, but she also had a bag. She opened it up, took out a flask before making a cup of Lapsang Souchong and handing the plastic lid-cup of the flask over to her employer.

'Thank you,' said Siobhan, taking the cup without looking, but sipping it instantly.

'How do you do this, then?' asked Kylie.

'I need to think like him.'

'He was your colleague, though.'

'Yes, and I need to think like him,' said Siobhan.

'But you could call Declan my colleague. I couldn't think like him. An idiot.'

'He's not an idiot. Just young. He's just keen. Keen on you.' Kylie turned her face up. 'Think like the person because you know who they were.'

'What do you mean, "know who they were?"'

'Eamon would have come here and the first thing that would have caught his eye would have been the water, not the fact that it's a waterfall, but how even it is. You're not drawn to one spot, it's the total effect. The calming presence of it. The endlessness of it. Continuing over and over. You can feel it soothe your soul. You can feel it . . .'

'Siobhan, you said this guy was a colleague, didn't you?'

'Yes, he was.'

'And you guys were spies.'

'We were operatives. We worked together.'

'Did you get into any dangerous situations?'

One or two, thought Siobhan, but she answered, 'On occasion.'

'Well, I take it you'd have had to lean on each other quite a lot.'

'Yes,' said Siobhan.

'And from the picture, he looked, well, he was reasonably attractive, wasn't he?'

In his day, he was stunning, thought Siobhan. *That chin, the way it jutted, the way he turned and looked at you with those eyes. The photo fit they had up of him didn't do justice to his eyes. Didn't do justice to the way he anticipated your need. Was always there. Didn't do justice to the way his arms rubbed your shoulders. The way his hand came round across your neck.* For a moment, Siobhan felt herself drifting.

'We got to know each other to a point,' said Siobhan.

'I think there was a bit more than that.'

Siobhan turned her head, staring at Kylie. 'What is that meant to mean?'

'He's dead. It's from the past, a long time ago. But he's left you a message. Why you? Why now? If he's still an operative, or if he was still an operative at that time, why would he leave it to you? I mean, you're retired. You're not in that Service. If he's doing something for the Service, he's going to talk to the people in it. He's surely going to have support. Why talk to you? He no doubt knew you were in Northern Ireland, so why didn't he drop by and say, "Look, Siobhan, I'm doing this; why don't we pop up together?" Or does he know that your husband's not long dead and doesn't want to intrude?'

'He knew Andrew and I were nothing.'

It had just popped out. Like Siobhan had felt she needed to defend her actions, but Kylie didn't know what those actions were. She insinuated that something of that ilk was going on, but she didn't know for sure. There was no need to defend the action. Defending it confirmed it.

'Well, if he knew that you and Andrew were nothing, that meant that you were close. You must have talked. Talked that special talk,' said Kylie.

'What do you know about special talk?'

'You might be older, but I've been there too. You know that. That bit where you say things. And I guess you would have had to talk about others in your life when you got that close.'

'You're wasted as a housekeeper,' said Siobhan. 'You read people well, Kylie. We were lovers, but that was a long time ago. Twenty years-plus. Andrew was happy enough with what he was doing. And I didn't really care because I was out doing what I wanted to do. Andrew and I were complicated. Or maybe we were actually simple.' Siobhan laughed. 'Two people that got married then realised that they didn't really want to be together but were happy enough because our lives never were together. But rather than create all the hassle, we just get on with it.'

'So where would he be planting this stuff?'

'Not here,' said Siobhan. 'Ultimately not here. He wouldn't ruin it. He wouldn't come here. This would be a place of solitude. This would be a place of calm. Not like the Causeway. The Causeway is expansive. This is small. It's tranquil. It's a haven away from everything. And it's somewhere you can pop to in a couple of minutes.'

'Well then,' said Kylie. But the next thoughts that she said were not picked up on by Siobhan. Across the falls, there was a man. He had looked at her several times. She stood up and walked a little, surprising Kylie, who followed. He was looking, and he was doing his best not to show it. She'd seen enough tails in her time. This was a tail, a tail looking for her. Not that look of a hopeful romantic.

'So where would that mean he would leave it?' asked Kylie.

'I didn't hear a word that you said. Sorry. Lost in thoughts,' said Siobhan. 'Shall we get some lunch?'

'If that's what you want,' said Kylie. 'Suppose we can always come back again. Nothing's going away after all.'

Chapter 10

'Are you all right?' asked Kylie.

'I'm fine,' said Siobhan. She had pulled down the sun visor in the car, flipped up the little opening for the mirror and was watching the road behind.

'But I'm doing the driving,' said Kylie. 'You don't need to look behind.'

'I'm just checking I look all right.'

Kylie seemed distracted and suddenly reached down, pulling her phone from her pocket, and handed it to Siobhan. 'Who's that?' she said.

'Declan,' said Siobhan, looking at the message. 'He's asking how we're getting on; wants to know if he can help. Why is he messaging you?'

'Does he have your phone number?' asked Kylie.

'Yes,' said Siobhan.

'Oh.' Kylie looked somewhat disappointed. 'I thought he was messaging me because that was the number he had.'

'No, he's messaging you by choice. I'm telling you, that boy has got the hots for you.'

'We're not talking about that,' said Kylie. 'Anyway, where do you want to go for lunch?'

Siobhan had given no thought to it, but she'd need to be somewhere open. Somebody was tailing her, and she wanted to find out who.

'There's a place further on down here.'

'Take me to it,' said Siobhan, not understanding where Kylie was talking about.

'Do you not want to know what type of food they do?'

'Sure,' said Siobhan.

'You'll probably get like fish and chips, stew, that sort of thing. Wheaten bread. Do you like wheaten bread?'

Siobhan hadn't eaten wheaten bread in years. It's one thing she missed from home. That and Veda bread, the malty loaf that they used to get. It was great toasted and buttered.

'Go there then,' said Siobhan, thinking that she could always say no if she wasn't happy with the venue. Open, that's what she needed.

It took five minutes before Kylie pulled up at a very modern, open-looking building. From a distance, Siobhan thought that the eating area had a lot of visibility. There were no pokey corners. There were a lot of tables and it all looked busy, but you could almost see through from the outside sitting in the car.

'This is perfect,' said Siobhan. 'Come on.'

She stepped out of the car, leaving her jacket behind, and let Kylie follow her in. It was one of those self-service, almost garden, centre-style eateries, but the food looked good.

'Have what you want. I'll get it,' said Siobhan, and she grabbed a tray and ordered steak and kidney pie for herself. She forced herself to have rice with it and not chips. Though the chips looked good.

Sitting down with Kylie and looking at Kylie's salad with a

little despair, Siobhan tucked into her meal, but her eyes were everywhere around the room.

'I shouldn't have given Declan my number. He asked for it. I thought it was to do with us coming up here. I didn't realise he just wanted to pester me on it.'

'Pester's a bit of a strong word,' said Siobhan. 'You shouldn't get so worried when a man likes you.'

'I've had five messages today asking how we are. He's got a flipping garden to do.'

'Indeed,' said Siobhan, glancing around again.

'It's a wonder he didn't try anything the other night when you made the two of us act like we were some sort of couple.'

'Indeed,' said Siobhan.

'Are you listening to me?' said Kylie.

'Yes,' said Siobhan, almost nonchalantly.

'You are not.'

'When you've something useful to say, I'll take it in properly. Until then, continue with your boyfriend troubles.'

'I haven't got boyfriend troubles.'

'It sounds like it.'

Over there, far table, thought Siobhan. *Two of them. Meant to look like a happy couple. Looking like anything but it. There's no touching of hands. No smiling. There's no nothing between them. Even husbands and wives who've been out together and whose fire maybe has died off still have something. There's still the odd little connection. These two have nothing.*

'I'll just eat my salad then,' said Kylie.

'Good,' said Siobhan. 'I was thinking, I'm not sure you are insured on the car.'

'What?' blurted Kylie.

'I said I'm not sure that you're on the car insurance.'

'And what, you just thought you'd drop that bombshell after driving all the way up here? If we'd had an accident, I would have been screwed.'

'I'd have been screwed as well, probably. You have my permission to drive. Do you have any insurance of your own?'

'I don't have a car at the moment, so no.'

'We'd have been screwed,' said Siobhan. 'Good job we haven't been. I'm going to phone Declan. Tell him to bring his car up.'

'It's a long way up. I could always get the bus back.'

Siobhan grimaced. There was no way she was letting Kylie go off on her own. Any decent agent or operator worth their salt would see that Kylie was nobody, and she'd let them go. But just in case, she didn't want her to be on her own. If Declan brought the car up, they could drive straight back to Donaghadee. He could drop her at the house, stay there with her until Siobhan got back later. He would just be doing his work. Although, in fairness, by the time he got up and back, it could be a while. Siobhan picked up her mobile phone and dialled Declan's number.

'You don't have to bring him up all this way.'

'Of course, I do. It's not right leaving you up here.'

'Why are you leaving me up here, anyway? Can't you just drive home? Why are we bringing Declan up?'

'Because I'm staying.'

'Why?' asked Kylie.

'Don't ask, please.'

Kylie started looking around her.

'Don't do that either. At the very least, just drink your drink, eat your salad, and shut up. Don't start looking around as if something's up.'

'Have you seen something?' asked Kylie.

Siobhan remembered the days when she was out on her own, doing this type of work. She could blend in anywhere. Nowadays, it might even be easier. She didn't look like the young filly running around, a strange sight on the Moscow streets. She'd had to go wherever the Moscow younger style were going, to whatever shops they were going to, even though she was not interested in the slightest. Middle-aged women had much more latitude; they just did what they did; they had a confidence about them that said we have our own style; we're not interested in what you think.

Nowadays, Siobhan did like fashion in the sense that she had her own, and she would maintain her own style. She'd shop where she wanted. But Kylie was a dead giveaway.

'Oh, Declan, good to hear from you. You've been worried about us and I think you need to come up. No, no, we're not in panic stations at the moment. We're at an eatery,' Siobhan gave the name. 'Come up here. We're just having a bit of lunch. Grab a sandwich on the way for yourself. Well, it's just a bit of a difficulty, that's why. No, it's not a problem, but I'd like you up here. Okay, see you soon.'

Siobhan put her phone away and Kylie stared over at her.

'Eat up, keep eating. You're going to have some pudding as well.'

'I'm not hungry for pudding.'

'You will be because it's going to be a while before Declan gets here. Even if he drove like a bat out of hell, it'd take him an hour and a half.'

Siobhan tucked into her steak and kidney pie, and it was tasty, but she wasn't thinking about the flavour. She was thinking about the trilby and suit comment. The sun's pale light as well. Why? It made no sense out there. Why would there be a trilby and suit around Dunseverick? Had she got the right place?

She had noticed nobody tailing her to Dunseverick. The people had been there the second time. She hadn't clocked them the first. Was that because she was slack? No, she wasn't that slack. They weren't that good in fairness; she spotted them easily. She'd have got them the first time round. Wouldn't she? She hadn't been out in the field recently. She hadn't been out in the field for a very long time.

No, Dunseverick was right. She felt it. They'd talked about it. Eamon would have loved it. And now he was here. He'd have popped along to it, wouldn't he? He'd have known that she would have guessed where it was. She would have remembered the conversation.

That's what they were good at, operatives, remembering conversations, recalling bits and pieces. They taught you that. They taught you to take the unique fact about the other person. That unique connection between the two of you and make something of it when you wanted to communicate. It would be like a code, a personal code, unbreakable because they'd have to know everything about you. They'd have to know you'd talked about Dunseverick, and it was miles away from Russia.

So, people being there, spotting her; if they hadn't had come with her, if they hadn't followed her there, they must have seen Eamon there. Had they? But now they were on to her. She'd have to shake them. There's no way she'd shake them if Kylie was driving. There was no way she'd shake them if Declan was driving. Would they follow them? Hopefully not. That could complicate things. Still, it would be a while.

'How's Declan on your car insurance?' said Kylie.

'What?' asked Siobhan.

'You said Declan was on your car insurance. He was driving the other day.'

'I'm not sure he is, but he's got his own insurance. He drives his own car. At least he would have been third party. He was driving with my approval. You haven't third party cover so it won't work you driving.'

'Why are you staying up here? asked Kylie.

'Let's get some pudding.'

The two women stood up, made their way over to the serving area again, and Siobhan took a large piece of apple pie. She took cream with it, sat down and mixed it all in together, like she would have done when she was a kid. Kylie looked positively disgusted and sat with her large piece of cheesecake, delicately picking bits off at a time. Part of Siobhan wanted to tell her just to stick her food in and eat it properly, but it meant things were going slowly and that wasn't a bad thing until Declan arrived.

Siobhan looked over again at the couple that weren't, and they were still there. They were still looking. There was another group of four people who had been in for a long time. Tourist-like, except they weren't. Tourists sat talking to each other, excited. These four were all looking around. You could understand one of them being bored looking off, but they were on holiday. They were on holiday and they were of an age where you would go on holiday together, friends. It wasn't a family with the rather belligerent parents just thinking we've got to feed the kids.

Instead, these people were looking around. She had at least six people on her tail. *Bugger*, thought Siobhan. *Six. Losing a couple would be hard enough. Losing six?*

She looked at her watch. *Come on, Declan*, she thought. *Come on.*

Siobhan sat with another cup of tea while Kylie advised that she'd probably wet herself if she drank any more coke. But this was a waiting game. Siobhan felt like she was on display. She was the prize in the window. But she needed to wait for the door to open and get out of their line of sight.

Chapter 11

The tea in front of Siobhan was cold, but she kept lifting it up to her lips, although she drunk very little of it. Kylie looked unsettled. The conversation had stopped. Once they got beyond discussing chores for next week and teasing Kylie about Declan, the two women found they had very little in common. Kylie was clearly brooding over the fact that Declan was coming up, and Siobhan was agitated, on edge, realising that the past had come back to haunt her.

She was being followed, and she'd brought two people into this. At first, she had thought it was just a one-off, someone covering the murder scene, the place where Eamon had died. Having been there, and not intending to go back, Siobhan reckoned that the heat would be off. They'd just spotted someone at random, but now she was being followed. Of course, they hadn't tailed her to Dunseverick. Someone had been there, so the logical conclusion was that they'd been following Eamon for a while. Was it the same people that had spotted her at night on the Causeway? Too many questions, not enough answers.

It reminded Siobhan of those early days out in Russia, not

understanding who was looking at you, and who wasn't. Was it KGB? Was it the other agencies? Possibly the Americans, maybe even the Germans. She ran a lot on instinct back then. Instinct and careful observation, seeing the minor differences between genuine local people and those who were out to do harm to you.

Having been an analyst for so long, she was rough around the edges. She hadn't lost the spy craft, it just got harder to reproduce naturally. Then again, she was getting to that stage of life. When she drove the car, she was safe enough, but at times, she did some bad things. She switched off too much. Arrive at places and not know why she was there. Not realise that she'd missed her turn. She wasn't going bananas, but she just wasn't on full cylinders either. It was a strange feeling.

But here, with people watching her, it wasn't strange; it was terrifying. And she had an innocent in front of her who she needed to get out of here.

'There's not a lot to Dunseverick Falls, is there?' said Kylie.

'No,' said Siobhan, looking around before picking up her tea.

'I mean, where would you put something there? You'd need a spade. You wouldn't hide it under a rock. And what sort of thing would you be hiding? Would it be another poem?'

'Don't talk so loudly,' said Siobhan, under her breath.

'We have to look like we're talking normally,' said Kylie, 'otherwise people will know we're being suspicious. They'll realise we're talking about things that we wouldn't want them to hear.'

'But if you talk about them loudly,' said Siobhan, 'then they will hear.'

'This thing that people are looking for, do you think it's

back there?'

'I don't know,' said Siobhan. 'If I knew that, I'd either leave the place permanently, or I'd find it. It's a rather redundant question.'

'You're very eggy at the moment. It's like the cat's got your tongue too. You don't talk about it.'

'We're in an open restaurant, so I don't want to talk about it.'

'I was wondering if you got it right. If it really was Dunseverick.'

'It's Dunseverick, trust me. It's a very personal thing between Eamon and me.'

'How personal?'

'Personal,' said Siobhan. 'What are you implying?'

'I'm just trying to gauge how close the two of you were. I was watching the thing last night, that new programme, *The Johnsons*. They were talking about what he and her say to each other, and she wouldn't say them. They were very personal, apparently.'

'And?' said Siobhan.

'Well, they said them after sex,' said Kylie.

Siobhan narrowed her eyes and almost pierced the girl with her look. 'We were good colleagues,' she said. 'Good colleagues, and the business we were in, we shared things, moments, okay?'

'Whatever you say.'

'Don't give me that,' said Siobhan. 'You know nothing about what it was like.'

'Of course, I know nothing about what it was like. You won't talk about it. And yet it's okay if you tease me about Declan. But hey, go into Siobhan's past . . .'

Yes, it took two to tango, but Kylie had tangoed. What had happened afterwards was unfortunate, especially about the kid. But, that being said, Kylie had made her own bed. I'm just making it a more comfortable place to lie. I certainly didn't deserve this sort of kickback from it.

'All I'm saying,' said Kylie, 'is you might be wrong. I mean, the falls. You could go up to Tollymore, there're loads of falls up there. I mean, did you ever talk about Tollymore? Did he mean somewhere that wasn't in the province? Did he mean somewhere back . . . wherever you guys were in the world?'

'He meant Dunseverick Falls,' said Siobhan quietly. 'That's where he meant. In the pale light. The sun's pale light. And he talked about a suit. I don't know what he means at the moment. I will do, and it will take time, but it will come. Declan will be here soon, no? You won't have to worry about me.'

'What do you mean, "You won't have to worry about me?"'

'Declan's going to drive you back. I've got something else to do.'

'I need the toilet,' said Kylie, standing up. 'Look, I'm not happy about this. I don't see why you're gallivanting off.'

'Because I'm your employer, and I get to do what I want. You're paid to look after the house.'

'Apparently, I'm also paid to disappear in the middle of the night to a local tourist attraction. I didn't see you telling me then that I should go back and do your dishes.'

'Just go to the loo,' said Siobhan. She stood up and followed Kylie, who glanced back at her, angry for being followed.

They pushed through the door of the ladies' toilets and saw a row of cubicles. Kylie picked the first one, and Siobhan stepped into the second one beside her. As she did so, she heard the door open again into the toilets. Siobhan locked her cubicle and dropped quickly to the floor. She looked out and saw a pair of boots with a pair of shoes following them. One walked along and went into the cubicle at the end. Another washed her hands.

The two women who entered spoke briefly to each other, something about a programme that was on that night, but a foreign accent was there. One problem was, you were in Northern Ireland, not an easy accent to copy, if an easy one to lampoon. Lots of people could stick their teeth together and give it the old, 'How now brown cow,' but if you wanted to speak like you were local, that's not how you did it. It took time to speak without moving your mouth, like they did close to Belfast.

Further up here, yes, the mouth moved a bit more, the accent possibly a touch softer. You could go out to Ballymena, which was a whole new dialect of its own. The two women who were talking were clearly trying to do an Ulster accent and failing badly. They would have been better just speaking in a normal English tongue of some sort.

Siobhan sat down on top of the toilet seat, pondering her next move. These two were part of the team watching them, she was sure of it.

'What do you want for tea tomorrow night?' said Kylie from the next cubicle.

'Surprise me,' said Siobhan. She didn't have time to be thinking about that.

'No, seriously, do you want some chops from the butcher? You're not keen on the sausages, are you? I could get a wee bit of steak.'

'Whatever you think's best.'

'Fine, I'll get something. Oh, by the way, I also found out why a couple of those flowers at the front have had petals falling off. There's a wee hallion from down the road walks along there, and he picks them off. I was going to give him a clip round the ear, but you can't do that these days. So, I gave him a bit of my mind. Told him I'd haul him down to his mother. I don't think she's ever in. Anyway, shouldn't happen again. Just don't go blaming Declan for it.'

Sticking up for Declan, thought Siobhan. *That's interesting. She was the first one to put distance between the two of them. Maybe she's softening on him.*

Siobhan flushed her toilet, though it didn't require it. She stepped out and washed her hands. Beside her was a young woman, possibly mid-twenties. She had blonde hair, tied up at the back with a bobble hat on. Strange, since they were indoors.

Having seen Siobhan emerge, she turned back and started washing her hands again. *She's already done that*, thought Siobhan. *I heard her.*

The woman turned round and asked the woman in the cubicle where they were going next. Portrush was the answer. They knew their business. Portrush was always a suitable destination for tourists, especially later on in the day, because they could make their way to the amusements. It'd been a family tradition back when she was little. You would pop up to Portrush, and you would head into Barry's. Nowadays, it was under a different name, one she couldn't quite recall. And maybe some things had changed within, but a lot was similar. Tourists liked to race off in the morning doing something different, but by afternoon plenty of them would be there.

Portrush had good train links too. You could get from

Belfast to it. You could take the car. Plenty liked to stay in and around it, but if you were posher, you moved out to Portstewart with its long strand. The beach that went on for miles. People took cars down there. This was a massive part of the Northern Irish tourist industry, and they seemed to be aware of what their cover should say. They just didn't pull it off well.

Where the heck is she? thought Siobhan as she washed her hands. *What is Kylie doing in there?*

'Are you having trouble?' Siobhan said loudly, turning and looking at the cubicle Kylie was in.

'I'm just on the loo, for God's sake.'

'They'll have cleared away our table by now.'

'No, they won't. I've left my jacket there. Your jacket's there too. They will not haul the jackets off, will they?'

'Hurry up. People are going to think you've got trouble.'

'What?' blurted Kylie.

It was one thing that people used to say back in the day. Maybe the younger generation didn't pick up on it the same.

'I'll be outside,' said Siobhan, and she would be very near. She wasn't happy about leaving Kylie in this cubicle with two suspected operatives there with her.

'I'm just coming,' Kylie said and flushed the toilet. Siobhan stood to one side after she dried her hands, letting Kylie come out and do the same. The operative was still there. She didn't even have the decency to walk into the cubicle and pretend she suddenly needed to go. 'I'm done. All right,' said Kylie. 'Look, all better now. No trouble.'

'Come on,' said Siobhan. She opened the door, letting Kylie walk out first, and they strode back towards their table. As they got there, Siobhan could see Declan outside, his car just pulling up.

'That's Declan. Come on, time to go.'

'What? Let the guy have a drink, at least.'

'No, we need to get you back. Get your jacket.'

'Why?' asked Kylie.

'Don't mess with me. Just go. Come on. Pick it up. Your jacket.'

Kylie was fuming, but she did as instructed, and Siobhan put her own jacket on before glancing around surreptitiously. When she'd done so, she went outside to see Kylie standing beside the car. Declan looked out of his own car and smiled over at Siobhan.

'I'm here, Mrs D. Where do you want to go?'

'You're taking Kylie back to the house. I've got something I need to do.'

'That doesn't sound right. You sure you don't need me with you?'

'No, Declan. I need you to take Kylie back to the house.'

'Why?' hissed Kylie. 'We've just sat in there for ages. You hauled me out this morning to go to Dunseverick Falls. Now you've hauled Declan all the way up here just to take me back. This isn't making any sense.'

'Give my head peace,' said Siobhan. Almost too loudly. 'Get your arses into that car and go back to the house. When you're there, I want you, Declan, to stay. I'll be back later. Don't leave Kylie in the house alone until I'm back.'

'Why?' asked a frustrated Kylie.

'All right, Mrs D. If that's what you want, that's what I'll do, but you owe us an explanation.'

'I owe you nothing. Get in the car; take her back.'

'Are you in trouble?' asked Kylie.

'No, I just don't need you with me at the moment. Go.'

Kylie frowned, but Declan opened the door for her. She got into Declan's car and he spun round to his own side before turning to Siobhan. 'I'll look after her,' he said, and Siobhan saw a mature side to the man that she hadn't so far recognised.

'I don't know what's going on,' he said, 'but if you need me to take care of her, I'll do that. Won't go anywhere until you're back. I'm on the phone if you need me.'

If I need you, Siobhan thought, *I'm in trouble, big trouble.*

'Thank you, Declan. Be safe. There shouldn't be any issues, but you can lock the house if you need to.'

'Right, you go,' said Declan. Soon he was driving off with Kylie, with a scowl that would scare a grown man.

Right now, Siobhan thought to herself, *time to see just who is on me, and how important I am to them.*

Chapter 12

Siobhan got into her car and turned away onto the Coast road. Approximately half a mile away was what she wanted: Dunluce Castle. There was a small car park, one way over to the castle and no other way back out. As she pulled out onto the main road, she saw two cars beginning to follow her. As she pulled into the car park, she saw the first one driving on past, but the second one pulled in behind her.

Siobhan parked up, got out of the car, and stood around for a moment. The second car had pulled into a parking space, but nobody got out. Siobhan got back into her car for a moment, then stepped out again. There was no movement from the other car. She took her jacket, wrapped it round her, locked her car, and walked towards the small bridge that led over to the castle.

On either side was a neatly mown lawn and a stone wall encompassing it. You could imagine back in the day approaching somewhere like this, the threat it was and the difficulty of overcoming it. Now it was a ruin. But the main walls were still there, although all the roofs had gone.

Siobhan entered it and saw some excellent stonework, wild patterns of shaded greys born from the ages. There was grass on the inside too, all neatly cut. When you stepped into the main building, you were walking across a floor made of different flat stones with the odd gully. This would have been for cleaning back in the day. The walls beside it were old, some of them lower than others, worn from weather and from people climbing on them. Although the day was dark, the sea beyond still looked foreboding.

As she reached the end of the castle, the part closest to the water, she could look down and see the cliff side. It ran, grass covered out to the water until a large rock stretched out into the sea. This was surrounded by little clumps that broke up the wild water. The sea churned back and forward as Siobhan turned to look back through the castle.

There were several people about, although it wasn't busy. The trouble with an attraction like this was that if it was cold and certainly wet, people didn't hang about it long. She did, however, see the two women who had been in the toilet. Siobhan wandered about, through this passageway and that, remaining as the rain fell.

One woman was wearing a pink bubble-like jacket with a white scarf on. She was wearing the bobble hat back in the toilet too. If she was an agent, she really had done little to change her image. She was either very amateur, or she didn't care. If she didn't care, Siobhan could be in trouble.

Siobhan walked to a part of the castle where she could look up at the car park. She saw the second car, the one that had driven off, initially ignoring Dunluce Castle. It had turned back round and now was in the car park. There would be someone covering her exit.

At the moment, the public was still here, so what was their plan? Siobhan could feel her stomach beginning to churn.

What had she got herself into? Well, she didn't know, did she? That was the problem. How did she treat this tailing of her? People who were just keen to know what she was up to, or an actual threat?

Siobhan wandered around, glancing at the signage that told the story of Dunluce Castle. It occupied a headland built between the 15th and 17th centuries and was there to protect the sea routes of North Ulster. She read the names of the McQuillins, the McDonalds, but they meant very little to her.

Dunluce Castle meant a holiday spot. Somewhere they would visit every time they came up towards Portrush. Maybe for half an hour, maybe for an hour, but in earlier days, this is where she would be. She remembered travelling in the car, picnicking in the boot. All the joys of home and yet this dramatically placed castle was always a favourite. It seemed bigger back then, but then again, she was a lot smaller.

And there it was. She was drifting. Back in the day, she never would have drifted. She'd have been focused entirely on the four people, who at this point in time were walking around her, watching her from a slight distance. Were they waiting to find a spot where there would be no other tourists? Aiming to kidnap her? Were they aiming to do something worse? It was time for Siobhan to be more positive about what was happening and not just wait for it to occur.

Siobhan strode here and there about the castle. It wasn't the biggest and it wouldn't be that easy to get yourself in a part all alone with one of them. She walked towards the larger keep, walking around the interior, disappearing through one entrance to a room and then into another. Her mobile was out, as she surreptitiously took pictures of her tail. She moved at speed, gradually seeing the four tailing her reduced to three, to two, and finally to one. The others were still about and as she stepped through one passageway, she walked into one, almost bumping into him. Siobhan apologised and kept moving.

It took her another minute to lose that tail and to only have one still on her. She was now towards the outside wall of a castle. She could see a small window that led down to the beach below. It would be quite a fall, but it was a gap and at the top of it was an iron bar fixed in the wall, on either side of the window. It ran across the top. Was it there for support? Who knew? But Siobhan reached out for it quickly, pulling at it. It was strong and was not going anywhere. She doubled back quickly just as one of those tailing her walked into the room.

It was the woman in the pink bubble coat with the hat, but she also wore a white scarf around her. As she strode into the room, Siobhan grabbed her scarf, pulling it towards her and throwing an elbow up into the woman's face. The woman was shocked, stumbling when Siobhan had grabbed the scarf, pulling it tight.

Siobhan wrapped a knot in it and then she hit her again, with an elbow to the face. Siobhan never punched well, but elbows were pointy. They were awkward and they hurt if you hit around the nose.

The woman's nose was bloody, but Siobhan wasn't stopping. She grabbed the woman by the hair underneath the bobble hat, pulled her across and drove her face down into the stones at the window. She reached up with the scarf, tying it quickly around the top bar while the woman was stunned. Unceremoniously, she picked her up by the knees and flung her forward. The woman fell and then was left hanging by the scarf.

The arms came out flailing, legs kicking towards the wall. *She won't die*, Siobhan thought. In time, she could probably get herself back up. Siobhan's purpose was not to kill her, but merely to draw the attention of the others.

Siobhan made for the door she'd entered through and stepped into an open room. She saw two of them, and Siobhan fled, hurrying, but never running. She thought at least one of them had run towards the other woman. Then there was a cry, and the one tailing her peeled off. *Good*, thought Siobhan, except it probably meant that the front entrance was covered.

There was one way in, across that bridge. It had a moat on either side with a reasonable fall. She could have thought about exiting, running down the side somewhere from the castle, but it would be tricky. She could have run up the side, but there was nothing to say that she wouldn't be spotted. As difficult as it would be, she'd have to face them. Whoever was on that bridge would have to be confronted.

It wasn't long before she reached it, and sure enough, standing, looking to one side, was a man in a large grey duffle coat. She recognised him. He'd been in the restaurant.

The key thing was not to stop. She glanced quickly around her. There were no other tourists. That meant the man could act in whatever fashion he wanted. Siobhan had hoped there'd be a couple walking across the bridge. She could have used them for cover, bumped into them, and snuck past the man. But no, he was just there. And as her feet echoed on the wooden slats of the bridge, he turned to stand across it. His right hand was holding a knife.

Never stop. Don't give him time to think about it. Don't give him time to plan his action. Siobhan strode straight at him. She stared, snarling slightly from her mouth. Although she was never good at showing anger in that way, her anger was usually wilder. How long had it been since she'd taken somebody on hand to hand?

She'd done a bit of training but it was over five years ago. She wouldn't be the way she had been back in the day. Someone like this wouldn't have been a problem. She reached into the pockets of her jacket. In the right-hand one was a banana. Siobhan had taken it earlier on in the day, thought she might eat it, but now it was slightly the worse for wear. She reached inside, removed it from the jacket, but kept it behind her, letting the man see her arm was in an unusual position. Clearly, she'd have something to throw.

She was still coming at a pace across the bridge. Siobhan could see him tense, waiting. She launched the banana at his head. Instinctively, he put his hands up. By the time the fruit had hit him in the hand, and he'd realised he'd been attacked with a rather dire piece of fruit, Siobhan was up close. The knife was up high across his face, where the banana had struck him on the hand as he protected himself. She drove an elbow into his side, pushing him towards the wooden banister on one side of the bridge. She reached down without hesitating, grabbed his leg, and yanked it as hard as she could upwards. He tipped over the top of the bridge. The knife dropped out of his hands as he desperately tried to hang onto the banister. Siobhan finished the throw, letting his legs go straight up. He cartwheeled over the top of the banister and held on briefly, sliding down to the bottom before then falling.

Siobhan didn't stop. She wasn't bothered. He had pulled a knife on her. If anybody from the public had seen, they'd have witnessed the knife, and this man certainly wouldn't want to get caught. Having to explain to the police what he was doing with the knife would open up a can of worms. She'd been the same in Moscow. You never wanted to get picked up, especially holding a weapon.

As she approached the car park, she saw a man step out of one of the tailing cars and look over towards her. She could see his calculating face. He was adding up the odds of what was going on. Was the tail still in place, or wasn't it?

She would have to walk past his car, be close to him before getting into her own. Behind her, they would run out soon. They'd have to undo the scarf. The man who had tipped over the side might crawl back up, might come running. She needed to use the confusion of the driver. He was standing with the car door open, and Siobhan checked the car park. There was no one else there. Would he do something? Would he react quickly, or would he watch? It would depend on what his brief was.

As she got closer, he stepped inside the car, closed the door, readying the car so he could follow her. She turned and walked towards his car, knocking on the window. He rolled it down, clearly unaware of what had happened, unsure where his colleagues were. He wasn't ready to break cover yet.

'Excuse me,' said Siobhan. 'See over there.' She pointed out of the passenger window of his car, and he turned, looking that direction. She reached down, grabbed the keys that were in the ignition, and went to turn away.

'Oi,' shouted the man, and the car door opened. He started to get out, and Siobhan turned and threw herself against it, slamming the door hard. The door hit his chin, and he was momentarily stunned. She took the keys and threw them over the outer wall towards the main road. Then she ran for her car.

Once inside, she started it, driving off quickly. There was somebody coming up from the bridge, but the man in the car park had also come out from behind his car, looking to jump in front of her. He was calculating whether she would stop. Well, she wasn't going to. He realised this slightly too late, and she clipped him as he tried to jump out of the way.

She was out onto the Coast road and away, her heart pumping hard. He'd drawn a knife. Just what was going on? Was that an abduction team? The man in the car had clearly not been the boss, or he would've been able to decide having seen her exit. He had paid for that, but she didn't care. Just what had Eamon got himself into, just what had he died for, and who were these people?

Chapter 13

'So now you're back,' spat Kylie, as Siobhan walked in through the door. She ignored the young girl, looking beyond her and saw Declan come out of the kitchen. 'Good, you're still here. Thank you, Declan. Happy for you to go home if you need to. You've had a long day.'

'Long day? He's had a long day. What the hell? You just dumped us. You just told us to go away. Why?'

Siobhan ignored the girl and marched through to her study before rifling through several drawers. She pulled out a mobile phone, looked down and then into the air for a moment. It was as if inspiration arrived and she dialled a number.

'You're not ignoring me. There's no way you're ignoring me after that today. Is there something wrong with you? Are you off your rocker?'

Siobhan put her hand up, showing she was not fielding questions.

'That's a bit strong,' said Declan. 'Off her rocker. She asked me to come up and pick you up. She was just looking after you. Keeping you safe.'

'Exactly. Keeping me safe. Do you know who I'm being

kept safe from? Do you know who she is?'

Declan looked bemused and gave his boss a questioning look. Siobhan ignored him, closing the door on them both. She spoke into the phone. The door burst open.

'Don't you close the door on me,' said Kylie.

Siobhan slammed the door shut and continued her conversation. The door opened again.

'I said, "Don't you close the damn door on me." I don't give a toss who you are. You can't just block somebody out.'

This time, Siobhan turned and kicked the door shut. She grabbed her chair on wheels, spun it over towards the door, and then wedged it shut. The door handle flexed several times, Kylie obviously putting pressure from the outside, but she couldn't open it. Siobhan gave a smile, but there were still voices from the other side.

'Open the damn door. You're being an arse now, you're being a complete arse.'

Siobhan knew Kylie was trying to provoke her, but she didn't care. She was talking to someone, someone from the past.

'She was a spy, Declan, a proper spy. This guy who they found down at the Causeway, she bedded him. She was in deep with him, properly. He's an ex-lover. That's why she knows stuff about him, and he knows stuff about her. It's all pillow talk. It's all stuff from after they had sex.'

'What?' blurted Declan. 'Are you for real? Are you both having a laugh at Declan's expense?'

'No, I'm not pissing you about,' said Kylie. 'It's her. She's been pissing us about. She's been pretending that she's nothing; she's just a little retiree. Well, she's not. Where do you think all the money comes from? It'd be from the spy work.'

'Just a moment,' said Siobhan into the phone. She reached over, pulled the chair away, opened the door and said, 'That money came from Andrew's window business. You don't make money at the job I was in, not on that scale. Now shut the hell up. I'm trying to find something out.'

She slammed the door again, pushed the chair up against it, but the handle kept turning.

'Sorry,' said Siobhan into the phone, 'please continue.'

There was some more banging, and then Siobhan thought they'd stormed off. She closed down her call a few minutes later. It had only taken this long because she had sent a photograph and uploaded files for the man on the other end to do some identification.

She wasn't sure of his real name, but his nickname was Faces, and he knew everybody. That was his job. He assessed everything, and if he didn't know a face, it probably couldn't be known. The fact he'd responded so quickly meant that these faces were certainly not under deep cover. She snapped the phone that she'd used in half, pushed the chair back from the door, opened it and walked outside into the hallway, looking for her employees. They were now in the kitchen.

'Oh, now you come out; now your little phone call's done.'

Siobhan walked over to the bin, and dropped the phone into it.

'That's not good for the environment,' said Declan.

'What's not good for my environment is people banging on doors when I'm trying to make a serious phone call and discover what's going on. Now would the two of you sit down and shut up.'

'No,' said Kylie, 'I've been telling Declan who you are, all about it. You need to level with us. You need to tell us what's going on.'

'Yes,' said Declan, 'I want to know all about him, about what he did, how he lured you into bed, what was said. I'm right behind Kylie, completely.'

The man was now standing behind her. He had his hands on her shoulders, and he was close. Siobhan got the idea he was doing this for more than just his own intrigue.

'Keep it in your pants, Declan,' she said. His reddening face showed she had scored an obvious hit. 'And as for you, stop being a drama queen,' she said to Kylie. 'It's not an episode of those programmes that you watch. This is my house, and I am a former spy. I am in the stushie at the moment and need to think. I also need to gather information. In the meantime, I'm trying to keep the two of you safe, so shut up and let me get on with what I'm doing. If you both sit down, maybe we can get somewhere.'

Siobhan took up one of the large stools in her kitchen. 'Are you sitting down or not?' she said.

Declan whispered into Kylie's ear. Although the young woman looked angry, she took up the stool. Declan sat down beside her, but only briefly, as Siobhan said to him, 'Go make the tea, Declan. I'm going to get some information, and then I'll come back, and I'll explain what's going on, or at least as best as I can.'

Siobhan disappeared back into her office. She opened up her floorboards, put her arm underneath, and pulled out a file. It was Eamon's file again, but there was also another one, one that pertained to Russia. She then walked through to see Declan standing beside the kettle, and Kylie still in a mood.

'When you were out in Russia, how did he come on to you?'

asked Declan.

'Declan, let me explain how this works. I'll tell you what I want to tell you. Yes, we were lovers. That's it. You're not getting how we were lovers, you're not getting details of any affairs we had, or any sexual activity we took part in. I am not in a documentary. I'm here to work out who killed the man I used to sleep with. So, I will not explain my deeds of the past, or indeed, my deeds in the here and now. You're only getting told this because I inadvertently dragged you into it, and I'm going to need you to do certain things for me to keep you safe.'

Declan seemed to swallow hard. He didn't like the words 'keep you safe'. Kylie was still glowering at her.

'Why did you send us home, though? Why?' asked Kylie. 'We could have helped you.'

'Kylie, when we had lunch, there were six people watching us.'

'What?' stammered Kylie. 'Where?'

'Table of four was sat off to your left-hand side within about ten metres of you. The other table was sat within about six metres, two people together. The foursome was two male, two female. The other was two men. Of the foursome, lady in pink had the chicken soup, vegetable soup was had by the other lady. The two men seemed to have a roast beef sandwich. Champ was had by the two men together. All were drinking coffee by the looks of it, although there may have been some fizzy juice as well.

'When we got up, and we went to the toilet, the two women followed us in. One stood washing her hands for the entire time I was sitting in the cubicle and then washed them again when I came out. She talked in a rather disappointing

Northern Irish accent and clearly wasn't from here, even though she tried to make out that she was from the province. Our compatriot, who never emerged from the toilet, was very similar. I wanted to get out of there quick, but I would not leave you behind in case anything happened. I had already contacted Declan because I needed to get you out of the way so that I could deal with them.'

'You killed them?' said Declan, a mix of horror and admiration.

'No,' said Siobhan, shaking her head. 'I didn't kill them, Declan. Dealt with them. I made sure who were the people who were following me and then I got them off my tail.'

'Did you kill any of them?'

'Declan, stop it.'

'You did then, didn't you?' said Declan, his eyes wide.

'I did not kill any of them, Declan, but I engaged them because I had to. I also got photographs of them. What I was doing in the office was sending the photograph to a person who knows faces. He has identified some of the faces for me. They are former Russian spies, young ones, but former Russian spies. I believe they work for a Russian businessman, Daniil Baranov.'

'Bullshit,' said Kylie.

'No,' said Siobhan, 'truth. Daniil Baranov. Stay there and I will get you some information about Mr Baranov because I need it to try to work out why his people are following me around.'

'It's probably got something to do with Eamon,' said Declan.

'You're a significant loss to the service, Declan. Of course, it's got something to do with Eamon, but what? Why? At the moment, we can't work out his poem. We found nothing when we went to Dunseverick Falls, so we look at it from a different angle. Now we know other people are involved. I'm going to go find and print some information. The two of you are going to sit here, have a cup of tea, and above all, not leave until I have spoken to you, and we have worked out what we are going to do.'

'You think they murdered him?' asked Declan.

'Stop being over dramatic,' said Kylie.

'Possibly,' said Siobhan. Kylie shrunk back as if she'd been chastised. 'I truly don't know. Somebody did. That's what bothers me and why I sent the two of you back here. If we have people who murder, you need to know how to handle them.'

'And you can handle them, can you?' asked Kylie disparagingly.

'I can handle myself, or go into hiding. I can also learn to avoid them, or call in other resources.'

'Thought you were retired,' spat Kylie.

'We've got a lot of Russian spies running around on UK soil. You think my former colleagues in the British Service are going to be happy with that? You think they will not help? Sure, they might take over, but they'll help.'

'And I'm just expected to just believe all this?' said Kylie.

'Previously, you were saying I was holding everything back. Now I am telling you stuff you refuse to believe. You are a loss to the Service, Kylie. You could have worked in the sceptics division.'

'What division is that?' asked Declan.

'It's just beside the division of I missed the joke. Declan, get the tea made, sit down with Kylie, and I'll be through soon. I need to get information.'

Siobhan walked to her office, sat down in front of the laptop and began typing, requesting information about Danill Baranov. She initially searched through Google, and got the generic results. She printed off the information to get an overall impression of the public life of Danill Baranov. Siobhan could then access some other sites, private ones, for a little more of his history. His criminal undertakings were available. Again, she printed these off.

'How long are you going to be?' It was Kylie, and she was outside the door.

'I don't know,' said Siobhan.

'Well, I'm gone when I finish my tea.'

'You're going nowhere,' said Siobhan. 'You can't walk away without understanding what we're in.'

'Well, tell me.'

'I'm trying to. I'm trying to find all the information I can and to bring it to an understanding. Kylie, I am not pissing you about. I am not messing about. I am probably looking after you in the best way I can. Kindly sit back down.'

'I'm just not taking this.'

Siobhan stormed over to the door, opened it, and let rip at Kylie.

'You will sit your arse down, madam. I don't care who the hell you think you are. I don't care if you think you understand everything. You're just a trumped-up little girl and if you speak to me like that again, I'll tan your backside and put your arse on the seat. Understand, I don't need to ask you to sit down. I could put you down in that seat and keep you there for weeks.'

Kylie looked slightly perturbed. She stared at Siobhan's face. Siobhan wasn't sure how threatening she looked in a rollneck jumper and jeans, but she raised her eyebrows, giving an invitation to challenge. Declan appeared in the hallway outside.

'We'll just sit down,' he said. 'Come on, Kylie. I think the least we can do is hear Mrs D out over a cup of tea.'

'Well done, Declan,' said Siobhan. 'I'll be through soon.'

Siobhan returned to the laptop, printed off more material, and then walked back to the kitchen, carrying it through about ten minutes later. Kylie looked up from her tea, while Declan pointed to one on the table.

'I didn't know whether to come through and disturb you,' he said. 'That's yours. It's probably cold by now.'

Siobhan could smell the smoky flavour and wished she'd been here for it. Instead, she took the reams of paper in her hand and dropped them in front of Kylie.

'Danill Baranov, Russian gangster, or as they say, business-man. Nasty piece of work. I'll take you through what's going on.'

Siobhan sat down, picked up her cup, took a sip, and pushed it to Declan.

'I'll take you through what's going on once Declan makes me a fresh one.' She watched him pick it up, turn, and shouted at him before he could take his next action.

'Not in the microwave. Pour it out, do the kettle. I want a proper-made cup.'

Chapter 14

ylie stared at the paper on the desk in front of her as Siobhan took various sheets and spread them out. There was a much more sombre atmosphere descending around the table. No more anger. More like a touch of shock.

'I'm sorry the two of you were involved in this. When we started out, I didn't realise it was something so deep. I thought that he'd left me a little mystery. Something small to find, pick up, maybe report back to the service. Maybe an item to get.'

'But you were a spy,' said Kylie. 'Surely you would have known.'

'Let's put this in perspective,' said Siobhan. 'I haven't seen Eamon in years. We had relations when we were out in the field together, and I was a lot younger. I thought he was dead. In my profession, you don't get to know if everyone's died. Sometimes people will fake their death. Sometimes people will be missing, presumed dead. Eamon was gone. The best word said he was dead.

'So, when I saw him actually dead, it was a bit of a shock. But when I say actually dead, I only saw a photo. I didn't see the body. So, part of doing this, I guess, was for me to confirm that it was him and he was dead, not that he had just left me a mark. Well, I may have got the answer to that. Because we were going to a scene that was cold, as they say, and that the police had already been over it, I didn't think there'd be anybody hanging about. When there was, it didn't seem like many people. At that point, I probably should have told you all to leave, but I was engaged then. I was excited. I was on the trail.'

'I think, in fairness, we'd have gone on the trail with you as well,' said Declan.

'Shush, Declan,' said Kylie. 'She's given us an apology and you're defending her.'

Siobhan gave a slight grin. 'When I went to Dunseverick with Kylie, things changed. I thought there was someone tailing us. I tried to see if they were. It turns out there were six people. I sent Kylie home because six people are a lot. I can look after myself, but looking after everyone with that going on? Difficult. I gave them the slip at Dunluce Castle. If you see a report in the paper about a man falling off a bridge or a bit of a kerfuffle, it'll probably be me.'

'You threw a man off a bridge?' said Declan. 'How?'

'How is that important?' asked Kylie. 'What on earth has that got to do with anything? Would you just stay quiet a minute!'

'I don't think you're getting the seriousness of this, Declan,' said Siobhan. 'I think you should stay here at the house.'

'What, stay at the lodge?'

'You're not staying with me,' said Kylie. 'It's small up there, Siobhan. I mean, it's grand for me, but Declan is not staying there with me.'

'It's all right,' said Declan. 'I can take care of myself.'

Siobhan raised her eyes across the table. The boy looked back, giving a glance of complete non-understanding. He could look after himself, after all. Siobhan stood up, disappeared outside for a couple of minutes, then came back into the kitchen. She held a handgun.

'Whoa,' said Declan. 'Have you got a permit for that?'

'A license, but it isn't important, Declan,' said Siobhan. 'I know how to use it. It's been a long while since I have used one, but I have it here because this is serious.'

'But the gun's always here,' said Declan.

'The gun is here to protect me from anything from the past that comes back. I guess something just came back.'

'You're worried they're going to come here,' said Kylie. 'But I—I'm at the lodge. I'm at the bed at the front. That's the nearest bed to the road. They'll come there first. How is it going to work if you're back here with the gun?'

'I'll know when they come. Don't worry about that. The two of you aren't a threat. I don't want to see you getting caught in the crossfire. Not that I'm intending for there to be any shootouts.'

'So, you want me to stay here?' said Declan.

'Ideally,' said Siobhan. 'Probably best if you stayed at the lodge with Kylie. Someone to give her some protection.'

'I'd rather you were there with the gun to protect me,' said Kylie.

'No, you wouldn't,' said Siobhan. 'Guns bring unwanted attention. Never produce one unless you know what you're doing with it. These people and these other Services, they don't kill you at random. You won't see them coming. Why leave a body when you can just knock somebody out? I want Declan with you because if they're in this house, he might get caught in the crossfire.'

'I don't have anywhere for him to sleep. It's a one-bedroom. I've got the lounge, I've got the bedroom, I've got the bathroom and the little kitchenette.'

'I can sleep on the sofa,' said Declan.

'Just sort it out,' said Siobhan. Leaving the room in a business-like fashion, she could feel herself going into that mode again. Back to the day of being an operative. Not the analyst, but the operative. She had brought out the gun to make a point. It was getting there. Until they saw something happen, the two of them would still think this was the TV. This was the movies. On her return, the other two weren't speaking.

'I hope you've sorted that.'

'He's been told he's on the sofa and he does not come into my bedroom under any circumstance.'

'Why would I come into your bedroom?'

'You know, you're a bloke.'

'Quiet,' said Siobhan. She sat down on the stool again and told Declan to warm up the cups of tea. When he'd done so, she put an array of the paper in front of her.

'Eamon was a wonderful friend,' said Siobhan. 'But he's got something to say. He's trying to communicate something with me. He thought it important enough that in his last moments before he died, he should do it. Hence, he left me the poem.

'By the waterfall in the sun's pale light, you fell for me in a Trilby and suit. But the wind is cold and howls at night where we used to listen to whispers abroad.

'The waterfall is Dunseverick. Understand that. The waterfall is Dunseverick. We spoke about it. Spoke about it after being intimate once as well. Yes, Declan. That's how close we were,' said Siobhan, noticing the boy's attention suddenly piqued. 'We have Russians involved. When they're involved, it isn't good. Eamon has paid a price for their involvement. Whatever he knew, whatever he wants us to know, is dangerous enough that he was killed for it.

'There's been nothing about working for the Service either. When I called in about the tail that was put on me, my man on the other end didn't bring Eamon up or talk about him. The Service could be fairly ignorant about this. Although if I've identified it from the news that Eamon is dead, so will they. Maybe they'll get involved. Again, not good. I need to keep you two out of it as much as possible until I can resolve it.'

'No,' said Kylie. 'That's not your choice.'

'Excuse me?' said Siobhan. 'I've just told you we have Russian people involved. I told you that Eamon paid the price of his life for information he's trying to pass on to me. You know I come armed to the teeth. I want the two of you to not be in this house in case someone comes. And you turn round and tell me you will not stay out of the way?'

'No, it's my choice. It's our choice.'

Kylie put her arm around Declan, and Siobhan shook her head. *That was mean. Let the boy make his own decision,* she thought. *Don't cuddle up to him knowing how he feels about you.* She was playing him beautifully.

'She's right, Mrs D. At the end of the day, you brought us into it and it's our decision whether to still be in it.'

'Why?' asked Siobhan.

Declan looked at Siobhan and then quickly threw a glance towards Kylie.

'Because it is,' said Kylie. 'It is our decision. We've got every right. You pulled us into it, so we're going to help you.'

'And exactly what help are you going to be?' asked Siobhan. 'Can you handle a gun? No. Do you have a clue about this lifestyle I led and about who could be involved? No.'

'I could drive the car,' said Declan.

'I can actually drive the car myself.'

'Not with the insurance thing, though,' said Declan.

'No, Declan, I made the insurance thing up. You're both able to drive my car. It's not a problem. It's fully comprehensive insurance. I just needed the two of you to not be there.'

'Right, Mrs D,' said Declan. 'Clever.'

Kylie was nearly swearing at Declan, but she was restraining herself.

'You haven't solved the poem either,' said Kylie. 'Although you slept with this man, despite the fact that he told you stuff after sex, he writes a poem and you can't identify it.'

'I identified it. Dunseverick, it's the falls there. I told you that.'

Kylie stood up behind Declan, put her hands on his shoulder, and placed her face right beside his, smiling at Siobhan. The girl knew what she was doing. She was going to take Declan along this line of the argument because in reality, he was too stupid to actually say any different. He was a likable kid. He really was. Talkative to a fault, but also friendly. Willing, but not the cleverest in the pack.

'The poem,' said Kylie. '"By the waterfall," you said it's Dunseverick. We'll have to take your word for that because we know nothing else about Eamon. "In the sun's pale light." So, it's somewhere where the sun shines, but it's at the start or the end of the day.'

'But Dunseverick is so open you will not get a beam of light,' said Siobhan.

'No, you won't,' said Kylie. 'But what if it's not about Dunseverick Falls, exactly?'

'I've told you it is.'

'No,' said Kylie. 'You've told me that the waterfall section is relating specifically to Dunseverick, so we have a location. We're in the right place. Yes? What if it's about where he's staying?'

Siobhan went to jump in. Wanted to tell Kylie she was talking nonsense. But actually, the girl was doing something very sensible. She was expanding an idea. Not hurling herself down one particular path, but throwing her mind open to possibilities. She didn't know Eamon, and maybe this was a good thing.

'What if,' said Kylie, 'there's maybe a photo in the place where he was staying? What if the light comes through the window? It would either come through in the morning or the evening. There's a window on one side and not on the other. We'll know which it is because it can only come in one.'

'That's if you're facing east or facing west,' said Declan. 'What happens if it faced north and south?'

'Declan, run with this, please,' said Kylie. Siobhan noticed she rubbed the man's shoulders as she did so.

'Okay,' said Declan. 'We got light coming in through the window. What about the suit? You think he's got a wardrobe with a suit in it?'

'Maybe he's got a photo,' said Kylie.

'This all depends on one thing, though, doesn't it?' said Siobhan. 'Where is he staying?'

'There were houses up by Dunseverick. Maybe one of

them's a guest house.'

'So, your plan of attack,' said Siobhan, 'would be what?'

'We go back up and inquire about accommodation. We see if anyone's staying there, see if anyone's disappeared recently. Did they go without paying their bill?'

'The police would have checked the area,' said Siobhan. 'Why is it that the police aren't spotting this? If Eamon had been staying fairly local to the Causeway, and Dunseverick's local enough. Given the low level of accommodation around the Causeway until you get to Portrush, Portstewart, or Coleraine, one of the bigger towns, I would say the police would have checked it.'

'That's if he's staying in a regular sense,' said Kylie. She was clutching at straws now, Siobhan could tell. Her line of thought had been good. Given that Siobhan had absolutely no other ideas, it would be something to do.

'Okay,' said Siobhan. 'We go up in daylight. We check, but we make sure that there's no one around us when we do it.'

'So, we'll take your car up tomorrow,' said Declan.

'No, Declan,' said Siobhan. 'You're going to hire a car in your name. I'll pay for it, and you'll drive.'

'So, we're in with you. We're a team now,' said Kylie.

'We're a team for the moment,' said Siobhan. 'But listen, I understand this business. I understand these types of people. You don't disobey me. When I say you get out, when I say that you go somewhere and I say you do something or I tell you to shut up, you do it and you do it straight away. Break these rules and you're not part of this anymore.'

'Deal,' said Kylie.

The girl had delight written all over her face. She was almost ready to jump up and down like an excitable school kid. She turned and kissed Declan on the cheek, bringing about a similar response from him.

'What time do we head off in the morning?' asked Declan. 'When do I move in?'

Kylie's face changed slightly. 'Sofa,' she said. 'You're not moving in. It's temporary. Only temporary.'

'Okay,' he said.

'Kylie's got the tea to make,' said Siobhan. 'Go hire a car, Declan. I'll give you cash.'

'You keep enough cash to hire a car?'

'Outside. I'll meet you there in a minute.' He left the kitchen and Siobhan started shuffling the papers in front of her together.

'Leave them,' said Kylie. 'I want to look at them. Thank you.'

'I have reservations,' said Siobhan. 'Understand that, and don't play him like that.'

'What do you mean?' asked Kylie.

'The shoulder rubbing, the close-in, making sure he followed with your line of attack even though he hadn't a clue where you were going with it. You were playing him, using his feelings for you. It was done well, but this isn't a two versus one vote, and it's not fair to him. He's going to be stopping in with you. Don't make him think that it's the first step to something else unless you're prepared to make that a reality.'

Siobhan saw Kylie's rather down-beaten face, and as she turned away, she threw back a cursory comment to uplift her.

'Did well with the poem, though. Thank you.'

Chapter 15

After Kylie had made a picnic to take with them and Declan had loaded it into the boot of his hire car, the three of them drove up to Dunseverick Falls again. The drive was over an hour but there was silence reigning. The day before, they had formed a team. Now, Kylie's reckoning was going to be put to the test. Siobhan had clarified that she didn't think they could bring a lot to the table, but Kylie had thrown in a crumb. If the crumb stuck, Siobhan could not very well deny they had helped. Declan of course, was taking on more of a physical role, shifting the picnic about and driving. Siobhan had held little hope for him being part of the intelligentsia solving the poem.

The day was bright and Declan took the car along the road past Dunseverick Falls. He drove up and down three times as the women counted the houses that were there. Close to the falls was a set of four houses, some of which had signs outside, making them available for booking. Two were occupied at the moment. Another one had what was a cleaning van outside, with the fourth one seemed unoccupied.

'These are fairly new, aren't they?' asked Kylie.

'I've been out of the country for how long and I've just taken up a new house,' said Siobhan. 'I don't have a clue.'

'No. Look at them. They're newish build—holiday homes, I guess.'

Siobhan stared at the houses. They were indeed new and were of brick construction. Double glazing on the outside, but each was modest in its size. Yes, you could fit a family in it, maybe four or five people. They looked like they had a couple of bedrooms upstairs. Maybe there were bunks shoved in a few of them so you could increase the numbers. There was no garage; however, a parking space was available at the front of the house.

'Okay then,' said Siobhan. 'You're thinking that there may be somewhere here that he stayed. How are we going to find out?'

'We get inside the houses,' said Declan.

'Thank you, Declan,' said Siobhan. She really should stop being so sarky with him. 'We know we have to get inside the houses, Declan. How are we going to do it?'

Kylie seemed stumped.

'Two of them have people in them,' said Declan. 'Okay. So, we might need to find out how long they've been there. One of them has a cleaner in it, so that would seem pretty good if Eamon had been there. Yes, it's been a week or two now, but at least you could understand that it was being cleaned. The cleaner would also know if the police had asked about it. Maybe we could just pop up and ask on the premise that we are trying to establish whether we can hire one of these.'

'Good,' said Siobhan. Declan was proving to be cleverer than she thought.

'And I was thinking, Mrs D,' said Declan, 'why don't you hang back? I could go up with Kylie. We could pretend to be a new couple, and we could talk to the cleaner. You could nip in. You're a spy after all, so I assume you know how to get inside without people seeing you.'

He's not that stupid, is he? thought Siobhan.

'What's this couple thing?' asked Kylie.

'What? We're going to go up and pretend we're brother and sister or something. That's not going to wash,' said Declan. 'Young couple checking out the house. We were driving past. We don't have to be married or anything. Just pretend we're here for a dirty weekend.'

Siobhan nearly burst out laughing. Especially because Kylie's face gave the impression that Declan suggested that this was a real occurrence. Not just some ploy to allow Siobhan to get inside the house.

'Make sure you look like a couple,' said Siobhan with a very straight face.

Declan nodded. 'She's right, Kylie. Probably best if I have my arm around you or something, or holding hands.'

'Holding hands. No arms,' said Kylie.

'We'll drive away a bit, not too far, and I'll get out,' said Siobhan. 'Best if I don't come out of the car to then go in. Just in case someone's watching. There are a few fields about. It's daylight but I can move in quickly.'

'Do you need camo gear?'

'Camo gear?' asked Siobhan.

'Camouflage,' said Declan. 'You know, maybe green army trousers or stuff.'

Siobhan looked down at what she was wearing. She had her grey jumper on, the one that had a roll-neck collar that hung down again. She was in blue jeans, along with her hiking boots. What was he expecting? She was going to nip into a house, not crawl through the fields down on her hands and knees? There was a cleaner in there and they were distracting her. That's all she needed.

'I'll be fine, Declan. I'll do the sneaking bit. You worry about doing the acting.'

'Do we use our real names?'

'No,' said Siobhan, 'just in case people ask afterwards.'

'Okay. Then I'll be Matt.'

'Matt?' asked Kylie.

'Yes. Like that film star.'

'You're Alan. She's Deborah. Okay. Alan and Debs. That's it,' said Siobhan. 'No film stars. You know, we're not a modern-day Charlton Heston here. It's not an acting role for the lifetimes. It's just distracting a cleaner while I get in. And ask her sensible, proper questions. Ones that she can give you answers to, that will also explain the history of what's going on in the house, such as, "Can we book it? Who's booked it before? Did they enjoy it? What did they feel like about it? Did they leave you a mess? Is that why you're here?"'

'I think I understand,' said Kylie.

'Good, and work as a team,' said Siobhan. 'Now up the road, Declan—drop me off.'

Half a mile away, Siobhan got out of the car and walked back towards the houses. She told them to give her five minutes and then approach the house. She had thrown her jacket on but not zipped it up, for the day was relatively warm for autumn. The sun was shining and Siobhan basked in its glow as she looked out over to towards the water. She was at one with the gorgeous coast that hugged the northeast of Northern Ireland.

She breathed in deeply. *This was home,* she thought. This

was home and yet it felt that something from away was trespassing. She had told them Eamon had asked her for a favour and she'd have to follow that through, but in truth, something was bugging her.

Russians in Northern Ireland. Why? It didn't appear to be terrorist-linked either, although she could rule nothing out at the moment. Part of her was itching to go to the Service, part of her itching to tell all, to get more resources. But she didn't know who was playing whom at the moment. Why had Eamon died?

The method of his death was brutal, but that could have been deliberate. It could have been set up by the British service or any other clandestine Service wanting it to look like an argument among paramilitaries. If they were, nobody was buying it. It's not what the papers were saying. Just a brutally murdered man.

Siobhan saw the car pass by her and sure enough, Declan parked it up and the pair got out. They were holding hands, Declan giving a smile and a laugh. Siobhan thought Kylie could do better. She'd given the boy some hope when she'd used him to make her arguments. Well, she'd have to pay the price for that. Siobhan just hoped it didn't end up in a mess.

Siobhan cut out across the field where it said a path was running. It was only a sheep trail, but allowed her to walk towards the rear of the houses. In the field behind, she checked the windows and saw no one at them, hopping a fence into the back lawn of the house. There was a small swing and a sandpit with a jacuzzi at the rear.

This was a holiday home, definitely a holiday home. The back door was lying wide open, as were the windows. It was a proper clean, by the looks of it. Siobhan entered the house to the smell of bleach. She looked down at a recently mopped floor, slipped off her boots, and carried them with her as she walked across the floor. As she reached the edge of the kitchen, she looked out into a hallway and an open front door where a woman was standing with a mop.

'Can I help you two?' said the woman. From the rear, she looked maybe in her late fifties. A woman who had obviously been cleaning for a long time, for she stood at an awkward angle. A life of manual work was not the kindest.

'Hi, I'm Matt.'

Siobhan rolled her eyes. What was he doing?

'This is my girlfriend, Shanice.'

Matt and Shanice, thought Siobhan. *Seriously?*

'We just wondered about hiring a place like this. I mean, is this one available?'

'It will be soon,' said the woman. 'It's had a problem for the last couple of months, so it hasn't been on hire. I'm just cleaning it out. It got fusty and that. There was a leak around the kitchen.'

Interesting, thought Siobhan. *Very interesting.*

But she couldn't stand there and just listen to the conversation. She needed to get about the house while the cleaner was at the front. She crept down the hall, and Kylie could see her behind the cleaner. The girl didn't move an inch of a muscle on her face and Siobhan stepped into the front living room.

There was a green sofa which matched the wall's colour. The curtains were off at the moment, maybe being cleaned. Siobhan could see several magazines and books of random sorts. There were games as well, a TV, a wide screen, board games in the corner. Everything said holiday home. There are random pictures up, none of them matching the other.

The people, all different.

Trilby and suit. Siobhan looked round at the photos. None of them showed anything like that. Would the sun come in here? She thought about the orientation of the house. It would come in here in the evening, not the morning. She went to the door of the living room, could hear the woman still talking, and shot up the stairs, treading on the outside to make sure they didn't creak. At the top, she took a left into the master bedroom.

She spun round. It was simple enough. A bed, chest of drawers, table with a mirror. There was a wardrobe too. She opened it quickly, but it was empty. No trilby and suit in there.

Then she caught the photo on the wall. It was small. There was a child at the front of the photo, but behind the child, not really involved in the picture, but walking, was a man in a trilby. He was wearing a suit. It was a shop-bought photo. Clearly, there was nothing there to say that this was anybody in the family. Siobhan took the photo and placed it inside her pocket, carrying her boots back down the stairs until she stopped halfway down.

'If that's all,' said the woman.

Siobhan crouched down quickly. She could see Kylie looking back up at her and Siobhan waved frantically, seeing the woman turn. Kylie reached forward and grabbed her arm.

'Any chance we could see inside the living room? You've been really helpful and I appreciate that you're cleaning at the moment, but if we could just pop in briefly with you.'

What was she doing? thought Siobhan, and quickly she crept back up the stairs. She heard the three of them enter the house and walk into the front living room.

'Oh, I like that sofa,' said Kylie.

'It's fairly new,' said the woman as Siobhan crept back down the stairs. The trouble now was she'd either have to leg it out the front door, but she could be seen through the window by the cleaner. She'd have to leg it past the living room, but they could turn at any moment. It'd be better if the woman was outside or if she was back in the kitchen. Siobhan would have a better exit then, although she wanted to go through the kitchen herself.

'What have they got on the telly?' asked Declan. 'Can you show us? It's just it's quite important.'

'Him and his telly. We've come away for a weekend and he wants to watch his telly.'

'Look, love . . .' said Declan.

Siobhan was halfway down the stairs now and could see into the living room. The cleaning lady had picked up the remote control and was switching on the telly. Declan had his arm around Kylie, pulling her close.

Siobhan didn't hesitate. Quickly, but quietly she got down the stairs, cut past the door of the living room where everyone had their backs to her, snuck across the kitchen and out the rear door. She popped her shoes on, tied the laces quickly and legged it out and over the fence at the back.

She then nonchalantly walked back along the track and out onto the road. When she reached the road, she stood there, looking back towards the houses and saw the pair of them come away five minutes later. Kylie spotted her up the road and the car pulled up, picking her up, and Siobhan went into the back seat.

'Shall we do the other houses?' asked Kylie.

'No,' said Siobhan, pulling out the picture of a man in a

trilby and suit. 'You were right. Sunrise, sun would have come through the window onto this picture. Man in a trilby and a suit.' Siobhan turned it over. 'There's a code on the back. Let's go have our picnic. I need to have a think about this one.'

Chapter 16

Siobhan told Declan to make his way towards Portrush and put a fair bit of distance between them and Dunseverick Falls. She was wary that people would be watching having had people previously pick them up and tail them from Dunseverick; she thought best if she was away from there. Had the Russians seen enough of her to follow her to her house? She didn't think so.

Siobhan had seen no one when she was infiltrating the Dunseverick house, but then again, people could have driven by when she was in the house. They had seen Kylie and Declan before, so a mere passing in the car and seeing the couple engaging the cleaning lady could have led to them being tailed. She was unsure but would find out eventually. She told Declan to make for Whiterocks Beach. After all, it was pleasant and there'd be quite a few people about, dog walkers and the like, others just out enjoying the brisk weather.

They got to the parking area, which was on two levels, and Siobhan pointed Declan to the lower one because there were toilets available. He said he'd take the food down to the beach, but Siobhan said no. They would eat in the car and she told Kylie to prepare the food from the car's boot. Siobhan sat in the front with the stolen picture in front of her, but turned it over and read the code on the back.

It made no sense. It was a load of letters and would need to be broken, but with what? What cipher? Siobhan pondered. Eamon and she had run a few ciphers in Russia and she'd need to remember the code replacement. Before she could get deep into it, Kylie had placed a sandwich in front of her and also a cup of Lapsang Souchong with hot water from the flask. Siobhan sat back in the car seat for a moment, sniffing the smoky aroma of the tea. She put it to her lips, almost chewing on it.

'I'm going to need to do a bit of work here, so might be best if you two did something else.'

'Probably a good idea if I look around,' said Declan.

'We don't want to go too far,' said Kylie.

'No, but he's right,' said Siobhan. 'What to do is, Kylie, you stand at the back of the car, pretend you're doing stuff in the boot, making more sandwiches, whatever. If that runs out, sit your bottom on the boot. Keep Declan in sight at all times and let him roam around the car park. Do not lose sight of him. Declan, do not lose sight of Kylie and me. If you see anything, shout.'

Siobhan sat with her head down, staring at the photo frame on her lap. The letters in front of her were standard, each one of them one of the twenty-six in the English alphabet. The order they were in made absolutely no sense. It wouldn't be a simple cipher. It wouldn't be one where you just change one letter for another. If letters were repeated, it would be a shifting code.

When they ran codes in Russia, they didn't need to have code books. They could read them, but Russia was twenty-odd years ago, twenty-five maybe. When you were running the codes all the time, it was easy. You got them in an instant. Your brain just clicked in, and you read it as you went along. Yes, it wasn't like an English sentence; it took a wee bit longer than that, but not much longer.

Siobhan stared and then put the picture with the man in the trilby and suit facing upwards onto the dash before her. She stepped out of the car and stretched. There was Declan on the far side of the car park, walking around. Kylie was sitting on the boot, watching him.

'You need something, Siobhan?'

'Resting my eyes. Just changing position.'

Kylie produced a banana to eat, but Siobhan wanted nothing to distract her. She sat down again in the car, flipped the photograph and stared at the letters. For five minutes, she didn't take her eyes off them.

Second year, she thought. *That's the second year. Has to be that code. Only Eamon and I knew it. Five in the ring, three were dead. It had been a rough year. Three of them had got caught except they put up a fight and had died before being lifted. I got away. I'd had to blag my way past three KGB agents and I'd impressed myself with my Russian accent. Now that code*, she thought, *what was it?*

She took a notepad from inside her jacket pocket and took out a pencil. She closed her eyes and thought back. It took ten minutes to put the code down on paper and then took a minute to actually read the sentence. When she'd done so, she ripped up the bit of paper, stuffed it in her pocket, put the notepad away and got out of the car. She saw Declan at the far side of the car park and waved him back over.

'Have you got something?' asked Kylie.

'I have. Let's go for a walk.'

Kylie closed the boot of the car and Siobhan grabbed her jacket, pulling it on. Together, they trudged down to the beach at Whiterocks. It was long and quite stunning. The golden sand rippled at first, but then turned flat where the tide had previously run in. All this was set before gorgeous white rocks that towered above them. There were a few families about, most wrapped up, and a couple of hardy souls entering the water in wetsuits. Siobhan turned left and walked down the beach.

'I've cracked it. It's a code that only Eamon and I knew because the other three people who knew it are dead.'

'Dead like Eamon?' asked Declan, 'or dead like Eamon is now?'

'Dead like Eamon is now. They died out in Russia, so he's definitely intending me to follow up whatever he's giving us.'

'So, what's the code?'

'Far too complicated,' said Siobhan. 'But what it says is the Saint Petersburg's princess is in the second chord.'

'What?' queried Declan.

'I said "the Saint Petersburg's princess is in the second chord". We need to know who the princess is.'

'And we need to know who the chord is. Or which chord it is,' offered Declan.

'No,' said Kylie. 'The second chord is the second part of the puzzle. We've only solved the start of the poem. There's another half to it we haven't cracked yet. This is saying that— or wherever that takes us.'

'She's right,' said Siobhan. 'That's how we work it, so we've got another location to find and discover.'

'So what do we do today, then? Do we head away?' asked

Declan.

'No,' said Siobhan, 'we take a walk. I'm going to ponder this. We'll walk another half mile or so down here, then we'll turn back. When I get something, I'll let you know. I don't want to go all the way back and then return.'

Declan walked off ahead of the women, insisting that he would scout and make sure that nobody was about. Siobhan simply nodded, and Kylie and she worked on the second half of the poem.

'"But the wind is cold and howls at night, where we used to listen to whispers abroad." It's tied into you again, isn't it? Where "we used to listen to whispers abroad." Is that back from Russian days as well?'

'Depends what it means,' said Siobhan. 'Is it we, me and Eamon, or is it we, the Service? "Cold wind and howls at night." Somewhere where the wind blows. Ah. Got a few of those places in my lifetime. I need to think more. I doubt you're going to get it,' she said to Kylie. 'This one's quite personal, though you did well with Dunseverick. Maybe when I get to the place, you'll be able to assist more.'

'Thank you,' said Kylie. 'Thanks for taking a chance on us.'

'It wasn't a chance,' said Siobhan. 'It made sense. You made sense. I don't take chances.'

'You don't, do you? Having Declan scan all around, that's a good idea. Good precaution.'

'No, it's not,' said Siobhan. 'It's keeping him busy. Trouble with Declan is if he's got nothing to do, he'll start doing something and get himself into trouble. At the moment, he thinks he's scanning the beach and looking for people.'

'He is, though, isn't he? He is scanning.'

'Oh, yeah, he's scanning. Looking for people, but he's not

finding any,' said Siobhan sourly.

Kylie looked at her, but then left the matter, as it was clear Siobhan was trying to think. They walked the length of the beach, the sun still shining down on the wintry day, and then came back up for the turnoff back to the car park.

'Have you got something?'

'I do,' said Siobhan, 'but we'll talk about it in the car. I don't want to talk about it here.'

'Why?' asked Declan. 'Fairly safe. There's nobody here except a few of these families.'

'Declan, there's at least six people watching us at the moment,' said Siobhan. Kylie's face went into shock. 'Six of them. You're a complete amateur with this, but you try hard.' Siobhan walked to the car and heard Kylie padding through the sand quickly behind her.

'Six. Will they attack?'

'They won't attack. Last time they tailed me, I had to attack them to get rid of them. They were probably going to interrogate me. They can't just grab me here. We're too open. Too many people about; people will see their faces. They're a different squad though from last time, which is very worrying. This man, Danill Baranov, obviously has enough money and resources to bring them here. You don't switch the squad over that quickly, yet he has. There's definitely KGB training involved here. Maybe he's got somebody from the old school looking after him. Most of the faces are very young, and although they're very good at evading the likes of Declan, they wouldn't evade anyone of my ability.'

'So, what do we do?'

'We go, and we'll discuss in the car about how we check out the places I believe are involved in the poem. But we have a tail on us, and we will need to get rid of the tail. That tail could be with us most of the day, Kylie.'

'When you say get rid of them, I take it you've got your gun with you. Are you going to get rid of them properly?'

Siobhan turned suddenly, looking at Kylie. 'What do you think I am? I didn't operate as the assassin. I wasn't there to take people out. Agent running was my business. We tried to not kill people because it caused too much of a fuss. There are other agents for that. I'm not the James Bond figure.'

'Well, no, you're not a man, are you?' said Kylie.

'I'm not even the Janet Bond figure,' she said. 'That sort of action brings a lot of heat, and that's fine if you're getting out quickly. If you are working a place and staying there and going to be there a long, long time, you knew they would know who you were, so you gave them no call to arrest you. They suspected most people in the embassy, and therefore you had to act as if you were part of the embassy. Not there to ruffle feathers, but obviously look after your own country's interest.'

'So, you didn't kill anyone?'

Siobhan looked away for a moment before turning back. 'Some things about the Service, I will never tell you or anyone else. I may be part of this team, but that's part of my history that must remain secret, and some of it for excellent reasons. Don't ask me questions like that.'

'Okay,' she said. Declan was padding up now behind them, too. 'I can't see them,' he said. 'Six people. Where the hell are these six people?'

'They're around, and they're tailing us, and I don't want them to know that I'm all over them. Okay? At the moment, you look like a clumsy fool. Which is great, but I'm not, and they'll know I'm not after what happened last time. We're going to have a lot of heat on us for the rest of the day, Declan. Just stay calm and we stay together.'

'But how do we visit these places you're talking about, that you've come up with, if we've got these people all over us?'

'All in good time, Declan. What we're going to do now is head to Portrush. You're going to find me a hotel, and one that's nice because I don't want to spend the rest of the day messing about in some dive. Instead, we'll make sure they spend money as well. Anyway, onward James, your lady wants to go to her hotel.'

Declan looked a bit bemused for a moment until Kylie told him, 'Back to the car, Declan.'

Chapter 17

'Okay,' said Declan, 'we're in the car, we're driving along and nobody else can hear us, so what's the deal?'

'Just pull over on the side somewhere,' said Siobhan. Declan looked at her and then around at Kylie. 'Just do as I ask,' said Siobhan.

Declan pulled over, and Siobhan stepped out, stretching beside the car. Several cars went past, and Siobhan clocked them. She saw two cars go by carrying the six people who she had spotted on the beach. Siobhan got back in the car and told Declan to continue driving.

'What was that all about?'

'Our friends from the beach just went past once. Some of them are going to be pulled over at the roadside in a minute. Others will do a loop around to see if they can come back behind us again. I mean, there are not that many turnoffs on this road towards Portrush. But they will pick us up again, and that's fine.'

'What do you mean, that's fine?' asked Declan.

'It's fine, Declan, because I need them to lose me at a time of my choosing. At the moment, I don't want them to lose me because I'm not going looking for something in the places I'm thinking of in broad daylight.'

'Can we know what you're thinking about?' asked Kylie.

'But the wind is cold and howls at night. Where we used to listen to whispers abroad,' said Siobhan. 'I think he's talking about Torr Head.'

'Torr Head? Don't people jump from there?'

'Has been associated with it in the past,' said Siobhan, 'but it's cold and the wind certainly howls around there. But more than that, I think we talked about it.'

'You think?' queried Declan. 'You're not very sure, for a spy.'

'Before we pass out opinions on my credentials as a spy, young man, maybe we should talk about your lack of ability to spot other spies.'

'Okay,' he said, 'fair enough.'

'But what's the second bit mean?' asked Kylie.

'"We used to listen to whispers abroad." I think it's talking about we, the Service, or the state, so to speak. There's an old listening station there from the Cold War era. That's not something we talked about. Torr Head is, but the listening station is well known. It's in the public forum. I think that could be the place he went to. He's just written it in such a way that it can mean lots of other things, too.'

'So, if we're heading out towards Torr Head, what are we doing with these people on our back?' asked Declan.

'We go to the hotel and from there we have a nice evening meal. Then, get ourselves off the bed and we disappear out in the middle of the night. We've done this routine before.'

'Somebody was waiting for us last time.'

'That's right, Kylie,' said Siobhan, 'but last time they knew where Eamon had been killed. They don't know where we're going this time.'

'But they were at Dunseverick Falls.'

'They knew he was there. There's nothing at Torr Head for him to have been there for. I think this is going to be a lot more secretive. Whatever it is, is going to be very well hidden. There's nothing in the poem that suggests an actual place other than the listening station.'

'How big is it?' asked Declan suddenly. 'Are we able to search it?'

'It'll be the size of a room or two, but that's a lot of places to hide things.'

Declan drove the car on in towards Portrush and carried on towards Portstewart to find a hotel. It was off the road to one side, not large, but it was definitely an upper-class establishment. When he parked the car, Declan jumped out of it, ran round to the other side, and opened the door for Siobhan with a curt nod. He said, 'Mrs D,' before stepping out of the way and letting her out. From the backseat, Kylie shook her head, but then smiled as Declan opened her door too.

'We have got no bags,' said Declan.

'No, we haven't. But we have some of the food in the back. If you zip up some of those bags, and we'll carry them in like we are staying overnight. We'll have to sleep alfresco, I'm afraid,' said Siobhan.

'It's a good job we're in separate rooms then,' said Kylie before Declan could say a word.

'Oh,' said Siobhan. 'I was booking you two in as a couple, just as cover.' Declan seemed to smile, but Kylie gave Siobhan a dig in the ribs.

'Excuse me?'

'Too easy to wind up,' said Siobhan. She walked on into reception and calmly asked for three rooms, all side by side. Having signed in under a false pseudonym, Siobhan led the two up to the rooms, where they put down the food bags inside.

'I suggest we go downstairs to the bar. After all, we could do with getting some food. I don't know about you, but I'm tired. I could do with a bit of sleep before we do any late-night escapades.'

'Food sounds good,' said Declan. 'Shall we meet down in twenty minutes?'

Twenty minutes later, Siobhan walked into the restaurant to see Declan and Kylie already there. The boy was beaming, but there wasn't much talking. Kylie looked over as Siobhan entered, and she was certainly pleased to see her.

'Be a good lad, Declan,' said Siobhan as she reached the table. 'Go up to the bar there, get what you want, what Kylie wants, and I'll have something like a spritzer.'

'A what?'

'It's wine with fizz in it. Sort of a concoction of wine and tonic water. A fizzy water or something,' said Kylie.

'Something like that, Declan, but a lot nicer sounding,' said Siobhan. Declan nodded, took an order from Kylie, and then walked up to the bar.

'He knocked on the door for me,' she said.

'Really? He is keen. He's not as daft as he looks, either.'

'Full of compliments today,' said Kylie. 'I noticed a few people check in when we came in here.'

'Oh,' said Siobhan. 'They've tailed the car and seen we're here. They'll book a couple of rooms. Another hour or two, and the rest of the contingent will join them.'

Declan returned with a pint of Guinness for himself, a vodka and coke for Kylie and some sort of fizzy wine in a glass. Siobhan tried it. It wasn't great, but it would do.

'Not too many more of this for either of you. You've got to keep a clear head tonight. One can ease the nerves, keep you steady, but too many and you become slack at what you're doing.'

'Is that an order?' asked Kylie.

'It is. You're on a team and I'm heading it, so yes, that's an order.'

They sat in silence for a moment, but then Declan asked Siobhan if she could explain a bit more.

'Why are you here?' he said. 'It's what I don't get. I don't understand how you've ended up back here and then involved in this.'

'I don't get how I'm involved in this. Eamon's brought it upon me. He's seeing it as being important enough for me to get involved, but he's had to lay a path to it that's cryptic enough that nobody else picks it up. That's a two-fold thing. He'll be trying to make sure that I understand what's going on, but also that nobody else gets involved who shouldn't. Probably failed him in that. After all, you two are involved.'

'We chose,' said Kylie.

'Glad you did. As to why I'm here, I've tried to explain this before. Andrew, my husband, ran a window business, glass replacement. During the Troubles, places would be bombed and if you were quick enough and you had it ready, the glass was put in later that day. So local firms who could react got paid a small fortune. Andrew was happy enough to take that fortune.

'He inherited the glass business from his father. Back then, it wasn't much. When I married him, it wasn't much, but it took off quickly and he got heavily involved in it. I, however, got picked up by the government and then got moved to an embassy. My background was from a top university. They were watching since I left it.

'I married a local businessman and was then travelling away. They trained me and I was able to use my discretion and wit to move up the ranks. I was away nearly all the time. However, I noticed Andrew had already started picking up other women to satisfy himself, so I lived a life away. We kept the name together, and, in truth, when I came home, we got on all right. Just never had a bed together.

'I didn't dislike him, despite what happened. Although we never really had a genuine marriage, he liked me. Hence why he left me all his money when he died. Before any of you say it, it wasn't a Service thing where we rehashed his will.'

'Do you do stuff like that?' asked Declan.

'No, we don't,' said Siobhan. 'We're above that. A little more classy.'

'So, then what?'

'Well, Kylie, then I've got too much money. He's died, and I thought I can get a chance at retirement. I told them I had a condition brought on. It took me a year and a half of walking incorrectly to convince them. But, anyway, they let me go. They didn't have to give me a great package. I didn't ask for much because I had Andrew's money.

'I always wanted to come down and live near Donaghadee. We used to walk all the way into it as a child. I love that coast. Just love it when the sun shines. I love the countryside around it and yet you're right beside the sea, too. I love Northern

Ireland for its compactness. And round near Donaghadee, it's really the epitome of it. Where can I not go in an hour, an hour and a half and not be in some of the best places in the world? Tollymore Forest Park, the Mourne Mountains, the north coast, Lough Neagh as well. Up to the lakes in Fermanagh, down to the countryside of Armagh, and yet you can jump on a plane and go elsewhere happily. I came home, you see; this is home.'

'But things didn't leave you.'

'No, they didn't, Declan. And that's bothering me. What's going on here? This is home. This is not a place where this should be happening. I'm not the operative I once was, I have to warn you. Can't handle myself in a fight the same way I used to. I was fortunate that I got some youngsters who tailed me the other day. They were pretty naïve. Probably thought the old woman wouldn't take much. I can handle myself. If we get an experienced operator against us, I'd have to be much more cautious. Don't be afraid to run, either of you, if things go south. I'll protect you as best I can.'

'Why don't you carry the gun with you?' said Declan, a little too loudly for Siobhan's liking.

Siobhan reached up and scratched behind her ear. 'Coming in at the moment,' she said, 'two of them. They're checking in for tonight. I know which cars are theirs. You'll both be coming with me. You need to understand that when we operate, we operate as best we can without weapons. Weapons are taken only if there's an extreme likelihood of having to use them. I do not intend to use weapons tonight. If people are there, we don't go in. Earlier on today, we infiltrated a house with no weapons. You ran cover with a cleaner. That's the best way to do things. Be a ghost. Make sure nobody knows you were there.'

'Do you miss it?' asked Declan.

'Miss what? The Service? In some ways.'

'I meant being an operative. You said you became an analyst, but now you're back to being an operative with us.'

'No, I don't,' she said. 'You don't understand. We had to run so many secrets. So many times, we were touch and go as to whether we'd get out. When you're young, your nerves can handle that. It was all a big game then. I'm afraid I see life very differently now.'

Siobhan turned and waved over to the man at the bar, indicating she'd like some food. He came round with menus, and they ordered. Between the three of them, they ate well and disappeared up to their rooms just a little after eight o'clock. Siobhan had told them to be ready, come one o'clock in the morning. Taking to her room, she quickly walked around, checking there was nothing untoward.

Siobhan then took a bath, letting her muscles relax in the hot water. Today's endeavours were felt a little more than they really should be.

She thought about what Declan had asked. Did she miss it? Oh, yes, she missed it. She had loved her time in Russia. Loved her time with Eamon. Retirement? That question was coming back to her again.

Siobhan was only just turned fifty. She had retired because she didn't want to be an analyst anymore. She was tired of being out of the game. But here she was, finding a game. She'd do it because it was the only game in town at the moment, but part of her was worried she'd miss it. Worried when this was all done, who would Siobhan Duffy be? Just a woman who had a history and who now fought to put the days in. This was the truth that scared her.

Chapter 18

Siobhan's alarm went off, and she blearily opened her eyes. Within two minutes, she was up and changed, ready to go.

She walked out of the hotel using her key to get out while making sure she was clear of any CCTV. It was an older establishment. Classy, but old. When she got to the car park, she produced a knife from the lining of her jacket. While not the biggest, it was certainly sharp.

Soon, she had slashed the tyres of most of the cars in the car park. She disappeared back inside, knocked quietly on the doors of her colleagues, and the three of them made their way downstairs. Siobhan told them to remain quiet for the night manager, or whoever was meant to be on the desk, was in the rear room, feet up and watching the television. She disappeared back out the door with Kylie and Declan, so quietly that he never moved. She started the car and drove off, keeping the headlights off until they were out on the road.

Torr Head was back along the Coast road. Out past Portballintrae, through Bushmills and up to the Causeway road past Dunseverick and Ballintoy. Eventually, you arrived beyond Ballycastle.

The whole time they drove, the sea was almost hiding in the dark. Occasional boat lights were seen going up and down, but the cloud cover was strong, and the wind had got up in the last hour or two. The old listening station that Siobhan had been thinking of was well before Torr Head. They turned off and parked a little distance away from it. Together they crowded together behind the car out of the wind while Siobhan gave some last-minute instructions.

'We'll walk up to it. If we see anyone there, we'll turn and we'll walk back, and we will leave. The one thing that we won't do is engage anyone. When we get closer, I'll tell the two of you to stop and I'll scout ahead to make sure there isn't anyone there. The two of you should stand together. Act like you're having a curt.'

'A what?' said Declan.

'A curt.' Siobhan looked at Kylie. There was a complete lack of recognition in her eyes. 'A snuggle. You know what that means? Act like you're a couple out here in the dark. It's the best cover, as it's the middle of the night. Why else would you be out here?'

'I will not do that,' said Kylie.

'You're part of the team. Take one for the team. If someone comes close, don't hold back. Make it look like it's real.'

'No problem,' said Declan, smiling. Kylie looked down.

'All right, let's get closer. No torches. Nothing with a light. No phones. I want to get close first and make sure no one's there before we use any light.'

They walked just under half a mile, and then they could see the building. It was located off the road, a small path leading up to it. Siobhan stopped the pair as she disappeared on ahead. In the darkness, Declan could barely see her move. It was ten minutes before Siobhan came back.

'It looks good. Come on.'

'Thank God,' said Kylie in a whisper.

Together, they walked down the gravel track until they stood in front of what looked like an expansive old garage. Some of the front doors were missing. There was broken glass in the window. Around it was a small wall, but as they got inside, they could see the ruin it was. There was nothing to show what it had been. Yes, there was the odd bit of electrics still there, but most things were ruined.

A crude metal gate sat across a large opening. From the front, it looked like three garages were slammed together, but the middle one had a higher roof. The roofs were flat. There was a pipe above the doorway of the central one that seemed to be redundant. It was rusted and stuck out abruptly on the left-hand side of the central unit. There was a metal rectangle on the side of the building. Right at the bottom was a rectangular hole into the inside of the building. The door of corrugated iron was half missing.

'It's not the best monument to work ever, is it?' said Kylie.

'No,' said Siobhan. When she stepped inside and switched on a torch from her phone, a rat moved in the corner, then it ran past her leg, causing Kylie to jump. Declan grabbed her in the dark, holding her tight, and Siobhan noticed Kylie didn't step back out of his clutches.

'It's only a rat. We can deal with them,' said Siobhan, and began searching the edges. 'You too look, as well. You've got a phone?'

'Yes,' said Declan.

'Good, but don't shine it out through the door. Make sure it's focused on the interior.'

'It's just merely rubbish on the floor, though,' said Declan. 'These windows are smashed. Why would you hide something in here?'

'Why wouldn't you?' said Siobhan. 'How many people do you think come in here and have a good hoke around, trying to find something of use?'

'You wouldn't know this had been a listening station, would you?'

'What do listening stations look like?' asked Siobhan.

Kylie shook her head. 'I have no idea.'

'Exactly,' said Siobhan. 'Just look.'

'Does the poem say anything about where it could be, though?' asked Declan. He was shifting rubbish now loudly.

'No,' said Siobhan, 'and keep it quiet. We might be a bit off the road, but if anybody passes us or comes close, they'll hear us.'

It was fifteen minutes later when Siobhan pulled them together.

'It must be here somewhere. It's hard to see in the torch-light.'

'I've moved all the rubbish,' said Declan.

'He won't hide it amongst rubbish,' said Siobhan. 'It's got to be somewhere safe. It's got to be somewhere you can access it.'

She switched off the light from her phone, walked outside, and tried to look at the front of the building. After having their torches on, it took a while for her eyes to adjust, but slowly, a thought formed in her head.

'Maybe we could get up there,' said Siobhan, pointing to the pipe above the door of the middle unit.

'I don't think I could leap up there,' said Declan.

'I was thinking more of you giving me a lift-up.'

'Okay,' said Declan, 'I can try that.'

He bent down on one knee, cupped his hands together, looking for Siobhan to put a foot on them. She did so, and he drove upwards. But her foot slipped, and she fell down with his hands in between her legs. Quickly, he parted his hands and put them away to one side as Siobhan fought to keep her balance.

'I didn't realise you were that heavy.'

Siobhan glared at him. 'You don't tell a woman that she's heavy,' she said. 'I didn't realise you were that weak. Kylie, come on, put your back into it too. You can pick one foot each and push me up. Once I'm up, I'll be all right.'

Kylie reluctantly came over. Siobhan first put her foot up onto the upturned palm of Declan before pushing herself up and placing her other foot on Kylie's palm.

'Now lift, the pair of you.'

Siobhan swayed as they pushed her up, but she got her hand up and grabbed around the top of the metal pipe that was sticking out of the building. With her left arm, she remained there while her right arm went inside the pipe. Declan looked up at her.

'Bloody hell, how strong are you?'

'Strong enough,' she said and took out her phone, activating the light. She looked inside the pipe, and she could see something stuck on the side. Putting her phone back down and the light off, Siobhan reached in and tugged at a piece of paper stuck to the side. Soon she was pulling out some sort of plastic bag. Pulling it, she threw it down, asking Declan to look.

'What's in it?' asked Siobhan, hanging now with two arms

and feeling her shoulders beginning to separate.

'There's a dead pigeon in here. Somebody's bagged up a dead pigeon and shoved it in there.'

Siobhan couldn't think about that. She couldn't wait. Instead, she drove her arm inside again, feeling around in the wet and the damp before something cylindrical came between her fingers. She took hold of it, pulling it out and dropping it down into the outstretched hands of Declan.

'What is it?'

'I think there's something inside, like a note. It's like a cylinder with a note.'

Siobhan slowly tried to let herself down as best she could before dropping about three feet. She felt it on her knees as she landed. That differed from all those years ago.

She turned to Declan and took the small cylinder off him. It was a cigar case, and she could open one end and pull out a piece of paper. She put her phone light on again and looked at the words in front of her. Truly, they were more like letters. She remembered the code she'd used before, but it wasn't correct. It just produced gobbledygook.

'What do we do now? Can you break it?' asked Declan.

'No, but that's okay. We'll go home and do it. For now, we get back to the hotel. We need to leave in the morning, but we'll need some new tyres before we do that.'

'New tyres? queried Declan.

'Yes. Come on, back to the car, everyone.'

The three of them left in the dark, lights off again, marching along and having to keep a close eye on the track beneath them. They were getting somewhere, Siobhan knew. As they arrived back at the hotel, the time now being around about three in the morning, she sent the others inside and Siobhan slashed the tyres on her own car. It was a hire car, and they'd come out with a replacement or something else, but it looked like somebody had done a job on everyone. Siobhan crept back inside the hotel with her key, made her way up to her room to see the other pair standing outside.

'What are you doing?' she whispered.

'Waiting for you,' said Declan. 'To see what the note says.'

'The note will say what it says tomorrow,' said Siobhan. 'I am tired and my brain's not working. Time for sleep. We'll have time in the morning to look at it because we're going to have to change the tyres on the car.'

'What do you mean?' asked Kylie.

'You'll find out in the morning,' she said.

Declan looked horrified, but Siobhan shooed them both to their rooms, let herself inside her own room, stripped off her clothes and climbed into bed. Her left arm was sore. She was strong, but she'd hung there for a while and now it felt like the shoulder was detaching slightly. It wasn't, of course, it was just a feeling, but it forced her to roll over and lie on her front, her arms up above her head, hugging the pillow.

She lay there tired, and for a moment, she remembered Russia. Siobhan remembered Eamon's hands on her back. She remembered how they'd be out chasing a lead, tailing someone, working a source, and then they come back to the hotel. All of a sudden, the pressure was off, and they would relax.

They always enjoyed the relaxation, but they were that age, young, when physical relaxation seemed to be everything. Nowadays, she'd like to relax up close. Less energetic, more just a sense of being together. But of course, there wasn't anyone. She'd turned her life from being an operative and constantly being on the go, to being an analyst and finding other things to keep her on the go.

Badminton, squash, any other sports, painting, everything. Would she be able to fill it now she was retired? She didn't know. How could she know?

Siobhan closed her eyes and tried to think about other things, tried to think about life and being normal and going to clubs and rotas and many things. Instead, Eamon kept appearing to her. They killed him. They had killed him for what he knew, and now what he knew was sitting so close to her. She'd find it out. She owed the love of her life that.

Chapter 19

The following morning, the front of the hotel was a mess. Siobhan had slashed the tyres of so many cars during the night, including her own when they'd returned. Now, the owners were waking up to a very expensive bill. There were protestations with the hotel staff. When they checked CCTV, they could only see a figure in the dark moving about. Whoever it was had used the cars to remain out of view to such a degree that it would be hard to identify them.

Siobhan joined the others at complaining to the hotel staff before she called up the rescue people. They eventually turned up with a job lot of tyres. In the old days, there would have been a breakdown truck towing everybody away to a garage to have the wheels changed, but now a couple of vans came out. Jacks were brought out from the van's rear and the tyres were changed.

That being said, it still took the best part of the morning before they were in a state to leave. Declan had made the most of it, enjoying a rather large breakfast, but Kylie had seemed more anxious. Siobhan wasn't, though, although they still had those who had tailed them staying at the hotel. Maybe it was because Siobhan handed the tyre man an extra hundred pounds when he arrived to do her tyres first. By the time Declan drove out of the car park, the tail was still waiting for their tyres to be looked at.

'Nice one, Mrs D,' said Declan as he drove along.

'Do you think it will deter them, though?' asked Kylie. 'Do you think they'll not know where we are?'

As they drove back, Siobhan stared out the window, her mind elsewhere. Declan put some music on in the car, but it was almost as if she didn't hear it. Kylie asked a few times, should she go shopping? Did you want any more food for the house? It took Siobhan three times to hear the question before she answered. Her mind was already on the code she'd found, trying to break it down. She was almost there, wasn't she? They'd found the first part of the message, recovered it, and now discovered the second part as well. Did they join up and make sense?

Siobhan was annoyed because she wanted to just stop somewhere, sit down, in peace and quiet, and work through the code. She didn't enjoy doing that when she was being driven. There was too much distraction, too easy to slip up. She'd get back to the house and she would lock herself in, set the others off on some tasks around the house. They were keen, but she needed to keep them at an arm's length.

It was too easy to get distracted by them, because you were looking after them, or because you were thinking beyond yourself. As an operative, she had thought a lot about herself, about her own particular mission, and didn't have to worry about colleagues around her. That was their issue. She couldn't say the same with Declan and Kylie. They weren't trained at that level. Heck, she wasn't at that level anymore, and she was having to scramble back years of training.

When they arrived back at Donaghadee, it was a cool day, but the sun had broken out, bathing the house in all its glory as they pulled into the drive. Siobhan stepped out, walked to the front of her grounds, and sat on the wall, looking back at the house. She was going to take a moment. She had worked a lifetime and was finally somewhere she wanted to be. At the rear of the property, she could hear the blue water lapping up, not crashing in as it did some days. Kylie was fussing with taking everything from the boot into the house, Declan giving her a hand before he approached Siobhan.

'Are we going to crack this, then?' he said to her.

'What bit of the garden needs done next, Declan?'

'Oh, Mrs D, we need to trim back towards the rear of the house. Going to shift some of that grass where you want to gravel it and form a path.'

'Can you get on with that now?'

'I thought you'd want to do the code?'

Siobhan looked up into a face that resembled a puppy dog. He just wanted to play, and Siobhan wasn't ready to play. Instead, she sent him back to his basket.

Kylie appeared over his shoulder. 'That's everything in. Shall we get on to the code?'

'Look,' said Siobhan. 'I appreciate your help, but I need to do this one on my own.'

'Why?' asked Declan.

'Two reasons. One, I need the space and the quiet because if I don't get that, I'll make mistakes. The second one is, I don't want you to see something that you shouldn't do.'

'What do you mean?' asked Declan.

'Some secrets can get you killed. Some secrets need to be

silenced. That's what I'm talking about.'

'It's a bit melodramatic, Mrs D,' said Declan.

Kylie didn't look so sure that it was melodramatic. She took Declan's arm, wanting to pull him away.

'Well, we've come this far.'

'And I thank you for that,' said Siobhan, 'but really, let me check it first.'

'Declan,' said Kylie. She pulled him away towards the house, and Siobhan stood up and let the light breeze pass over her face in the sunshine. She'd have to go back inside to her office. That's where there'd be peace and quiet. That's where she should separate herself from everything, but this was nice. She would be doing more of this, she decided. She would get a chair out, sitting on the lawn, smelling that fresh sea air. *There was nowhere like this, really, was there?* she thought.

Siobhan walked inside her house and her eye caught the false door to the side of the main one. She'd had it built specifically into the house, and it reminded her that the past never went away. *Forever,* she thought, *I'll be looking over my shoulder. Forever, I'll be on the lookout. Even here, at my retreat, at a place away from time, a place away from Russia, a place away from that crazy world. Even here it's found me, through the newspaper, through Eamon's call in a time of need.*

Entering her office, Siobhan shut the door, sat down, wheeling her chair up to the desk. She took out the coded note, sat with it in front of her, and took out a pencil and a pad of paper.

What codes, she thought, *what codes did we use?* She began scribbling some down, then reading the code, trying to transfer it across. The first one made no sense. The second one looked like it might when the door opened.

'I thought I'd bring you a cuppa. See how you were getting on,' said Kylie.

'I'm going to have to check this again,' said Siobhan. She smiled and looked up at the girl. 'Thank you.' Siobhan sniffed the smoky tea, and it was comforting. Kylie stood, holding the tray in one hand now.

'How's it going?'

'It's not done,' said Siobhan. 'Thank you for the tea, but I need quiet.'

'Okay,' said Kylie. Siobhan turned back and started again on the code she was working on. Three minutes later, there was a knock at the door.

'Come in,' said Siobhan. She had just got going on that code again. Declan entered the room.

'I just wondered if you want to come and have a look at the cut of this path. Just . . .'

'Whatever way you want it, Declan. You understand the garden, you understand how it needs to be. Just do it.'

'I don't want to cut into the soil and then you'll come and say, no, the path should be . . .'

'Declan, I need some peace and calm. Okay? If you really want me to do that, you're going to have to wait and move on to something else.'

'Well, it's kind of in . . .'

'Declan, can you just get out? Okay? I need to work on this. I really don't need to be disturbed.'

'Okay, Mrs D,' he said. 'How's it going?'

'Slowly,' said Siobhan. She pushed the chair back and stood up. Siobhan wasn't a small woman and could easily come eye-to-eye with Declan. She put a hand on his shoulder and forcibly, but reasonably gently, pushed him out the door.

'Peace and quiet,' she said, 'and I will be done soon.'

She closed the door. They always taught you in a spy environment to remain cool. Control your nerves, control your anger, think. Siobhan realised she was failing in this regard because if they came in again, she was liable to string them up. She walked back across, sat down on her chair, wheeled into the desk, and thought again about the second code she had come up with.

Replace letter, not letter, change that letter over. That one's back. Two forward. Down three. The code was running through her head, taking in every part of her, except she could hear something. There was something there. Somebody at the door. She pushed back the chair, stood up, looked around the room, and then lifted a rather heavy paperweight. Slowly, she walked to the door, her back up against the wall beside it. She reached down and turned the handle.

The next motion was quick and fluid. The handle went down. She threw the door open, turned around, and stopped half an inch from Declan's face with the paperweight. Kylie was standing beside him.

'What?' spat Siobhan.

'We were just . . .'

'Wondering if it was done? I told you. Go away. Frankly, piss off and do what I've asked you to do.'

The language was extreme, but Siobhan thought she was going to put the paperweight into their faces if they didn't move quick.

'That neck vein's coming out, the one when you get angry,' said Declan. 'You upset, Mrs D?'

Siobhan swore little. She might have used what her mother would've termed coarse language. But she didn't use what was universally acknowledged even in this modern day, as pretty strong. Certainly not the F-word. However, it slipped out, and the door was slammed shut before she'd even finished the second word—'off'.

She turned, marched back to her desk, dumped herself into the seat, wheeled it over to the desk, picked up her pencil, and puffed. Siobhan tried to relax, breathe in, breathe out. She heard a noise. *Are they still bloody well there? Were they?* She pushed the chair back, stormed over, opened the door to no one. She breathed in deeply and then realised that some people had hidden over at the kitchen door.

'I will take this paperweight and I will shove it down your throat if you do not give me peace,' she said. Siobhan breathed in again. 'I know you're excited, know you want to know what's in this, but we won't find out unless you sod off and leave me alone. I will call you when I'm done. Kylie, sort some dinner out. Declan, make that path. I swear if you're at this door again, I will sack the pair of you.'

'Yes, Mrs D,' said Declan, walking out of the kitchen. Kylie made no such move.

Siobhan breathed in again and then out and then slowly closed the door. She walked over, sat down, pulling the chair in, and picked up the pencil. It took her another five codes before she realised that she wasn't looking at a message. She was looking at two names, Charlotte McGee and Ken Vegas. She checked the Vegas four times, and it still was Vegas. Who on earth was called Vegas? She was going to search them up on the laptop, but she reckoned she needed to repair relations with her two employees. She opened the door of the office and shouted that she was ready. The young pair appeared from the kitchen and were at her office inside of five seconds.

'You were meant to be out doing the path.'

'Just stopped in for a cup of coffee, Mrs D. I know you don't like coffee, so I started it in the kitchen, away from you.'

Siobhan glared at him, grabbed the laptop. 'Let's sit in the lounge to talk about this.'

'We'll be all right in the study, Mrs D,' said Declan. Kylie had already turned away.

'She doesn't like anyone in her office. She doesn't like a hoard in there. That's her space, Declan. We'll go to the lounge. Don't forget your cuppa if it's still warm.'

Siobhan looked over at her cup. It was full, and it was cold. Sitting down in the lounge, Siobhan looked at the young pair. Declan was still like a puppy ready to go, but Kylie was like some stroppy teenager trying to pay it cool, even though she wanted to know all the information.

'Two names. That's all that code was. Two names. Charlotte McGee and Ken Vegas.'

'Charlotte McGee and Ken Vegas' said Declan. He turned his chin up as if he was thinking. Siobhan couldn't work out if he was being thoughtful or just trying to cut a figure that showed he was intelligent. If it was the latter, he was failing.

'I know the name, Ken Vegas. My uncle Samuel's a journalist. Heard those names from him.'

'Really?' said Siobhan. 'He's definitely heard of them?'

'Yes, but I'm not sure Vegas is actually a real surname,' said Declan.

'Maybe I should meet your uncle.'

'I'm not so sure. He's not the most sober. He's a bit of a hack.'

'All the more,' said Siobhan. 'Take your uncle somewhere where I can meet him inconspicuously. Somewhere random.

Yes? I need to find out about Charlotte McGee and Ken Vegas. If he knows, that's a good starting point.'

'I could, of course, just type up the search bar on the internet,' said Kylie.

'Go on then,' said Siobhan.

Kylie spun the laptop round to her, and first typed in Charlotte McGee.

'Anything?'

'Loads. Too many.'

'Type Northern Ireland in with it. What do you get?' asked Siobhan. Kylie did as asked.

'Less, but still very wild and wide-ranging.'

'Exactly. Try Ken Vegas.'

'Nothing. Just Vegas and some guy who went to Vegas called Ken.'

Did she not think I might have looked? thought Siobhan.

'Now, Declan's uncle sounds like a good start, especially as he's a journalist. There's a story going on. Journalists usually have them. Set it up, Declan.'

'Will do, Mrs D.'

Chapter 20

Declan announced the next day he'd contacted his uncle on the phone, and they would meet him in a ten-pin bowling alley. Declan had booked a game for Kylie and himself and would drive Siobhan over to let her chat with his uncle as two older people watching them. Siobhan shook her head at the fabricated situation, but she didn't complain.

The day had turned to rain and Siobhan felt a coldness in the air. It was close to winter, after all, and the trees had a gorgeous goldenness about them. You saw the occasional green, the touch of yellow on those leaves, but the others were a fiery brown, the reddishness coming through. You also saw the bare gnarled trunk of the trees, the top of them having no leaves and giving a spiky crown. Autumn was beautiful, as long as you were well wrapped up.

The rain was still on and off when they got out of the car at Dundonald. There were many distractions for children here and as they entered the bowling alley, they found it to be extremely busy. Declan went up to the front desk, telling Kylie to come and get her shoes. Siobhan thought he was less interested in what his uncle would say and more about taking

Kylie bowling. It wouldn't be a bad thing, though. She could talk to this uncle, interrogate him properly, not be worried about offending Declan.

'Where is he?' asked Siobhan, staring around the room. Before Declan could answer, she knew who it was. There was a man sitting half sprawled in one of the plastic chairs at a table. He looked decidedly the worse for wear. He had a shirt with a tie that was pulled half off his neck, some stains down the front of it, but still had a suit jacket. If you were looking for an old-time traditional hack, you would have to look no further. *Did he still have a job, looking like that?*

'Shall I introduce you?' asked Declan.

'Don't,' said Siobhan. 'Take Kylie bowling. I'll get the biz.'

'The what?'

'Biz. The information,' said Siobhan. Surely, she wasn't that old. 'I mean, the biz.' She shook her head. Siobhan wandered over and sat down on the plastic chair beside the sprawled individual. Her leg touched his because he was over on her side of the seating and he hauled himself back up into a fairly upright shape.

'Yes?' he said.

'Siobhan Duffy. Your nephew said we should talk.'

The man stopped for a moment, looking her up and down.

'Indeed,' said the man. 'He said you weren't bad for an old bird.'

Siobhan raised her eyebrows.

'Though you're not that old, are you? That's the trouble with the kids. They think everybody's old. He's not far wrong with the looks, though.'

Siobhan wasn't sure whether to be offended or to take a compliment. She didn't need one. She had a confidence in the way she looked. Yes, she didn't have Kylie's flush of youth, and she'd had the odd battering over the years in the Service. There were lines on the face, a few bags here and there, but she was in good shape. She could be fun. Lively.

'You don't mind if I smoke?' he said.

'I don't, but they might,' said Siobhan, nodding towards the reception desk.

'Bugger it,' said the man. 'It's always the bloody same, isn't it? You can't get a fag anywhere these days. I could do with one as well. I could do with a drink. Why did you want to meet here? Was this your idea?'

'No,' said Siobhan. 'Declan set it up. Decided it was a brilliant cover. We would watch the youngsters bowl.'

'He's an idiot,' said the man. 'Even the coffee's crap.'

'Do you want to go outside and talk?' said Siobhan. 'It is raining, but I'm sure we can find somewhere.'

'Will do,' said the man. 'Come on.'

He stood up and looked like he might not make it to the front door of the building. Siobhan saw Declan looking over as Kylie was putting on bowling shoes. She gave Declan a quick thumbs up, but his face looked slightly alarmed. His cover story was going up in smoke.

The man hobbled his way outside, coughed a lot, and looked around. 'Rain's coming that way,' he said. 'If we go around the side of the building, it'll be all right.'

'Lead on,' said Siobhan. The man hobbled round, stood upright on the other side of the building, and took out a cigarette. Siobhan walked beside him and waved her hand as he offered her one.

'No, you look too good to be on these,' he said. 'Never start smoking. They're crap for you.'

'I won't,' she said. 'What do you know then?'

'You tell me first why you want to know,' said the man. 'No offence, but Declan's an idiot. I could be talking to anyone.'

'You could indeed,' said Siobhan. 'Basically, an old contact of mine got a message to me, said that something was amiss and, long story short, gave me two names. Charlotte McGee and Ken Vegas. When I told Declan these names, he said he thought you knew them or at least had heard of them. I want to know who they are.'

'Are they in trouble?'

'Don't know. I'm ex-service.'

'Military woman?' he said. 'I wouldn't have guessed you were military. You're quite thin. Narrow. You look like you have a bit of shape to you, but you don't have that bearing.'

'No, secret services,' said Siobhan.

The man stopped for a moment, took a drag on a cigarette. 'And you're telling me that because?'

'Because I'm retired and nobody from the Service is going to come after you, hound you, or get any information from me. I'm doing this to find out why a friend's dead. Nothing more, nothing less.'

'Okay,' said Samuel. He pulled out another cigarette, lighting it. The first one was underneath his foot being stamped out. 'Charlotte McGee and Ken Vegas are hacks like me. Well, actually, not hacks like me. They were good. Ken was more like me. Smoked like a trooper.'

'Were they working on the same story?'

'Look, I'll tell you what I know. I'm not sure if they were working together or not, but they told the same story. There's a new hotel deal in the midst. Up near the Causeway. It's going to be an enormous complex, lots of money. It's going to cost a lot to do. Ken thought it was being railroaded through. Lots of money passing hands. Charlotte saw the same, but Ken, Ken said that people were getting taken out. Killed.

'This is Northern Ireland. People have been killed before with shady deals, but paramilitaries aren't involved in this,' said Samuel.

He turned and spat on the ground. Siobhan found him distasteful, but certainly a compelling character. He put his hand across faded and thin grey hair. He stood with his shoulders tilted, hips also not square. Siobhan actually wondered if he was in distress standing like this, and then he coughed before dumping more expectorant on the ground.

'Ken's not stupid,' he said. 'He looked into it. He's able, with some of his contacts, to check what the paramilitaries are doing to a large degree. Not stuff he'd always print about, but he'd know. But they're not involved. He was saying it was a different connection, but he was struggling. Charlotte didn't get so far.'

'Where are they now?'

'Charlotte's off doing a feature in South America. Says it'll take her two to three years. Says it'll take her until at least that centre's built and done. She's got out of the way, made sure that certain people understood she would do nothing, say nothing. I think she was threatened directly. Ken tried to find out by who. All he said was it wasn't the paramilitaries. Look, I can't say much more. I can't get involved in this. You can't get information from me that can be traced back to just me. Whoever's doing this is a nasty piece of work.'

'I know somebody that's involved. Russian businessman.'

Samuel threw his cigarette on the floor, stamped it. 'Look, lady,' he said. 'You want to get involved? You want to find out about this? Do me two favours. Keep Declan out of it. He's not clever enough for this. You might be. I don't know you. Second, keep me out of it. I want nothing to do with it. I want to get to where I retire and I'm able to sit in my bookies. Sit and have my fags or whatever. Even take up a nice wee caravan by the sea. I don't want to end up with a bullet in my head before my time.'

Siobhan watched him lighting another cigarette and reckoned the idea of having a caravan by the sea needed to be a very near prospect. The cigarettes would get him.

'I need to see Ken,' said Siobhan. 'Where is he?'

'Ken's out as well. Don't see Ken. Don't go near him. He knows more than I do. If they got wind that you were seeing him, talking to him, Ken would probably be dead within a matter of days. I don't know who these people are, but they're brutal.'

'I'm sitting on a dead end talking to you,' said Siobhan. 'That means I have to see Ken.'

Samuel lit another cigarette and drew in several times. 'Okay,' he said. 'I'm saying this for Ken's sake. To protect him. Don't check it. Don't clarify it with him. Please, don't go near him. Promise me that.'

'If what you're saying is worthwhile checking out, I'll leave him alone,' said Siobhan.

'Okay,' said Samuel. 'Ken had witnesses. People who had seen the dodgy dealings. They were Jenny Goldsmith, Simon Redburn and Lauren Muntz. They're all dead. Ken wouldn't say anything to me about how they died. I got the impression it wasn't nicely. Certainly, wasn't with family sitting around as you bless the young ones, if you catch my drift. I think it was rather painful. They were all ready to talk to Ken. All ready to give more information. They ended up in these strange accidents. That's when Ken stopped looking.'

'Jenny Goldsmith, Simon Redburn, Lauren Muntz,' said Siobhan, and repeated them internally to herself to make sure she wouldn't forget. 'Thanks, Samuel,' she said.

He gave a cough, threw his cigarette on the ground, and stamped it out. 'I'd better get back inside,' he said. 'Before Declan worries too much about his cover.'

When they returned inside. Siobhan took up a seat with Samuel, watching the two younger people. Declan was enjoying himself, but Kylie kept looking around, almost as if she wanted to know if Siobhan had found out anything.

Kylie made her way over as Declan stood up to bowl.

'Are we good?'

'You're very good,' said Siobhan. 'Got all I want. Tell you on the way back.'

'Good,' she said. 'I don't know what I hate more, the bowling or the fact he's always looking at me when I step up to bowl.'

'He just likes you,' said Siobhan. 'Nothing wrong with that.'

'No, there's not,' said Kylie. 'The trouble is he grows on you, doesn't he?'

Siobhan gave a smile. She whispered in Kylie's ear. 'He told his uncle that I was good looking.' She laughed. 'That's the men we need around us.'

'Well, at least he didn't say you were some sort of cow.'

'Why would he say that?' asked Siobhan.

'I don't know,' said Kylie. 'But he didn't, did he? So that's all good.'

Kylie turned because it was her turn to bowl again, leaving Siobhan wondering what the two of them had discussed about her. Did they ever mention she was being a bit of a cow?

Siobhan sat down and watched. Bowling looked quite good. All the dark and the lights down the far end. Maybe this was something she could do. As long as her joints stayed good.

That was the key thing, wasn't it? Get this done and retirement was on the way. She had that in common with Samuel. It wasn't quite a caravan by the sea. It was a house. She would enjoy it. That's what you did when you retired. You stopped, you settled down, and you enjoyed it. As soon as she stopped, she would do.

Chapter 21

That evening in the house, Siobhan sat with Kylie and Declan, pondering over the information they'd received. She would have to look into Jenny Goldsmith, Simon Redburn, and Lauren Muntz. Kylie was desperate to go onto the internet, start finding out what the situation was, but Siobhan said they should be more careful than that. After all, all three of them were dead. If they were to investigate, they would need to be extremely cautious. Siobhan knew firsthand how cold and clinical Russians could be, and if Daniil Baranov was involved, it made sense that he was silencing people.

Samuel's exoneration of Ulster's paramilitaries gave Siobhan serious thought. How quietly were things being done as well? She found it strange that local paramilitaries would be so easy with Russian businessmen coming in. Maybe there'd been a deal done; maybe they weren't on speaking terms; maybe there would be kickbacks to come later down the road. Either way, she trusted what Samuel said and also heeded his warning to not get heavily involved.

'What I don't understand,' said Siobhan, 'is why the Service isn't investigating this. With everything that's gone on and the death of one of our own, you would think that they would be all over it. At least monitoring it, but I've seen no one from the Service about during our whole time.'

'Maybe there's no evidence,' said Declan.

'This is the Service. These are the spies and all the people that work in the dark, Declan. We never needed evidence, not like the police need evidence. We just need to know that something's going on to be investigating it. I think I'll spend the rest of the evening trying to contact some of my former colleagues, to see if anybody can put a light on it. It's difficult, because if they're not involved, they won't know about it anyway, but I should be able to do a reasonably wide sweep. I was actually liked in the Service,' said Siobhan, smiling. 'But I'll need to do it without you guys in the phone's background. They won't trust that type of call. They still have phone boxes around here?' she asked.

'Few,' said Declan. 'We don't have the need for them anymore.' He waved his mobile.

'I just don't want to go through so many pay-as-you-go phones. Costs a small fortune if you're calling everyone,' she said.

'Can't you just do it on your normal mobile?'

'No, because if the Service is involved in this, and I'm not seeing it, it can cause trouble later down the line. I'll be back. Don't open the door to anyone. Check before you do.'

Siobhan stood up. Kylie gave her a look. Do you really think it's that serious?'

'It could be,' said Siobhan. 'That's why I've told Declan to stay here. I won't be far. You've got my number. If you see anything, set all the alarms in the house to go off. Phone me straight away.'

Siobhan left the room and disappeared to pick up a weapon. It was a small handgun. She took it with her to the car, placing it underneath the passenger seat. She was wrapped up in a large coat as well because it was blooming cold. Siobhan drove off to find a payphone.

It took two and a half hours of making phone calls to get nowhere. No one seemed to know anything, or at least they weren't letting on. It was harder, of course, not meeting them in person. She wondered were they just blanking or did they genuinely not know anything? Siobhan could read people's faces, but it was very difficult to read a voice over the phone, especially one from the Service, because they were trained.

Siobhan got to the end of the evening and thought about one more person. She'd been avoiding calling him because, well, when you were in the Service, you got people who were friendly to you, colleagues who worked with you. Sometimes you got people like Eamon, people you fell for, but who also knew the lines. Who could, to put it bluntly, give you a love life without expecting a life of commitment afterwards.

Julian Patterson, however, was different. Julian admired her, to say the least. She always felt that he wanted much more than that. He asked her at times what she would do after she left the service, where she would go. He was a decent enough person. Very upright. He played the Service game well, not in a dirty fashion. Because of that, he didn't get put on certain tasks, ones that required a lack of limits, and she guessed his weren't bad limits to have in a person. With no one else talking, though, she needed to establish contact again.

Siobhan dialled an ancient number and heard a voice at the other end pick up.

'It's Julian.'

Siobhan had not realised how she would feel. The trouble with Julian had been, she had liked him as well. A thoroughly decent bloke in a rather bizarre world. You didn't get many of them. Someone who could hold integrity and level of decency, when so often you were having to compromise. Julian could find a way around it.

What he hadn't been able to mask was his raw desire for Siobhan. Not just sexual desire, but how much he admired her. Julian loved her as a person. She didn't have that, not from her husband, not from Eamon.

Eamon was wild and passionate, but he didn't love her. She was a colleague. A kindred spirit. Her husband had just been a man who wanted a trophy wife, and ended up with one that didn't give him any bother, either.

Julian. Julian was the first person Siobhan could truly say loved her. And that's why she'd stayed so far away from him. Love in the Service was not something you went into lightly. It could cause you to have to go against the Service. And that wouldn't be good.

'Julian, it's Siobhan. I need to talk to you. Some things are going on.'

'And no one's saying anything to you,' he said. 'I'll meet you. Where are you?'

'I live near Donaghadee now,' she said.

'Gone home,' he said. 'I could see you being there. You loved the water, but I would have put you on the Strangford side. You always mentioned it quietly.'

'I'm not sure what's happening.'

'I'll come meet you,' he said. 'Tomorrow, three o'clock, down by the pools in Donaghadee, by the harbour.'

'See you then,' said Siobhan, and put the phone down.

On return, she told her pair of cohorts that she'd be meeting a man tomorrow who could help. They seemed excited. Siobhan was worried. Julian wasn't wanting to talk over the phone. That either meant he was going to say something daft to her about getting together, or he had something he needed to tell her in person.

The following morning had been awkward. Kylie started building a dossier with what she could find out about the three names Siobhan had gained from Samuel. It was awkward putting the pieces together. And Siobhan gave a hand where she could. In truth, she had a bit of trepidation about what was about to happen. She disappeared for a shower around about one, and then stood in her bedroom, deciding what to put on.

Siobhan had a denim shirt, which she wrapped around a white t-shirt, with some black trousers underneath. She didn't wear heels and she would not start now, so she wore her hiking boots. Twenty minutes, she spent on her hair. She sprayed a little perfume around her neck and on her wrists.

'Someone's getting done up,' said Kylie suddenly from the doorway.

'Got to look the part,' said Siobhan.

'You haven't looked the part like this since I came to this house. Is this an old flame?'

'It's an old admirer,' said Siobhan. 'I never kindled it.'

Kylie went to speak, but Siobhan walked straight past her, and put on a long black coat. Three o'clock on the dot, she walked along the seafront at Donaghadee and saw a man sitting on a bench by the small pools. In summer, kids would play in and out of these. Families would be shrieking. But today was cold.

As she approached, he stood up. He was wearing a long coat with gloves and had a wide-brimmed hat on top.

'Siobhan,' he said, 'it's been too long.'

He reached out with his hand, took hers, pulled it up to his mouth, and kissed it.

'Always the gentleman,' she said. 'It's good to see you, Julian. You're the only one who would talk to me.'

'Well, I've always tried to look out for you.'

'You've always been a friend,' she said. 'At times, you've gone up over and above, back in the day. I know that when I was with Eamon, that hurt you.'

'That was your choice,' he said. 'And I won't deny I was jealous as hell. But look at you. Free woman now.'

Siobhan gulped. *Was he seriously coming to talk to her about that?*

'Sorry,' he blurted. 'You'll be thinking I'm here to kindle something. But I'm not. I'm here to keep you safe. Always. Shall we walk?'

Siobhan nodded, and they strolled side by side until they got to the harbour wall. Once there, they climbed up on top and strolled along it, looking out at the lough beyond. There was a stiff breeze blowing. And Siobhan felt cold. She wrapped her coat around her.

'Maybe we should go for coffee somewhere.' He stopped himself. 'Lapsang Souchong. Do they have it here? Many cafes do it?'

'No, I'm an awkward woman to please,' she said. Julian stopped. Siobhan turned, facing him. He put his hands up on her shoulders. 'Listen, you need to stay clear of this.'

'Why?' asked Siobhan.

'Everyone's keeping their head down,' said Julian. 'I don't

know what's behind it. I don't know why. But everyone. I can't get anything about it from anyone. Many people don't know and those who should know won't talk to me. Maybe that's because they know I'll look out for you. Why wouldn't they look out for you as well? Something high up stinks. That's the only reason that everyone is keeping their head down.'

'People have died in this. Eamon died,' said Siobhan.

'I can't even find out what he was looking into. I'm not sure if it was done by the Service or not. Eamon was more freelance towards the end.'

'You didn't like him, did you?' said Siobhan.

'That's not true,' said Julian. 'I was jealous as hell of him because of his time spent with you. But I actually thought he was good. An operator in the Service. There were very few better than him. And he had the Service at heart, although he did things I wouldn't have done.'

'It's always what I admired about you. Your limits. You could always work around your limits. Some of us had to compromise ours.'

'Sometimes you've just got to find other ways,' said Julian.

'I guess I disappointed you in that,' said Siobhan.

'No,' said Julian. 'I never held you up as the perfect person. I just . . .' He bowed his head.

'What?'

'I just thought there was a time when we may have given it a go. Some of it worked, but you were with Eamon. And I would have wanted more than that. I would have wanted . . . well, you had a husband, too.'

'I had a husband. I didn't have a partner. Well, he was a partner, more of a business partner,' said Siobhan.

'It's not what I came to talk about,' said Julian. 'Look, just keep out of it.'

'I'm not sure I can,' she said. 'I owe Eamon.'

'I'll do what I can,' said Julian, turning and beginning to walk again. Siobhan followed him. 'I'll see what I can find out. I'll see what I can put in place to protect you. But be so very careful, won't you? I don't say this lightly because you might take it the wrong way and I never want to hurt you. But you are not the operative you were.'

Siobhan was taken aback. Julian said very few negative comments about her.

'Meaning?' she asked.

'You're not as quick; you're not as sharp. You are vulnerable in that sense.'

She looked at him. 'Vulnerable?'

'We all are. Happens when we get older. We're vulnerable when we're young because we don't know stuff. Don't know what our limits are. We don't know the rights and wrongs of things. We learn a bit, and we get to a peak. Maybe in our thirties, we actually understand what we're doing. Yet we're still learning.

'Then when we get older, we think we know it all. We think we know how to do it, how to be safe. But then our body fails us. Don't get me wrong,' he said. 'You're the most beautiful woman I've seen in this world to date. You still are. I was captivated by you a long time ago. But I'd be lying through my teeth if I turned around and said you were as good as you were then. Don't trust your abilities to get you through. You have friends,' he said.

Siobhan stopped him walking, held both his hands in hers.

'I think you're more than just a friend,' said Siobhan. She

reached forward and gave him a gentle kiss on the lips. 'There's few I worried about hurting in the service,' she said. 'You were one. I hear you. I understand what you're saying to me. But I've got to do this. Any help would be greatly appreciated.'

She turned and walked away before stopping and turning back. 'I still have retirement to manage after I get this done. Maybe that's the time and place when we could find something out. See just how compatible we would be.'

'I'm not retired yet,' he said.

'Would you retire for me?'

'You know the answer,' said Julian. 'I'll try to keep an eye.'

She mouthed a thank you to him and turned. She knew the answer all right, and that's what scared her. No one had ever been prepared to commit so much to her. The Service didn't breed people like that. Julian was a one-off and a damn fine one-off, just not one she could explore at the moment.

Chapter 22

Y ou're looking fine,' said Kylie, as Siobhan walked back into the house. She simply smiled, took off her black coat, and hung it up. She strode across towards her study, opened the door, and plopped herself onto her seat. Delicately, she manoeuvred in beside where her laptop was and began typing into the search bar the word Jenny Goldsmith. Kylie appeared at the door. She said nothing, but shuffled over and stood behind Siobhan.

'I've already done that. She works for the environment agency.'

'You got a home address for her?'

'No.'

'Okay. Let's get one.' The woman was on the electoral register. After checking a few different sites, some of which were only available to the Service, or those who had left and still had connections. Siobhan wrote the address of Jenny Goldsmith.

'Seems she lives with an . . . or rather, lived with an Alan, Alan Bartholomew. Maybe he'll be there when we get . . . We should try the house first rather than her family.'

'Can you trace her family off that connection as well?' asked

Kylie.

'Yes. Let's have a look.'

Ten minutes later, Siobhan had worked out that Jenny's father had died, but her mother was still around. However, there was no address for her.

'Well, I think the first thing we do is see Mr Bartholomew. You come with me,' said Siobhan.

'Me?' said Kylie. 'I thought we were all going. If it's a man there, do you not want Declan? Just in case he gets a bit annoyed or . . .'

'Kylie, I can handle myself better than Declan can. No, what we need is someone who he's going to be more likely to open up to.'

'Well, you're there. You're his age.'

'What age do you think he is? Jenny was only twenty-five, according to her birth certificate. Alan's probably that or below on that basis.'

'Okay,' said Kylie, 'but I won't say much. I'm not good at the questioning.'

'You don't need to be good at the questioning. You need to be good at the thinking,' said Siobhan. 'You think right, the questions come. No time like the present, though.'

'I was just going to go make the dinner.'

'Leave that. Declan can make us a late one or we'll order in. Come on, we're on the move.'

Siobhan stood up, went to stride out of the room, but Kylie stepped across in front of her at the door. 'This person you went to see. What did they say?'

'Oh, that?' said Siobhan. 'Basically, that nobody in the Service is touching it. Everybody's keeping their heads down. Could be trouble from higher up. Maybe somebody there is involved. We don't know exactly.'

'Okay, and because the Service are not involved and aren't touching it, you suddenly come in bouncing around like you've got springs in your feet. I wasn't born yesterday. Who is this guy you went to see?'

'Julian,' said Siobhan, 'Julian. Nice guy.'

She moved Kylie out of the way, walking past and grabbing her coat. 'Declan, we're off out. Probably going to have takeaway for later. Make yourself something if you're hungry. Remember, don't answer the door unless you know who they are. You can get me on the phone; you can . . .'

'I'm right behind you,' said Declan. Siobhan turned from putting her coat on. 'Oh, so you are. Anyway, watch the match or something on telly.'

'There isn't a match on. You don't have sports channels.'

'No, I don't,' said Siobhan. 'Good point. Do something useful. Come on, Kylie,' she said.

'Where are you two off to?' said Declan.

'Keep up, Declan,' said Kylie. 'Off to see the partner of Jenny Goldsmith.'

'Shouldn't I come?'

'No,' said Siobhan. Before Declan could react, the front door had been closed with Kylie and Siobhan on the other side of it.

* * *

There were several new estates in Northern Ireland, and this one was on the outskirts of Belfast. The houses looked smaller. When they told you there were three bedrooms, they didn't look like it. Two and a half bedrooms, something like that, but they were a pretty penny.

Belfast was very different now to the days of the Troubles. People wanted to be in Belfast. Buildings were being erected that Siobhan didn't recognise anymore. She remembered the days of going shopping and having to go through checkpoints, people scanning your hand baggage as you went in, purses being opened. Men standing while electrical wands were swept in front and behind you.

She remembered the bomb threats and moving three doors down to shop elsewhere. People were so resilient. Normal life was resilient in the strangest of places. She'd seen that in Russia, too. She'd heard about it from the guys who had worked in other war zones, but now Belfast was on the up, and she hoped it'd stay that way.

It meant more houses, areas getting taken over. She drove through Bangor and it was two to three times the size it had ever been in her day. On the Belfast Road, however, there were still the larger houses, almost little mansions with estates around them. They seemed expensive enough to maintain an aura of the countryside.

Siobhan rapped the door of Jenny Goldsmith's address, with Kylie standing beside her. It was opened a few moments later by a gaunt-looking man, maybe in his early thirties. He wore a large jumper, a pair of jeans, and gave the feeling of an academic.

'Is it Mr Bartholomew?'

'Yes,' he said. 'We don't do Jehovah's Witness visits.'

Siobhan glanced at Kylie. Of course, she'd come with a trap, hadn't she? Older woman, younger woman.

'I'm not here to give you any religion, Mr Bartholomew. I'd like to talk about Jenny if I may.'

'Why's that?' he asked.

'I've come to talk about how she passed.'

He peered out through the front door, looked left and right. 'Come in,' he said.

Siobhan walked in but kept her coat on as she was led through to a front room that had a large gas fire going. She wasn't offered a seat. Instead, Alan Bartholomew pulled the blinds on the large window to the street outside.

'What is it you want?' he asked.

'Just quite simple. We don't think that Jenny's death was natural.'

The man didn't seem surprised. Instead, he looked more confused. 'Who do you work for' he asked.

'I'm sorry?' asked Siobhan.

'Who do you work for? Coming here to talk about Jenny's death. Are you . . .'

'Just some concerned citizens,' said Siobhan, knowing that was the worst line going. You could sense the man was tense. He wouldn't be very responsive. Kylie stepped up beside her, and the man turned to look at her.

'I'm really sorry. I've had people like Jenny die before, friends of that age in a similar fashion.' For a moment Siobhan thought Kylie was dragging him in. He became suddenly less defensive.

Siobhan used the opportunity to step past him. She saw the word address book on a small tome sitting on the side. She glanced over. Kylie was still engaging him. Siobhan flicked the book open, looking for an entry for Goldsmith. She went to G and saw an Amanda Goldsmith, and noted down the address.

'When did you first find out about Jenny's demise?' asked

Kylie.

No, no, no, thought Siobhan. *Too strong, too direct.* She looked at Alan Bartholomew. His open and almost warm demeanour towards Kylie changed in an instant.

'I don't get who the hell you two are, but get out,' he said.

'We're just people trying to help, Mr Bartholomew.'

'I don't need any help. Jenny's dead. Just leave me alone.' He went to the door and opened it. Siobhan nodded at Kylie to follow. As they walked past him, he said, 'It was sudden heart failure. Don't forget it.'

Siobhan had the door slammed behind her. She trudged to the car. When Kylie got in beside her, she saw the girl was almost in tears.

'That was horrible,' said Kylie. 'And we got nothing from it.'

'We got the address of his mother-in-law,' said Siobhan. Kylie looked at her. 'While you were engaging him, I looked through his address book and found it.'

'You only had about thirty seconds.'

'Yes, should have got more. Maybe I am losing it a bit. Anyway, she's over towards Newtonabbey. Let's go.'

Kylie looked cheerier. When they arrived at the address for Amanda Goldsmith, however, she looked a little wearier.

'What do we do when we get the same reaction?'

'We won't. Trust me,' said Siobhan.

She knocked on the door of a rather small house. This one was in a terrace, and looked like a two up, two down. The red brick was classical of its time, with the lintels above the door and the windows painted white. It was a common trait around Belfast, even this far out. The green door opened. Siobhan was appraised by the wily eye of a woman who was maybe slightly older than herself.

'Can I help you?'

'I'd like to talk about your daughter and about the unresolved questions regarding her death.'

'Are you a reporter?' asked the woman. 'Because the reporters generally don't talk to me. So you're a what?'

'Let's say I'm a friend. A friend of a friend of the reporters. Someone who looked into it. He's dead now, too.'

'Come in,' said the woman. She closed the door quickly behind them. The living room they entered was tiny. Siobhan stood while Kylie sat down beside the woman on a small sofa.

'Who are you?' asked the woman almost immediately.

'I'm going to level with you. My friend was investigating into issues going on up on the Causeway Coast. I believe Jenny may have been connected to that, certainly her death. My friend died because of it and now I'm investigating. My name is Siobhan. This is Kylie.'

The woman nodded. 'What do you want to know about Jenny?'

'I believe she didn't die of natural causes.'

The woman shook her head. 'I tell that to my blessed son-in-law. It's not fair, though. He won't have it. Whoever has got to him, they haven't come to see me because I'm just the bloody old idiot of a mother-in-law, a mother who can't take it that her child's died. That's what they tell you.'

Siobhan could see the tears in the woman's eyes.

'Tell me about it,' said Siobhan.

'There's not a lot to tell,' said Amanda. 'You see, she worked for the Environment Agency. She was asked to look at that proposed hotel complex. I didn't understand the issues, but she put protests in about it, saying that some of the environmental aspects weren't right. She came around and told me about some of it, but I didn't understand it. She was the clever one, not me. They removed her from the case, apparently. Then she lost her job. Just like that.'

'How did she take to that?' asked Siobhan.

'She went to the press.'

'Do you know who?'

'Somebody, Vegas,' she said. 'She told me he had warned her to keep her head down. She thought she had made a mistake. Then she died at home. They said it was sudden heart failure. She'd only just got going,' said the woman, tears now coming from her eyes. 'She was twenty-five. Somebody shut my child up at twenty-five. Somebody killed her.'

'They killed my friend too,' said Siobhan. 'He was older. They still killed him.'

'I talked to the police about it, but they said there was no sign of anything. Alan just keeps his head down because somebody went and spoke to him. I know it. He doesn't speak to me now. He won't come. I'm his mother-in-law. I just lost my child, his partner's mother, and he won't come and speak to me. It's not normal, is it?'

'No, it's not,' said Kylie.

'Don't blame him,' said Siobhan. 'The people that did this are nasty pieces of work. I need to get proof. I need to get authorities involved, which means I need to understand who's behind it all. Do you know anything else?'

'Only that they lied,' said Amanda Goldsmith. 'They lied and they killed my daughter. They bloody well killed her. Then they covered it up.'

'When she died, what happened to the body?'

'It was taken to a morgue. As far as I know, up in the city.'

'Did anyone examine her from a police point of view?'

'Police told me there was no evidence. She went to the morgue, they had a brief look at her and said she died of sudden heart failure.'

'I will look into it for you,' said Siobhan.

She heard somebody sniffing and saw Kylie almost in tears. She'd have to get a better backbone than that if she was going to question people. As heart-breaking as the woman's story was, there was stuff to do.

'If anyone asks,' said Siobhan to the woman, 'you didn't hear my name, you didn't hear her name. We don't exist. If I get the truth out of it, if I resolve it, I'll be back to tell you and explain. Try to give you some closure. Until then, I won't come near you. It's too risky. Keep your head down. Let me look at this.'

A minute later, they were back out and in the car. Kylie was in absolute tears.

'It's not fair. How can they do that? How can they just . . .'

'They did it to Eamon as well.'

'Well, he was in the Service, and he seemed to be part of it. This woman was only doing her job. She was only twenty-five.'

About your age, thought Siobhan, *that's why it struck you. You've just realised what she's missed in life.* Siobhan leaned over and let Kylie put her head on her shoulder. 'Let it out,' she said. 'Let it out. You might find there's a lot more of this before we're done.'

Chapter 23

The day was frosty but crisp as Siobhan looked out on a new morning. She threw her dressing gown on over her pyjamas and walked through to her kitchen to see Declan munching on some cereal. Generally, Siobhan didn't have cereal in the house, but as Declan was staying, it wasn't a surprise that he brought his own. The surprise was he was eating in Siobhan's kitchen and not up with Kylie.

'To what do I owe the pleasure?' asked Siobhan.

'I think Kylie just needed some space.'

'Why?'

'I was asking her about the people you saw yesterday. She didn't really take that kindly to it.'

'When you say asking,' said Siobhan, 'do you mean pester? Just keep on, keep on until you get an answer. You do that sometimes. In a friendly fashion, of course.'

Siobhan walked over to the sink, filled the kettle, pressed the switch and stood waiting for it to boil.

'I don't pester. I don't pester you, do I?'

'Declan, if you're asking me for the third time when I told you twice already no, you wouldn't get a chance to pester me.'

'Are you all right there, Mrs D?'

'Just be careful. You're both sleeping in the same house at the end of my drive. It's not a big house. There's not a lot of room. Kylie's used to having it on her own. She's used to evenings being quiet.'

'I thought she'd like the company,' said Declan.

Siobhan tightened her belt on her dressing gown, took a cup down and placed a tea bag of her smoky tea inside. She filled it with hot water as the kettle had just clicked. Taking the cup to her lips, she sipped on the boiling water.

'Declan, can I give you a bit of advice?'

'I've got a feeling it's coming anyway, Mrs D.'

Siobhan smiled. Declan had that ability to show you when you were in the wrong, but ever so gently. She didn't really have any right to give advice, but she was sure the boy could use some.

'I think Kylie likes you. I'm not sure she wants to, but I think she does.' Declan looked somewhat confused. 'I can tell you're sweet on her.'

Declan suddenly blushed. 'Is it that obvious?'

'Um, yes. It is,' said Siobhan. 'But just take it easy. A girl like Kylie, she needs to take her time, be happy in what she's doing. Sometimes us women think we need a certain type of guy.'

'All right. What type of guy's that?'

'Well, it depends on the woman, doesn't it?' said Siobhan. 'I guess it's like you guys. Sometimes you think you need that woman with the great figure, the large bust, and hair that's never seen a bad day in its life. But then, you realise that, actually, no, what you need is a friend, first and foremost.'

Siobhan stopped suddenly. She thought about Eamon. Eamon was what she thought she needed back then. He was exciting to be with, but ultimately, Eamon moved on. He didn't care about her. She thought about Andrew. When they'd married, she thought he was the one. A good marriage, a sensible marriage. Then she thought about Julian.

'Mrs D, you were saying something. Something about girls with big boobs.'

Siobhan snapped back into the conversation. 'That's not what I was talking about.'

'You did. You said girls with figure, and boobs, and hair.'

All women have those, thought Siobhan. 'No, Declan. I was saying you need a friend. A friend's the most important bit. I think Kylie realises that. Just take your time with her. You're also younger than her.'

'I'm two years younger than her. What's that got to do with it? It might have been in your day, but . . .'

'I'm fifty, Declan. I'm not dead.'

Declan slumped his shoulders slightly, letting his head droop before he looked up. 'Sorry, I didn't mean to offend.'

'It's all right. You guys forget people like me are still . . .'

'Relevant?' Said Declan.

'Away and catch yourself on. Relevant? What the hell word is relevant?' raged Siobhan suddenly. Declan looked as if the world was about to end and his worst fears were coming true.

'Just understand this. You young guys come out with all these words and you think, "Oh, this is what this is. This is how I should speak. This is the thing that all the oldies don't understand." I understand what the word relevant is and maybe you guys should understand the word, irrelevance.'

Siobhan stopped suddenly. *That is a word, isn't it?* Then she carried on.

'You guys get into your twenties, and barely into your

twenties, and your generation has done diddly-squat. Yet already, you're gobbing off about this, that, and whatever else. Frankly, Declan,' Siobhan stopped herself. She wouldn't say that word. That word was not a good one to say. 'Sod off, Declan,' said Siobhan with as much restraint as she could muster.

'I thought it was rough up there with Kylie,' said Declan. 'Bloody hell. I'm going to go back to breakfast with my father.'

Siobhan took her tea, walked out of the door and nearly burst out laughing. It was hard to dislike Declan. Even though he had hit a nerve, Siobhan was in good spirits as she walked into her office. It was half an hour later when Kylie entered the kitchen. Siobhan had showered and Declan was awaiting the next verbal bashing from the two women.

'We need to visit the morgue,' said Siobhan.

'The morgue? Why are we visiting the morgue?' asked Kylie.

'I need to see where Jenny was examined. I need to get information from there.'

'Can't you just break into their systems?'

'Declan, I'm no longer in the Service. There were people there that did that. I've got a few things that can lift stuff off laptops, but I need to be there, and I need to plug them in. Auto programs that will find stuff, but I have to be inside the building.'

'Okay,' said Declan. 'What are we going to do? You want me or Kylie to die so we can get in?'

'It won't need to be like that,' said Siobhan. 'But we'll get ourselves in. What we'll do is, you two will pretend to be students, pulling a prank, pushing a dead body around. You'll get yourself in there, then we'll cause a commotion. Then you'll run, get yourselves back out of there. Everybody will think it's a prank, but by that time you'll have left the body somewhere and this body will have got up and gone hunting.'

'What?' blurted Declan. 'If you ask me, it sounds like the script of a bad horror film.'

'We're going to be students; we're going to get Siobhan in and then we're going to get out. That's it,' said Kylie.

'You'll be all right once you're in, Mrs D?' asked Declan.

'I will be. Trust me, Declan, I've done a lot of this in the past. But make sure you look casual. Not too smart. What do you students wear?'

'Some of them wear all sorts of nonsense,' said Declan. 'I'm not wearing that.'

'Jeans and t-shirt will do,' said Kylie. 'Jacket or something.'

That afternoon they went up to Belfast, where Siobhan walked past the morgue several times. It was part of one of the large Belfast hospitals, with its own section down deep in the building. Although not the busiest place in the hospital, there was still a reasonable throughput of bodies.

Siobhan decided to wait until late in the evening. After all, students would pull a prank late at night, wouldn't they? A couple of beers on them. She took the pair out for dinner, making sure everyone was well fed before coming back close to eleven at night. They found a gurney in the hospital and Siobhan stole a couple of sheets from a linen cupboard down a lonely corridor. She jumped up onto the gurney and let them cover her with the white sheets.

Declan and Kylie pushed the trolley along the white corridors and the posters explaining who wore what colours among the hospital staff. Arriving at the morgue doors, they watched someone walk out. He glanced at them, but then walked on. Maybe he wasn't staff. Maybe he was going home and didn't want any hassle.

Kylie was able to get to the doors, standing between them and forcing them to open again. Declan pushed the gurney inside. There was a small reception area, and they continued to walk on past the desk and some cabinets, before arriving at another door. Although they couldn't see through the door, they were sure there were rooms beyond. It was at this point that someone from inside these rooms looked out through a window and gave a shout.

'What the hell? Who are you two?'

Declan looked at Kylie. She looked at him and shouted back, 'Student chopmeisters. We're here to cut her up with ye lot!'

'What the heck?' said the man. 'Come here.'

Declan and Kylie turned, running back out and opening the double doors beyond. Siobhan could hear someone run past the trolley. He was shouting, at first, loudly, and then it sounded as if he was further away. His diminishing voice sounded outside of the morgue.

Quickly, she pulled down the sheets, hoping she was right. Siobhan looked around a spotless room with several filing cabinets on the wall. There was a computer facing her at a desk. Rolling off the gurney, she walked over and moved the mouse, illuminating the screen. In front of her came a message about putting in your login and typing your password. Siobhan took out a USB stick and shoved it into the USB port at the side of the computer.

Siobhan wasn't totally au fait with how these things worked. She knew the programme ran, broke its way in, and got out again. This was an NHS system. It had its defences, but nothing that the Service guys couldn't get past. The programme she had was maybe six months old, so she was fairly confident that it would do its magic.

She'd fed it previously with the name of Jenny Goldsmith, and all Siobhan had to do now was wait. As she stood in the quiet, Siobhan could hear someone in the corridor outside. It sounded like the man again. He would be in shortly.

She looked around the office. She could go through to where the dead bodies were. There were lines of compartments where they stored the bodies. Or she could try to hide in the office. There was the desk, but she could be seen behind there. Anyone walking about in the office would catch you. She could go back on the gurney underneath the sheet, but that, again, would prove difficult if he checked if the students had nicked a real corpse.

Siobhan entered the main morgue area. It held what the public might call the slab or the table on which they examined the bodies, and all the storage facilities alongside. You could see through from the window to the office outside. Siobhan ducked when she saw the man walking into that office.

'And they put this bloody gurney here. Let's see who owns this.'

She watched as the man took the gurney outside into the hallway, and she breathed a sigh of relief. She waited, wondering if he'd come back. The invasive computer programme would need twenty minutes to be effective. It wouldn't show anything on the screen, not unless you pressed the mouse button, left and right keys in a certain fashion. Then it would show you its progress. Surely, it wouldn't be ready yet.

Siobhan felt the cold for the morgue was kept cool by a whirring air conditioning unit. But not as cool as she felt when the man walked back into the outer office, rubbing his hands as if ready to get back to work. She looked around her and pulled out one of the long drawers that stored the bodies.

Looking up at her was a cadaver. A middle-aged man, from what she could see. When she looked, there wasn't any room to get in beside him. There was nowhere else to hide in here.

She closed the door and opened the one next to him. It was empty. Siobhan clambered in and, using her arms, pushed the drawer backwards so that it rolled shut. As it did so, she heard the man entering the room. Siobhan was in the dark, but she'd rolled it just enough so it hadn't fully closed. She was hoping he wouldn't notice, as she was in the bottom drawer of a large cabinet.

Siobhan felt a chill. She remembered once when she'd had to hide amongst bodies. It was one of her worst days as an operative. A cull in an Eastern European land, they'd come for so many operatives of varying nationalities. They'd thrown a lot of the bodies into a pit, and she'd hidden in there.

It had been dark, about four in the morning, when she'd got herself out. They were going to fill the shallow grave the next morning.

She thought that was another reason she was leaving the service. It was the reason she'd become an analyst instead of an operative.

Siobhan heard the man take out a body, put it on the slab and start talking about it. He was making notes as he examined it. She felt cold, and hoped that her knees wouldn't knock together. Carefully, she wrapped her arms around herself.

When did this guy go for lunch? It was the middle of the night, of course. It must be now, what? Getting close on to midnight. She wanted to reach down for her watch and look at it, but she couldn't. Everything was just too cramped.

'Are we doing dinner together today?' asked a voice.

'I've just wrapped this one up. I'll be along.'

Siobhan hoped he wouldn't be too long at all because she was deeply chilled. She'd come in wearing only her jumper and jeans with a small light t-shirt underneath. She wanted nothing that was too ridiculous on her. When she heard him leaving, she waited five minutes and then slowly, she put her arms up against the top of the confined space she was in and pushed. The drawer slid out, and she saw the lights of the morgue. She squinted and quickly clambered out, closing the door behind her.

Walking through to the other room, she tapped the mouse in an intricate sequence of clicks. The screen clicked on. 'Completed,' it said. She pulled the USB and shoved it in her pocket. Looking at the window to the corridor, she saw no one. She walked out along the corridor to hear a man shouting at her.

'What are you doing down here at this time of night?'

She looked up and saw a security guard. She ran to him, flung her arms around him, put her head on his shoulder. Forcing tears, she wept bitterly.

'He's gone. They took him in there. In there.'

'Come with me, ma'am,' the guard said. He helped her to a lift and took her up to the front reception of the hospital. There, she saw Kylie and Declan and waved them over. They had concerned faces, for Siobhan was crying her eyes out. Before they could speak, she flung herself forward, putting her arms around him and saying, 'Dad's down there. Dad's in the morgue.'

'Oh, I think you should take your mother home. Obviously, been a rough day,' said the security man. 'But she can't really be wandering around. I'm sorry for your loss.'

'We will,' said Declan. 'Come on, Mum,' he said. 'Let's get home. We need to go home.'

Siobhan turned round one last time as if she was ready to reach back towards the morgue. Kylie grabbed her.

'No. No. We go home. Thank you for your understanding,' she said to the security guard.

The man was rather plump and gave a big smile. 'That's all right. I know how hard this can be,' he said.

The three walked out to the car, putting Siobhan in the rear seat. Declan drove out and once they were clear of the hospital grounds, Siobhan reached inside her pocket and pulled out a USB stick.

'Well, if she's in that computer, this little baby's going to have got her.'

'You're something else, Mrs D. Do you know that?' said Declan. 'I actually thought you were properly in tears there.'

Kylie looked over, first at Declan, and then at Siobhan, and then she smiled. *She does like him*, thought Siobhan. *Doesn't she?*

Chapter 24

It was three in the morning and Siobhan was sitting in front of her laptop; the infiltration program plugged in via the USB. She told the other two to wait in the kitchen while she worked on this.

The programme had pulled out information about Jenny Goldsmith, including the report from the morgue about why she had died. The autopsy revealed that everything looked in place for a sudden heart failure. Her body had been taken away, and she'd been cremated after a family service. The certificate which showed that she'd been handed over to the undertakers gave testament to that.

Siobhan pushed herself back from the laptop and walked through to the kitchen. 'So, what's the deal, Mrs D?' asked Declan.

'We go forward,' she said. 'According to the autopsy, she died of sudden heart failure.'

'Maybe she did,' said Kylie.

'No,' said Siobhan, 'but I'm thinking that it would be difficult to have got it wrong. If they killed her, even if they injected her or something, or they nicked an important artery, an autopsy is likely going to find it. We need to check out if the man who did the autopsy is mixed up in this.'

'You think that could be done?'

'Yes, Declan. These people are threatening and killing. Our journalist friends were quick enough to step back because they realised that threat. It wouldn't surprise me if they got hold of one consultant at the morgue to do the autopsy. Fudge It. If you can fudge that bit and you know that she's been taken away with suspected heart failure, no one's going to argue, and you get the body cremated. If you can control the disposal, so to speak, you'll be in the clear, but plenty of people will know not to mess with you.'

'Who did the autopsy, then?' asked Kylie.

'Signed by a consultant, Ernie Savage,' said Siobhan. 'I'm thinking we need to keep an eye on Ernie for a few days. Then we'll pay him a visit in the best way possible to extract information from him.'

'Do you have an address?'

'Fortunately, enough,' said Siobhan, 'because Mr Savage was mentioned in the autopsy report, the program lifted information about him. He lives in a rather expensive part of Belfast, so tomorrow we hunt him down, spend a bit of time finding out about him, then we'll lure him in. The key thing at the moment is that we remain incognito, that people don't realise we're looking into things. They know we're about, but they don't know where we've got to. If we can get evidence established before they find out what we're doing, we would have a better chance of making it stick. A better chance of getting it to the correct authorities.'

'And they don't come after us,' said Declan.

In some ways, he was a simple soul, and yet, in others, he was very astute. That was the key issue that Siobhan wanted to take care of. To make sure they didn't know where the team was and what the team was doing and therefore, not to wind up dead. Siobhan hadn't mentioned it in that fashion because she didn't want to scare the other two. She'd scared them enough, showing them guns and telling Declan to remain on the premises.

The next day, the team observed Ernie Savage. He was at work for most of the day, but in the evening, they followed him home and realised he was living alone. Did he have a wife? Was she away? They didn't know until Siobhan checked local death records and found that his wife had died three years ago.

That evening, Savage disappeared in a taxi, which they followed to a nondescript building in the centre of Belfast. The door was guarded by a single man, large and impressive. Though the building's fascia showed signs of nothing important, the team sat and watched the entrance. They noted that several single men entered.

Occasionally, a small group of girls would enter too. Siobhan put them maybe in the eighteen to twenty-two-year-old section. At least she hoped they were eighteen and over. They were dressed in rather revealing clothing, too. They had bare legs. Occasionally, she saw the bottom of a dress, up round their rear end, as people used to say.

She sat back in the front seat and turned to Declan. 'What do you think's going on in there, Declan?' He looked a little embarrassed.

'You ever been in anywhere like that?' Kylie asked him.

He went a little red and turned away.

'Where?' asked Kylie suddenly.

'Not like that. I have been in a strip joint.'

Siobhan almost laughed. It must be the guy's worst nightmare. The girl he's interested in asking him if he'd been to a place like this and another woman sitting in the front with him who could almost be his mother.

'Don't worry, Declan, I've been in a few in my time as well.' Siobhan saw his jaw almost drop.

'I didn't know you were that way inclined,' said Kylie.

'I'm not,' said Siobhan. 'It was with the job. High-powered men and even some high-powered women seem more drawn to dangerous sexual activity. I think that's the correct way to put it. So, you end up chasing them, you end up setting up honey traps for them and you end up seeing where they go.'

'I'm not sure I'd be any good at that job,' said Declan. 'Not in these surroundings.' He'd gone red again.

'Anyway, I've seen enough for tonight,' said Siobhan. 'Let's go home. We'll tail him for another few days.'

Over the next two days, they found that Ernie Savage returned to this building twice. After the last day of tailing him, they sat in the kitchen, ready to discuss what to do next.

'I don't know if you're up for this,' said Siobhan, 'but I want to set a honey trap.'

'A what?' blurted Declan. 'You mean get a woman to . . .'

'Get a woman to lure him somewhere. Yes. Back in the day, they would have killed him. That's what the honey traps were for.'

'We're not killing him,' said Declan.

'No,' said Siobhan, 'of course we're not. What I want to do, though, is lure him back to the car. When he's there, we can put a gun in his back. If the Russians are involved, I think they'll be the ones who have paid him the money to cover up the autopsy. I think he needs a visit from Russian friends to say that things don't look so good. See if we can get him to blurt out what he did. See if he'll drop any names. If we can do that, we might have somewhere else to go with this.'

'Where are we going to get a honey?' asked Kylie. 'We need someone to lure him in. What does he like? Young girls. Someone eighteen or nineteen, prepared to dress up like that. Lure him in. Is it risky?'

'No, it won't be risky. I'll keep an eye on you,' said Siobhan.

'Me?' said Kylie.

'Kylie?' blurted Declan.

'Why do you think it shouldn't be me?' retorted Kylie.

'You don't want to be doing that,' said Declan.

'You think I don't look good enough?'

'No,' said Declan. Then Kylie suddenly turned on Siobhan. 'You think I should do it? You think that's the sort of person I am?'

'Whoa,' said Siobhan, 'hang on for a minute. You're having a go at him for saying you're not good-looking enough and you're having a go at me for saying you are.'

'I didn't say she wasn't good-looking enough. She just shouldn't be doing that. She's not that type of girl.'

'Siobhan here thinks I am,' spat Kylie.

'No,' said Siobhan. Things had been easier back in the service. People were trained for jobs and you didn't have to make do with what was around you. You could get a specialist if needed.

'I'm saying you're a talented actress, Kylie. That's all. You wouldn't have to do anything with him, either. Just dress up, catch his eye, offer him a good time, tell him to go back to the car and we'll head for a hotel or something. That's all. When he gets to the car, I'll be there. I'll play the Russian.

'Of course, you don't have to do it,' said Siobhan. 'But if we go outside the team and get somebody else to do it, that opens a link to us. We want to stay as tight as we can so they don't get what we're up to.'

'Okay,' said Kylie, 'I'll do it, but it doesn't go beyond the car. You better be there.'

'Of course, I'll be there,' said Siobhan.

'So tomorrow I'd better buy an outfit because I don't have the stuff that they were wearing in my cupboard.'

'I'll take you,' said Declan.

'No, you won't,' Kylie said suddenly. 'Just because you want to have an ogle at me.'

'I was just going to drive the car,' he blurted. Siobhan watched the guy's face, realising he'd dropped himself in it, but he hadn't done it deliberately. He was trying to help.

'That's decided then,' said Siobhan. 'Come on, off to bed. We go tomorrow night with this. If he heads back to that club or whatever he's at, we'll intercept him before he gets there. In my experience, these guys like something new. It's the thrill, the risk, the danger. Someone new, someone they don't know. Getting to do it without a bouncer there to keep tabs on you.'

'As long as you're my bouncer,' said Kylie.

Next day, Kylie did her shopping, and Siobhan checked how she looked when she came back. The skirt was obscene. The top too, along with the bubble jacket. Siobhan gave Kylie a quick lesson on what not to do. She'd have to open her jacket, she'd have to show him the honey, so to speak, but then to zip back up to make sure he understood he had to go elsewhere with her.

She was nervous, but she was brave too, and Siobhan made

a point of telling her that Declan would be in the car nearby to where Savage had his. If he took a taxi there, they would use Declan as a nearby taxi driver.

That evening, they were at Ernie Savage's house at five, watching him return from work at approximately six o'clock. He re-emerged at half past seven, this time taking his car. He threw them off their plan as he drove to the local supermarket.

Bugger, thought Siobhan. *It must be his night off.*

'I can't wait another night,' said Kylie. 'Shall I just go for it?'

'How?' asked Siobhan.

'I'll wait by his car. Tell him one of the girls from the club said he was a good mark, paid well. He's got money, hasn't he?'

'That's true, but you can't get in the back of his car here.'

'Why not?'

'CCTV,' said Siobhan. 'Too easy to get spotted. You'll need to convince him to go elsewhere. Take him up to the Craigantlet Hills, up to one of the car parks. Tell him you like it outdoors. Tell him anything but get him to the car park up there.'

'Which one?'

Siobhan took out her phone and, using Google Maps, showed Kylie where to go.

'We'll tail you,' said Siobhan. 'Keep an eye on you, but if we lose you, you're going there. I've always got your location tracer, anyway.' She'd put this on recently when she saw the increased threat. She could trace the phones of both, Declan and Kylie.

Kylie stepped out of the car, and Siobhan watched Declan's startled face as she marched across. High heels and bare legs. It was so unlike her. The girl was good-looking, yes. She had the advantage of youth, but she wore her jeans, leggings, baggy tops. She wasn't this sort of girl at all. Yet she was striding across, owning the character.

It was five minutes before Ernie Savage came out of the supermarket, and she must have been frozen. The night was bitter, but Siobhan watched as Kylie approached Savage. His face was a picture. When she opened her jacket, Siobhan thought he was almost licking his lips, looking like some hungry wolf eyeing up Little Red Riding Hood. Boy, he was sick.

Siobhan had to stop Declan from starting up the car before Savage had begun his. He drove past, was about to head out of the car park before Siobhan told Declan to turn his own over. They followed at quite a distance, knowing that they were heading off into the Craigantlet hills.

Sure enough, Kylie had got him to park up. The car park was dark, and from a distance, Siobhan watched Ernie Savage's car go dark too, the interior light switching off. She moved quickly, covering her face with a balaclava. She opened the rear door of Ernie Savage's car.

'Good evening, Mr Savage,' she said in her best Russian accent. She could feel him shake. 'There have been complications with the work we authorised you to do. People have been tracing us; people have been asking questions.'

Kylie had opened the door, stepped out of the car, was walking back over towards Declan.

'I want to know that you did your job properly. I want to know exactly what you did. In the case you've dropped us in it, we will kill you. If they come for us, we will kill you. We paid you good money.'

'I did the records as asked,' blurted Ernie. 'I did it, everything. There was no mention of anything in her system. She has a record; you can check. Sudden heart failure, an anomaly. I found the problems within her system that caused it. Totally natural; was going to happen at some point. I told them all, I've told all my colleagues the same. None of them got to examine the body, just me. It was routine. They took her away, and they burnt her. I don't understand. They didn't get it from me, not from me.'

'Somehow, they have come asking. Somehow, they know it's us.'

'Maxwell, it must be Maxwell who's at fault. Maxwell, go ask Maxwell. It's not me, please. Please!'

'If you tell anyone I was here, I will come back and kill you. If you tell anyone anything about our arrangement, we will kill you. Our reach is long.'

'I won't tell anyone.'

'Good. Wait here for ten minutes, then leave.'

Siobhan stepped out of the car, gun still trained on Savage. She hurried back and jumped into the front seat beside Declan.

'Go, no lights until we're clear of here.'

Declan drove off on the road until Ernie Savage could no longer see them, and then flicked on the car lights. Siobhan turned round, looked at Kylie. 'Are you okay?' she asked.

'Yes,' said Kylie. 'God, he was horrible. Horrible. Just before you got in, I had to push him off, talk about money and things, so he wouldn't.'

'Good girl,' said Siobhan. 'I told you I'd be there, didn't I? I had your back.'

'Did you get anything, though?'

'Maxwell. He said, "Maxwell could be at fault." I don't know who Maxwell is, but we'll need to find out.'

'Is that it?' said Kylie. 'It doesn't sound worth all these last lot of days.'

'Maybe. It may not be. We'll have to wait and see, but we've looked into Jenny Goldsmith's family. Time to look into Simon Redburn's.'

Siobhan noted that the other two were deflated. 'Hey guys, easy. These things take time, and sometimes things don't come through straight away. You've got to keep battering on. First things first, let's get you back, get you out of that clobber you're in,' said Siobhan. 'It doesn't suit you.'

She saw Kylie smile at her, but then the mouth waned a bit.

'I don't know,' said Kylie. 'It could be fun in the right situation.'

'Yes,' said Declan. The two women glowered at him, but he turned and stared at the road. The entire way back to Donaghadee, Declan said nothing.

Chapter 25

The next day, Siobhan told Kylie to have the day off to pick up some shopping and rest up after her previous night's exploits. She took Declan with her instead to follow Simon Redburn's widow. They found her house on an estate in Newtownards, which was at the other end of the housing market from Ernie Savage's house.

These communities were sometimes harder to infiltrate because they were more suspicious. They noticed strangers. Fortunately, they spotted Amy leaving the house and tailed her, first of all, to the supermarket. She was buying flowers. As they left the supermarket, Siobhan thought there was another car nearby that seemed to follow her. She told Declan to pull back and watched as the other car maintained a distance behind Amy.

Siobhan rejoined the pursuit and was interested when Amy pulled off towards one of the local graveyards. The other car kept going, so Siobhan told Declan to pull into the driveway of the graveyard as well.

Siobhan stepped out, wrapped up in her black coat, looking solemn, and told Declan to accompany her. They watched as Amy took flowers and walked into a heavily wooded spot of the graveyard. There was an old church, but the area Amy was walking to was freshly laid out, ready for gravestones, and that of Simon Redburn was one of only a few in that corner.

Siobhan pretended to limp, so it was taking her more time to arrive than Amy, and watched as the woman knelt down in front of the headstone and placed flowers there. Siobhan spotted a modern headstone, turned, and stood in front of it. Whoever George Smith was, he was now her temporarily lost husband, and Siobhan stood with her head bowed.

From the corner of her eyes, she could see Amy beginning to weep. The woman was small, maybe five-two, and had long red hair. She was wearing a waterproof jacket, kneeling in jeans and trainers. There was nothing prim and proper about her. Nothing that said here was class or money. Siobhan's heartstrings tugged because the woman looked deeply sorrowful. She felt like a vulture preying on the woman's sadness to find out more about her husband.

Declan pulled up close, putting his arm through Siobhan's, and leant in to whisper, 'There's somebody else here.'

Siobhan didn't turn, but whispered back to Declan, 'Tell me about him.'

'The man, he's about as tall as me, if not a bit more. He looks quite stocky. He's wearing a black coat, but he hasn't gone towards any of the gravestones. Seems to be slowly making his way over towards Amy Redburn.'

'Okay, just stand here with me,' said Siobhan. Not turning her head, she cast her eyes to the left, seeing Amy easily. Then, at the corner of her vision, the man Declan had been talking about walked slowly into view. He had black gloves on and a black coat. His hair was greying at the sides but was black on top. It was trim and neat, but what really spoke to Siobhan was the way his feet made no sound as he walked.

There was little sound when he crunched the odd piece of gravel, and he walked lightly. People were trained to do that. Siobhan cast her mind back because something about the man was familiar. Something was telling her, he was Service. She had seen him before.

It was asking a lot to work out where, even though she was trained in recall. She hadn't worked with him on any missions. She hadn't been stationed with him. Those people she knew straight away, but sometimes when you were back at headquarters or you had to go somewhere, you crossed paths with people. They were maybe in another room. You didn't get to know their name, didn't get to know what they were doing, but with the sort of mind she had, she clocked that she'd seen him before.

'Shall I try to take a photograph?' said Declan.

'No,' whispered Siobhan. 'You're not skilled enough for that, and he'll be watching. He doesn't consider us to be any sort of threat because he's approached her, but he'll be watching us. So, we do nothing except mourn.'

Siobhan watched him out of the corner of her eye again. *Frame, build. Yes,* she thought, *I do know him, know him from where? Where was it? Where was it?*

Siobhan's face showed no emotion as her brain worked overtime, racking through images of places.

'Hungary! she thought suddenly. *Hungary. I was passing through. Did a courier drop. I was just dropping something off at the embassy and he was in the background. He was a lot younger though,'* she thought, *'and I asked who he was and they said no one. So, he was clearly someone on his way up. They weren't bothered I'd seen him, so he was Service.'*

She remembered she'd mentioned him to Eamon, and Eamon had said . . . what had he said? He hadn't given a code name. Just said that was a guy to watch. He was on his way up and I might bump into him one day at the top end. That was right. He was from Hungary, or at least that was where she'd seen him.

Siobhan watched Amy stand up when she suddenly realised someone was there. Maybe it was a sixth sense, that feeling of someone being close. The man reached out with an arm. He didn't put it on Amy's shoulder, rather he gripped her shoulder in his hand, staring at her, looking up and down.

The woman was in tears, and yet he didn't embrace her in a kind of helpful, comforting way. Instead, he pulled her roughly towards him. His hand was down on her backside, and he seemed to push his mouth at her. She was tilting her head away, but he was strong, much stronger than she.

'Declan,' whispered Siobhan, 'walk over there and ask if she's okay. Just as a concerned person, okay? If they break off and say they're okay, come back over. Don't push it any further.'

Declan peeled away from Siobhan, striding over, and halted before the man and the woman. 'Excuse me, but are you okay?' Declan said to Amy.

'Of course, she's okay. Why wouldn't she be okay?' asked the man.

'I'm talking to the lady,' said Declan. 'Are you okay?'

The man's hand slipped away. He said one word to her. 'Later.' He walked towards Declan and roughly banged his shoulder into him.

'I am now,' said the woman. 'Thank you.' She turned, crying, and knelt again at the grave.

'I'll stay here,' said Declan, 'just in case he comes back. You take your time with whatever you need to do there, okay?' The woman looked up and smiled at Declan.

'Thank you,' she said. 'That's really kind. Thank you very much.'

When Siobhan looked over, Declan looked like he was a sentry. Arms were down by his side, his chest was out and his neck was up straight. As he scanned left and right, Siobhan made sure that the man was gone, disappearing off in his car, before she walked over to the grave.

'Amy Redburn,' she said suddenly, catching the woman off guard.

The woman suddenly looked frightened. 'Yes,' she said. 'Who are you?'

'No one you need to be frightened of. My name is Siobhan Duffy. I know your husband died under unusual circumstances. I know he had something to say about the hotel to be built up on the Causeway Coast. A friend of mine also passed because of these circumstances. I just wanted to let you know I may be able to get that man off your back if you can tell me what's happening.'

'How do I know I can trust you?' she said. 'Is this your son?'

'No, that's my associate, Declan. You can trust me because you don't have anybody else to trust. I've worked amongst these sorts of people before. I can get things done,' said Siobhan. 'But I need information. I can get justice for Simon if that's what you want, or at least I can try. Certainly, I can get that man off your back. He doesn't look like a man who's trying to extort money from you. He looks like a man who's seen something he fancies.'

'Maxwell? You can get Maxwell off my back. I know what

he wants,' said Amy. 'He said that no one would believe anything I was saying about Simon.'

'Did Simon die suspiciously?'

'Simon died suddenly,' said Amy. 'Simon was fit. There was nothing wrong with Simon. The next thing—Heart failure. Sudden heart failure. I know it happens in people sometimes, but this was different. Simon had gone to the newspapers, had told people.' The woman was in tears, crying.

'Take it easy,' said Siobhan.

'Maxwell wants to . . . he wants me to be his plaything. He wants me to be his kept woman. He's already said he'll pay for everything. Put me in a better house. Take me off the estate.

'We were moving off the estate. Simon was doing well. He was stepping up in the architecture firm. But he got involved in the bids process and then, after that, he died. He was uncomfortable. He never told me exactly what, but he was uncomfortable with what was going on. I could tell. He was up at night. He wasn't himself. I said to him, "You need to sort this out." He told me he was going to. A day and a half later, he's dead. I killed him. I pushed him to . . .'

'You didn't kill him,' said Siobhan. 'Maxwell or his cohorts or one of them killed him. My friend died too. I'm going to sort it out, but I need your help.'

Amy looked up at Siobhan. 'What can you do? Forgive me,' she said. 'You look like a fifty-year-old woman. Your friend here was very kind, but I don't think he could have stood up to Maxwell if he had turned round and did something.'

Siobhan bit her lip. Everywhere she went at the moment, everyone looked at her and everyone thought she was nothing. Everyone underestimated her. Just because you were getting older. If she had told people she was a secret agent, suddenly they all would have expected more. A good agent didn't tell everyone who she was. A good agent didn't reveal she could fight.

'Amy, I have friends,' said Siobhan. 'My friends can do a lot.'

Currently, her friends were Declan and Kylie. They weren't really that much superior to Amy. Outside of that, it was Julian who wasn't doing anything. Siobhan didn't have that many friends. But if it got Amy to believe . . .

'Okay,' she said. 'I'll have a talk with you. You can explain to me what we need to do or what you want from me,' said Amy. 'But I'm not saying yes. You seem a decent person, and I have got nowhere else to go and I'm scared. I'm scared that man is going to take me and use me. He's already told me the police won't help. If I go, I think he'll kill me like they killed Simon. I don't know if you're any good, lady, but at the moment, you look like all I've got.'

Siobhan smiled. With votes of confidence like that, how could she ever fail?

Chapter 26

Siobhan took Amy to Mount Stewart, former home of Viscount Castlereagh and frequent day out for the local populace. It was located along Strangford Lough from Newtownards and close to her home. Once there, they took a walk in the gardens. The paths that spread out past the main house gave the chance to be secluded away from others. Yet because they were on the move, you would struggle to creep up on them.

She told Declan to walk a bit behind and Kylie a little in front. They were to stop, turn, or catch up if someone was approaching. Amy was nervous by this behaviour, and Siobhan didn't blame her for that. She wasn't used to the techniques which Siobhan used, but they were there for a reason.

'This Maxwell guy is clearly involved,' Siobhan said to Amy, 'but I need to find out more about him. I hate to ask you this, but he seems to be infatuated with you, or at least, there's some sort of connection.'

'Well, I'm not giving him that connection. I'm not luring him in.'

'I think we're both women of the world. We don't need to

lure men on. Often, it's usually just what they see or what they think they see, but he clearly has a fascination with you.'

Amy was reticent to answer, so Siobhan continued.

'It's not your fault. There's nothing to be ashamed of. It's just what is, but I'd like to use it against him. He may open up a bit more to you. It's a folly that most men have. They think just because they like a woman, they can impose any sort of will on her. She will automatically go along with whatever they want, and more than that, has become an ally, not just some sort of frightened partner. I think I know where he's from originally. And given his background, I wouldn't think to penetrate his defences in other ways. I'm sorry, but you're our best option. I'd like you to say yes to any proposals he makes.'

'Any proposals? I'm not going to bed with him,' said Amy.

'No, it won't be that unsubtle. You were alone in the graveyard,' said Siobhan. 'You'll find he'll ask you out for dinner first, maybe a hotel restaurant. He's not a man who's just going to take what he wants. He's got some sort of decency in him if you want to call it that, or maybe a man who likes the challenge of making you succumb willingly. Maxwell will woo you to some degree. That's part of it. You've been anti, you've been against him. He'll want to see it as winning you over, not simply using you.'

'And that's a good thing, is it?' asked Amy.

'No, it's not,' said Siobhan, 'but you're young. Maybe he likes the red hair, maybe it's the fact you're not that tall. Maybe it's something else. I don't know, but whatever it is, he wants you, and I think we can extract information from him.'

'So, you want me to go for dinner with him or something?'

'Whatever it is he offers. You'll tell me about it, but if it's too risky, I'll say no. We will be somewhere where we can watch, and we can be close at hand. We'll also be disguised so he can't recognise us. He's seen me now. He's seen Declan. Maxwell certainly won't forget Declan's face. But whatever happens, we'll protect you.'

'Can you, though?' asked Amy. 'Can you really? Simon's dead. They didn't hesitate to kill him. What's to say that they won't hesitate to kill me?'

'Well, Maxwell wants you alive. If he thought you were a threat, you'd be dead, or else he thinks he can bend you to his will. I don't think it's Maxwell that's killed Simon, more like a combination of other things. I believe there may be Russians involved—they're more likely to kill. They're on foreign ground, more difficult for them to operate with the law, bend it here and there, influence it. If they think someone is going to be taken seriously with information against them, they'll just kill them. Unfortunately, I think your Simon was a victim of his knowledge.'

'Okay,' said Amy, as they continued to walk. 'I'll go with it, but it's somewhere safe and you're watching me.'

'Agreed,' said Siobhan.

The path rose towards a large pool with trees around it. With winter here, it wasn't looking like the glorious greens that she remembered from childhood. Rather, it was cold, the water murkier than crystal clear. The ducks were playing, and Siobhan thought about taking retirement walks here; not taking this poor woman for a secret conversation and promising to protect her.

It took only two days before an offer from Maxwell came to Amy, asking her out to dinner. He had spotted her out by the grave again, and this time had been more discreet. His hand apparently had gone to her shoulder. He'd even kissed her on the cheek. She had at first refused, but on encouragement had agreed to go.

Siobhan told her to wear something that was attractive but not too overt. She wanted to give the idea that she was coming round to his advances, not gung-ho out for a night of rampant joy in a bedroom somewhere. The balance was key, lest he suspect anything.

The Belfast restaurant was at the base of a hotel, and Siobhan liked it because there was a large amount of glass at the front. Passers-by could see in, so Maxwell couldn't make a move inside the restaurant. He would have difficulty in forcing Amy anywhere.

Siobhan had disguised herself with a blonde wig and more makeup than she had ever worn in her life. She'd aged Declan as well. He looked more like a forty-year-old, with grey streaks running through his hair. Kylie waited outside in the car.

Siobhan sneaked a look at the reservations list, spotted the name of Maxwell, and then asked for the table only two away.

Siobhan was staring into the eyes of Declan. When Amy walked in with Maxwell, he had his arm around her, not through her arm, and a hand up on the shoulder, pulling her close. Her coat had been taken, and she had a dress with a moderate neckline.

The woman did good, Siobhan thought. *Attractive' A hint of moving towards the man's ideas, but not so much that he would be suspicious*. Amy's hair was brushed out to its fullest extent. Siobhan had worried that Maxwell would spot her, but he was fully engrossed in Amy.

They sat and dined, and Siobhan made what was meant to

be small talk to Declan, talk about the kids and where they were. All of it was a total lie. She listened, picking up what she could from Maxwell. He was boasting to Amy he would soon be rich, and he wanted, as he put it, a fine filly to share it with. Siobhan never understood why some men, usually older men, wanted to compare women with a horse. Didn't come over well. Horses were dominated, controlled by their reins. The rider told them where to go, what to do. Women didn't want that.

Amy, however, was smiling, and Maxwell seemed to have a genuine fascination with her. This wasn't an afterthought; he had seen this woman, and he clearly wanted her, even though he was probably involved with the murder of her husband. He certainly would have been aware of it. Amy asked him a few times where the money was coming from and he told her, investments, always investments. She asked if it was hotels, and he said amongst others.

Declan had disappeared off to the bathroom. Something Siobhan told him to make sure he did. They wanted to look like a normal couple having dinner, not people fixed on their seats, having a listen in. There was a cup of coffee in front of her she was forcing herself to drink. It was always a good disguise to have something that you didn't like yourself, but you had to make sure your face didn't show it.

As she sat there listening to Maxwell witter on to Amy about previous financial conquests in life, Siobhan glanced around. She saw something that bothered her.

There was a table of gentlemen, four of them, sitting opposite Maxwell. They were talking, but she noticed that several of them kept looking towards Maxwell as if they were waiting for a sign. The table on the other side had two women and two men, but they too kept glancing over. Maxwell wasn't doing anything over the top or interesting, he was just blabbering on about money. If he was hoping to entice a woman, he was wrong. Yet Amy was playing her part, smiling at every word.

'Why don't we have some alone time?' asked Maxwell.

Amy's face changed. 'I'm not sure I'm ready for that,' she said. 'Maybe another night. Why spoil it now when it's been such a wonderful evening?'

'The excitement has only just begun,' said Maxwell. 'I think you'll find it will be a night you'll remember.'

Ignoring the ridiculous cliché, Siobhan scanned around Maxwell and saw the two other tables rise.

'Don't make a scene,' said Maxwell. 'We're going to go upstairs.'

Siobhan prayed Amy didn't look over towards her, even if she knew she was there. Siobhan had deliberately not told Amy how she was going to look or where she would sit. Maybe Amy was in the dark that she was only a couple of tables across. Even more scary for the woman.

Siobhan checked those with Maxwell. There were too many. She wouldn't be able to get to Amy quick enough. She'd have to do this another way. If she fought now, she would get herself engaged with a two or three-person fight, and Maxwell would be off in a car somewhere with Amy. At least he was going upstairs, albeit not for anything good. Declan came back from the toilet and sitting down opposite Siobhan, had a worried look on his face.

'I think it's about time we went for a stroll or something,' said Siobhan.

'Oh, yes,' said Declan, and stood back up. Siobhan turned

and sent Declan over to pay the bill. As she wandered out behind Maxwell's large party, she saw them move to the lift. She watched as the elevator light changed through the different floors until it said third. She walked over to the reception desk.

'Excuse me. I've just been talking with a man, Maxwell, said he was up on the third floor. I don't know if you have his room number. It's just I forgot to pass on some detailed information that he's going to need.'

'Maybe we could.'

'No, no, no, no,' said Siobhan. 'I need to do it myself. It's to do with company business. I can't give it to anyone else. If you just give me his room number, I'll pop up and do that.'

'Okay,' said the woman. 'Mr Maxwell is Room 317.'

'That's excellent. Thank you very much.'

Declan came back from paying the bill and Siobhan said to him, '317, that's where they've taken her. Come on.'

Declan walked over to the wall and picked up a gigantic sword that was hanging there.

'You saw how many of them there were,' he said, under his voice to Siobhan.

'Put that back, dear. You can't just take stuff off the wall. I admit, it is a terrific sword.'

Under her breath, she said to Declan, 'You'll only get yourself hurt trying to use that. You do not know how to use a sword.'

'I suppose you do,' said Declan.

Siobhan had been involved in fencing, although she thought this sword would be too heavy for her. Instead, she pointed over to the lift, and with Declan entered it and pressed floor three.

'When we get there, follow my lead. Stay back. I may throw you Amy at some point. If I do, grab her, run down and get in the car with Kylie. If I'm not out, go. Take her back home. Lock the door until I come back. Understand?' Declan nodded. 'Don't get into a fight, Declan. You're not trained for it.'

Siobhan gave him a smile, then turned, and with her handbag on her arm, smiled at the elevator doors as they opened slowly in front of her.

In front of them was a large man, but he smiled politely as he said to them, 'I'm sorry, but you can't come onto the floor. There's been a minor incident and we need to keep it clear.'

'But I have a room here,' said Siobhan.

'It'll only be an hour. Here,' the man handed over a twenty-pound note to Declan. 'Have a drink while you're waiting.'

The man stepped back and the doors of the elevator went to close, but Siobhan put her foot forward. The door hit it. For a moment, the doors froze, and then they moved aside again. The man's face changed from one of conviviality to one of anger.

Chapter 27

You need to leave the floor. You can't come in at the moment. We have a problem,' said the man. 'Please leave the floor.'

'I have a room here. I have booked a room, and I have paid good money,' said Siobhan. She stamped her foot down on the lift and the man reached in to press the button to make the lift go down. Siobhan slapped him across the wrist. He glowered at her.

'You don't manhandle me down,' said Siobhan.

'You talk sense to this bitch,' said the man suddenly. 'The two of you are going down in the lift, because if you don't, well, let's just say you will be probably a lot sorer than you are now.'

'How dare you,' said Declan. 'How dare you!'

'Dare me?' The man swung his hand across and slapped Declan's cheek hard. It was only the back of his hand, but it caused Declan to stumble into the wall of the lift. 'That's a little measure,' said the man. 'Not much. I can do a lot worse than that. Now, time for you lot to move.'

'Well, I shall complain to the management,' said Siobhan. She pretended to sniff and opened up her handbag. Reaching inside, her hand moved through the various items.

The man blocking their path now stepped into the elevator and went to press the button to take them back down to the ground floor. He noticed too late that Siobhan's hand had emerged from the bag holding a needle. She drove into his neck, pressing down and driving the dose of the liquid inside. He reached up with a hand to grab her, but as it reached her throat, it went limp. There was a loud thud as he collapsed onto the floor.

'Tommy,' said a voice from outside the lift. 'Tommy, are you all right?'

Siobhan reached inside her bag, took something out, ripped it open and put the contents in her mouth. She then tossed her bag to one side, turned to the man who was on his back, and jumped on top of him.

'Start counting,' she said through gritted teeth to Declan. He looked at her for a moment and as she appeared to be pressing down on the man's chest, he began.

'One, two, three, four, stop. One, two, three, four, stop.'

Siobhan shook her head. What the hell was that? That wasn't how you did compressions, but she had to go with it. What Declan was making up for in enthusiasm could be destroyed by his complete lack of knowledge.

Tommy's friend came running into the lift. He stood for a moment, then looked towards Declan.

'He just collapsed. Literally, just collapsed. She's working on him. She's trying to get—'

'I can see what she's bloody doing,' said the man. He knelt down beside Siobhan. 'How is he? Is he responding?'

Siobhan turned, faced the man and spat what was in her mouth into his face. The liquid half-shot into his open mouth.

For a moment, the man was stunned, wondering what had just happened, and then he collapsed onto the floor. Siobhan stood up, stopping her compressions.

'It's bloody hard to speak with that in your mouth. Don't worry about these two. They'll be out for hours.'

Declan was still standing, looking down. 'I thought you'd killed them.'

'Declan, you don't kill people unless you have to. I mean, really. You just don't.'

Declan again looked bemused, but as Siobhan strode out of the lift, he followed her. Siobhan was wearing a long skirt, but it wasn't tight, allowing her to move freely. She was happier in her jeans, if she was honest. Jeans and a jumper, cup of tea in hand, watching the day go by. She had to dress up tonight, but fearful that she may have to take action as well, she was wearing a skirt she could at least run in.

'317, 317,' said Siobhan. She ran along the hall and then she realised Declan wasn't with her. She turned and looked back.

The hall had several shields and swords strategically placed along it. Looking at them, Siobhan had thought them to be replicas and not good ones at that, but Declan had taken one sword off the wall.

'I told you. Put it back if you don't know what you're doing with it.'

'I'm unarmed,' he said in a half-whisper. 'I'm unarmed. Look at the size of the fellas we're trying to take on.'

Bless him, thought Siobhan, *he's actually willing to take them on. Doesn't he realise the last thing you'd do is fight them? They're too big.*

'Room 317,' said Siobhan. 'Come on, 317.'

She strode along the corridor, found the door, and listened

carefully. She couldn't hear anything from inside, so she rapped the door, announcing, 'Room service.'

There was a grunt from inside, and then the door was cracked open.

'What are you doing?' asked the man. He was taller than Siobhan and looked like he would be wide through the little of the door that Siobhan could see.

'Did Tommy not tell you?'

Sometimes the thing to do was to take them by surprise. Siobhan threw everything she had into the door. It caught the man in the face knocking him backwards and Siobhan carried through her advantage despite the pain she now felt. The man, although he stumbled two, three, no, four steps, righted himself again. Siobhan was stuck in the small entrance to the room with nowhere to go and an angry man looking back at her.

'You're going to regret that,' he said. He drove a fist into his open palm and stepped forward towards her.

'Declan, the bloody sword.'

'You said.'

Siobhan had already turned, had two hands on the sword Declan was holding, and snatched it from him. She turned round, crouching a little to fit the sword under the ceiling during her swing to the man's face with the flat of the blade. He tumbled sideways once. She followed it up with another flat of the blade to the head, and then to his side.

As he hit the ground, she heard something from the toilet beside her. The door was closed, but the light was on underneath. She heard somebody standing up as if they were fumbling quickly with their trousers. She stepped beyond the bathroom door, turned, and held her hand up so that Declan wouldn't come any further in.

Quickly, she reached down into her bag. Picking up a needle from within her bag, she stepped up and onto the bed so that she would be hidden from anyone exiting from the bathroom.

She heard the man cry out, 'What the hell?' Then, 'Was that you?' She assumed that the man had stepped out of the toilet, seen his fallen colleague, then had looked at Declan. Siobhan jumped off the bed and drove a needle into the back of the man's neck. He turned, flinging an arm towards her that knocked her back, and she spun across the bed and onto the floor. Then she heard him fall. Declan came over to her side quickly.

'Mrs D, are you all right?'

Siobhan took a deep breath. The tumble had knocked the wind out of her, but she had to think. This was 317. This was Maxwell's room, but he'd taken her elsewhere. Of course, if anything had gone wrong, the last thing he needed to do was to be in this room.

'Come on, he's somewhere else on the floor,' she said.

Siobhan stood up, stepped over the two prone men on the floor. As she exited the room, she turned to make sure Declan was following. He, however, had picked up the sword again, clearly impressed by how useful it had been. Siobhan didn't have time to tell him to leave it.

Siobhan indicated Declan should be quiet. 'Listen, go to the far end of the corridor, and we'll go along listening, see if we can hear them.'

'Hear them doing what?' asked Declan.

'Declan, he's taken her to have her, you know, sex. It'll probably be noisy.'

Declan nodded and tore off down the corridor. Siobhan

ran up and down, listening, but she couldn't hear anything. She may have been wrong, of course. Maybe sex wouldn't be loud. Amy may be gagged. Maybe she would—Siobhan had to drive the images out of her head. Now was not the time to think about that. Now was the time to act and to get this right. Siobhan met Declan halfway back up the corridor on the landing.

'We're going to have to go in every door. We're going to have to rap on every door.'

'Okay,' said Declan.

'I don't want to,' said Siobhan. 'If I do, it gives them a warning. It gives them . . .'

There was a sudden, loud, piercing shriek, but it wasn't a voice. It was an alarm. A loud alarm that kept going off.

'Is that a fire?' asked Declan.

'No,' said Siobhan. 'Which room? Which room? That's a rape alarm.'

She looked up and down the hall. It was further up, back towards Declan's end. It must have been. Siobhan tore up with Declan following her, and then she stopped.

'Declan, fire hose, fire hose. There!' It was an older hotel. It still had a fire hose. 'Bring that with you.'

'You said it was a rape alarm.'

'It is. Just bring the damn hose and make sure it's on.'

Chapter 28

Siobhan rapped on the door of the room loudly. 'This is the police,' she said. 'Open up. There's clearly a disturbance. Open the door. This is the police.'

She turned to look behind her, where Declan stood with the fire hose. He had the throttle in his hand and was about to open it, ready to let the water come out. The door didn't move, so Siobhan thumped on it again.

'Open up or we're coming in.'

She heard the unlocking of a catch and then slowly the door opened. Siobhan stepped out of the way and Declan opened up the throttle at the front of the fire hose. Water gushed out, hitting the door and sending it left, right, and centre, but the door was driven backwards into the man who opened it. As the door opened further, he became the target of the hose, throwing his hands up in front of him in a desperate effort. The power of the hose was so much that he just stumbled backwards, tripping over his own feet and eventually hitting the floor.

'Hose off,' shouted Siobhan. Declan turned it off, and Siobhan pushed the now-closing door back, stepping inside the room.

It was a standard hotel room. Bathroom on the right through a very short, almost corridor feature. From this, the room spread out with the table on the left, bed on the right, and a window at the far end. The difference in this room was there was a man now sprawling on the floor by the table. Meanwhile, on the bed was a half-dressed Amy. Her clothes had clearly been removed against her will, some of them ripped.

Maxwell was towering over her. He'd got out of his jacket, but otherwise, he was still in the suit he'd been wearing at dinner. On seeing Siobhan, he slapped Amy hard and then turned quickly, running towards his jacket. Siobhan wouldn't reach him in time. And if he was going for his jacket, he was going for one thing, his gun.

Siobhan started forward. The man on the floor kicked up at her, hitting her on the knee, stopping her momentarily. Maxwell continued to his jacket, and then a voice behind Siobhan shouted, 'Here, catch!'

She turned and saw the sword from the wall being thrown towards her. Siobhan caught it in midair and turned with it, swinging it low and catching the jaw of the man on the floor. He twisted in pain, rolling to one side. Maxwell had now reached into his jacket, was reaching inside, and began pulling a weapon out from within.

Siobhan stepped forward quickly and lunged with the sword, covering the extra distance. As Maxwell turned to shoot, she hit him in the middle of the chest with the sword. It was blunt and didn't slice into him, but the force of it drove him backward, sending his firing hand up into the air and a gunshot into the ceiling of the room.

Siobhan then swung at the hand holding the gun, clattering

it on the side of the sword, and the gun fell to the floor. Siobhan turned, reached out with her hand, grabbed hold of Amy and told her to come on. She saw Maxwell fumble for the gun again but tore out of the room past Declan.

As soon as the women were clear, Declan opened up the hose again, hitting Maxwell right between the eyes. He spluttered as water enveloped his mouth. Trying to stand, he was driven back to the floor again as Declan turned the hose repeatedly from him to his associate and back again.

'Declan,' shouted Siobhan from down the corridor, 'we need to go now.'

Declan nodded and dropped the hose, the water continuing to pour from it. None of the doors were opening on this floor, suggesting that guests weren't on it. The noise of the water gushing out, the gunshot, everything would have made people panic. Maxwell had clearly enough influence to take over the entire floor.

Siobhan reached the fire exit and began descending the stairs, hauling Amy behind her. The woman was still in a state of distress, tears falling from her eyes, her clothing half hanging off her. Siobhan found it slow going because she felt she was dragging Amy at every turn and Declan was soon catching them up. As they reached the second floor, Siobhan heard men from below and decided rather than descend, she would cut onto that floor.

Here in the corridor, there were guests, looking out of their rooms and asking what was going on. Halfway down the corridor, water was falling from the ceiling.

'Don't stop for anyone,' said Siobhan and belted down the hallway, Amy in tow and not waiting for Declan. Siobhan reached inside her handbag, pulled out her phone, and pressed a button for Kylie. She could hear the call ringing as she ran. Once it was picked up, she said three words. 'Hotel front, now.'

Kylie wouldn't know what she was walking into, wouldn't know what had gone wrong, although she may have heard the gunshot. With a gunshot being fired though, the police would be here soon, and the last thing Siobhan wanted to do was to explain away what was happening. Amy was an obvious candidate to be spoken to, but the police would just bring up questions about Siobhan. Questions she didn't want to deal with at this time.

A man stood at the far end of the corridor where the lift was and stepped across Siobhan's path.

'You're best staying put, you don't . . .'

Siobhan clattered him with her forearm and the man spun off to one side. She didn't have time for that, didn't have time to be nice. Reaching the end of the corridor, she found stairs down, but they also ran up as well.

Where are they? thought Siobhan. *Where's everyone else? Maxwell would be back on his feet. He'd be coming for them, or would he simply be clearing out? Surely too much to let them simply get away.*

Siobhan decided she needed to go down rather than up, because up was the third floor. It would be full of water, and only full of Maxwell's men. If she went down, she'd be amongst people, and possibly Maxwell's men as well. Siobhan raced down the stairs, stopping at each corner to listen and see if anyone was further down. She kept going. When she saw a crowd milling around towards the base of the stairs, she made for it.

The door into the foyer was open with people in a state

of mild panic, and she pulled Amy close to her and walked out into the crowd. The noise was incredible. People were desperate to know what was happening.

And then the fire alarm went off. This was Northern Ireland and there'd been a gunshot. One thing about locals in Northern Ireland is they know if gunfire happens, just get away. You certainly don't look to see who's firing.

However, there were guests here from other countries and they were desperately seeking the concierge to find out the situation. As far as Siobhan could tell, the concierge had left his desk. He was probably halfway across the road outside the hotel, seeking any safe ground he could find.

She pushed through the crowd and then saw a man making his way towards her. He was broad-shouldered, dressed smartly but also looked fierce. Unlike everyone else who was in a panic, he was making a beeline for them. Siobhan reached inside her handbag and withdrew a tiny knife.

It was like moving through thick treacle with everyone around moving in totally random directions. Some were pushing for the door, some pushing back towards the concierge, slip-sliding off each other, and the large man got closer. As he did so, Siobhan couldn't keep the distance between them and the man brought a firm hand down on Amy's shoulder. Declan tried to jump from several people away, throw his hand onto the other man's hand. The man brought a fist down on top of Declan's head and he went straight to the floor.

Siobhan saw two hands now go onto Amy's shoulders and she stopped, turned and drove the small knife down into the wrists of the man so quickly he couldn't react. He screamed, his hands lifting off Amy, and Siobhan stepped past her to get closer. Her arm snaked around another person in front of her and drove the knife into the gut of the man. He stumbled and fell down. Siobhan pocketed the knife back into her handbag. She reached down for Declan.

'Just get out,' she said. 'Follow Amy, get out and get into the car with Kylie. I'm coming.'

Declan grabbed Amy's hand, and he was more adept at swimming through the crowd than he was with handling any of the goons. Siobhan followed, but she was scanning the room, looking for the next assailant. When they reached the doors, the crowd was breaking and there was more room to manoeuvre. Siobhan saw across the street her own car with Kylie inside it, waving at them.

Seriously! Kylie's telling everyone where the escape route is!

'Go, go, go,' said Siobhan as she saw two goons coming towards her. Although it was easier to move, there were still plenty of people about. As the first one arrived, Siobhan grabbed an older man and shoved him straight into the arms of the goon. She then reached into her handbag, took out another needle, and as the second one arrived, she threw herself into his clutches, slamming the needle into his side. Siobhan felt the squeeze. She felt like her ribs were going to be compacted, and then the grip loosened. The man dropped to the floor.

The other goon had pushed the older man away and was now reaching for Siobhan. She fainted to attack him, causing him to stop momentarily, and then she turned to run.

Declan was now showing Amy into the back seat on the far side of the road, and Siobhan shouted at them to go. Kylie started the car, and it was creeping forward.

'Roll down the window,' shouted Siobhan.

As she ran towards the car, she saw the window slowly descending. The car was getting quicker. Siobhan ran as hard as she could until she reached the car and threw herself in, head first, through the open passenger window. She found her midriff catching on the window's edge and her legs were sticking out, waving frantically. Reaching forward, her hands grabbed the seat belt connection on the far side of the seat. She put two hands around it as tightly as she could and shouted, 'Drive, drive,' at Kylie. Off they went.

The cool air brushed over Siobhan's legs because her skirt was falling. Who knew what sight she was giving any of the locals, but she didn't care? Kylie drove away, turned one corner, turned another, and kept going until Siobhan said, 'Would you stop the damn car so I can get in?'

Maybe in her younger years, she would have been able to scramble in. Not these days. The car stopped. She let her legs fall, hit the road, and extracted herself from the window before opening the door and getting inside. Kylie looked at her in almost disbelief.

'Go,' said Siobhan, 'they'll be coming, just go.'

'Where?' said Kylie, as the car drove off.

'Back to the house. Yes. Back to the house, we need to have a chat.'

Siobhan lay back in the seat, breathing deeply. She turned and looked at Amy. The woman was shaking. Was it cold? Was it panic? She'd seen a gun go off. A number of men had come for her. She'd also seen Maxwell try to have her on his own terms. No wonder she was shaking.

It didn't go well, thought Siobhan. *That did not go well*, but she needed to sit and think through the evening. She needed to ponder the conversations she'd heard. No, it didn't go the way she wanted. Amy had been taken upstairs, but Maxwell had made a connection. Maxwell had spoken. He had said something to Amy, and now, after the heat of battle and running around, Siobhan needed time to just stop and think.

Questions were running through her mind. *Were they safe? Could they stay at the house? Had they got away with no one noticing who they were?*

When, 'Unlikely,' came up as the main answer, Siobhan felt worried. Maybe it was time to take more extreme measures.

Chapter 29

Siobhan had sat Amy down in front of the fire in the living room. The woman had first showered before taking some of Kylie's clothes, for she was nearer to her size than Siobhan's. Then she'd sat in silence, just staring at the fire.

It was past eleven at night, and Siobhan needed to have a discussion. They were going to have to do things differently. This current situation of investigating from the house couldn't go on. They'd have to hand it over to someone else or she'd have to operate from a remote location, somewhere that gave them a chance to remain out of sight and out of sound.

Siobhan stood in the room's corner, looking at the three people with her. Amy was petrified. Kylie was too, but she was hiding it, trying to put a brave face on for Amy. Declan wasn't petrified. He had a confidence. Maybe unwisely, one that was born of naivety rather than understanding the current situation.

Siobhan was troubled. If it had just been her, she may have continued to operate from the house, but under very different protocols. Instead, she had these three to think about. Bringing her cup of tea with her, she sat down on her table in front of the fire. It was a low glass coffee table, and normally, she didn't sit on it, but she was feeling the cold and wanted to be in front of that fire.

'We need to talk,' she said, 'about what we're going to do.'

'We should go to the police,' said Kylie. Amy nodded.

'No,' said Declan. 'We must have enough, haven't we? To put it out to the press. ' He saw doubtful faces. 'But we're on top. We've got them rattled. We can still get enough on them to expose them.'

'We could have got Amy killed tonight,' said Kylie.

Siobhan was going to interrupt, but Amy had been out of her view for too long, and if Maxwell had have taken the notion, Amy would have been dead. *Operating with amateurs isn't easy*, thought Siobhan.

'I don't think we can go to the police,' said Siobhan. 'Going to the police won't keep us safe. We also have nothing.'

'What do you mean, we don't have anything? What about the autopsy being wrong?' said Kylie. 'Being faked?'

'I put a gun to a man's back to get him to confess that,' said Siobhan. 'They won't take that as admissible. I broke into somewhere to find out those facts. We need to expose this on a different level before we can go to the police. I don't believe that's the solution.'

'We must have enough,' said Declan.

'We don't. What do we know? There's a plan to bring a development to the coast. One of my colleagues was killed. I can't reveal that to the police that Eamon was one of my colleagues. If they don't know now that Eamon was in the Service, the Service isn't telling them and they will not believe me. The first thing they'll do is go for clarification to the service. If it's a spy murder, the police don't want to know.

They want to know that the Service will sort that out.'

Siobhan sighed. It had been a rough evening, but she continued.

'The three deaths that happened, Jenny Goldsmith, Amy's Simon, and Lauren Muntz looked like normal deaths. They were signed off as normal deaths. We need to get our consultant Ernie to confess. He's got every reason not to. He's got every reason to keep this in the dark. If we get him lifted by the police, the Russians will try to get him before they can move him anywhere. Justice is going to be very poorly served if we go to the police. It's not that sort of justice we need. We're going to need to expose this. We need to show the corruption. Not just simply bring it to the police with ideas and that, but actually show it. Put it wide out in the open so people can't miss it.'

'I just want it all to go away,' said Amy. 'I've already lost Simon. I want no more of this. Do you realise he—?'

'I'm very aware of what he could have done to you,' said Siobhan. 'And I'm sorry.'

'You said you would be there for me. You said . . .'

'I did. I totally underestimated the size of the operation. And that's why we need to talk about how we operate now.'

There was a ring from the doorbell.

'Just a moment,' said Siobhan. She stood up and started walking towards the front door. *Who would call it this time of the night? Nobody ever did. Had the police seen the number plate? Were they following her here?*

She approached the door and then thought better of it, stepping to the side and the alcove where the false door was. She looked through a peephole. There was a man there, tall and strong.

'Just a minute,' said Siobhan to herself. The man's face wasn't covered, but she didn't recognise him. He looked cold and passive. The night air would have meant that anyone standing there would have been shivering, or at least trying to keep warm. If you weren't, then you were probably determined to do something. You had other things on your mind. Siobhan reached round from the alcove with her hand and caught the lock on the front door. She turned it and slowly let the front door swing open. Through the peephole, she saw the man start to lift a gun.

Siobhan opened the secret door to the side. She saw the man's face go into shock just as she reached forward and scrabbed his face. She dug her nails deep to feel the flesh beginning to peel and the blood trickle out. With her other hand, she knocked his wrist hard, causing the gun to fall.

She drove him back against the wall, nails digging in deep, before he shoved her backwards. Her head hit the wall, but he turned and fled, rather than jumping at her. She looked down at the gun and watched as he tore off up her driveway, out onto the Donaghadee Road. A car door opened, and he jumped inside.

Siobhan looked at the blood on her nails. If she'd still been in the Service, she'd have collected some of that blood, to see if there'd be a match. The man was a professional hitman, but in saying that, he was far from the best she'd seen. He'd not be dumb enough to stay in town and finish the job, especially once he'd lost the element of surprise. She would have recognised him again. He'd have scars from the damage she'd done to him.

She reached down, grabbed the gun, and contemplated it. Siobhan cocked her head, looking inside the house, thinking about the three people sitting in front of the fire. She could tell them about this, but they were scared enough. Instead, she turned, took a short walk down through her garden until she could see the water lapping up against the rocks just beyond her boundaries.

She drew her arm back and threw the gun as hard and as far as she could. She didn't see it hit the water, but she heard it, a faint plop, before she walked back to the house. Once inside, she closed the alcove door and the front door, and locked up again.

He wasn't that sloppy though, she thought. He beat the perimeters. She checked her surveillance system and found that the perimeter alarms had been disabled. It was time to move, time to work from somewhere else. Siobhan walked back into the living room, where the three of them looked up at her.

'Who was that?' asked Declan.

'Nobody important.'

'It's after eleven at night,' said Kylie.

'Like I said, nobody important.'

Siobhan gave a look, showing that any further conversation on the subject was banned. 'I don't think we need a discussion,' she said. 'I think we need to leave and go somewhere else. That's all that's left to us.'

'Keep the fire piled up,' she told Kylie. 'And then the rest of you go get some sleep.'

'What are you going to do?'

'Pack,' said Siobhan. 'In the morning, we're moving out.'

'Hotel?'

'No. Not a hotel, somewhere safer.'

Siobhan could see the worried looks and the murmurs from

the other three in the group, but she told Amy to have her bed that night, and she would make do with the sofa. Kylie was going to return to her own small abode at the front of the property, along with Declan. But Siobhan told them not to.

'Take my spare bedroom, Kylie. Declan, there's room on the floor in one of the other rooms.'

'Where are you sleeping?' asked Kylie.

'Don't worry about that,' said Siobhan. 'Off to bed. I need all of you refreshed for the morning. Some of you will have driving to do, and we'll need to pack up properly and quickly.'

Siobhan watched them all disappear before walking through to her study, and reaching down to a place underneath the floor. She pulled out a handgun and a large shotgun, and brought them through to the living room, where she sat in a seat by the fire. The shotgun she placed in her lap. The handgun she put in the side of her trousers. She would doze, but lightly. The place had already been compromised, and there was no way she was going to sleep until she knew they were safely elsewhere.

The night was long, and Siobhan had many thoughts running through her mind. This was retirement. This was her switching off. Yet she'd become embroiled in something again. *Damn you, Eamon*, she thought. He brought her excitement and adventure back in the day, and he brought excitement and adventure again. But she didn't want excitement and adventure. She wanted retirement, didn't she? Wasn't that the point?

She didn't come to the Donaghadee Road, looking to tear things up. Siobhan came to settle down. She came to find sports that were easy-going and community-based. Ones where you could talk to people while you played. Maybe take a painting class. Yes, she wanted to do exciting things, but not like this.

Amy could have been killed tonight. Back when she was young, that would have excited her. That level of danger, that level of risk. Now, it worried her. She knew Kylie could see the danger as well. Unlike Declan. Declan seemed to think everything would be all right. Siobhan had enough experience in her life to know that things didn't always go that way.

'Just take it to the police'. That was Kylie's idea. Not that easy to prove things to the police or the courts. Better if it could be resolved outside of that. Better if she was still in the Service. They had ways and means.

Those ways and means had already come to haunt her tonight, though. A hitman. *They sent a hitman for me. They really don't know who I am*, she thought. Part of her wished she could have got hold of the hitman, for she hated that kind. To kill people in cold blood you didn't know just for money. She'd have taken the knackers off him.

Siobhan stood up and walked around the house, checking each bedroom. Amy was sleeping fitfully. Kylie, much better.

When she saw Declan lying on the floor, she could see he was still awake. He was awake from excitement, not fear.

'Get some sleep.'

'And you,' said Declan. 'You need it too, Mrs D.'

'Indeed, I do.'

Siobhan made her way back to the living room, sat down, and looked at the clock. It was four in the morning. Another three hours, she'd pack up and then move out. As for where they were going in the morning, she didn't know.

Chapter 30

At seven o'clock, Siobhan woke the rest of the house up. She went through to her own room to pack a bag and also several small weapons. Siobhan didn't let the rest see the shotgun or the handgun that she'd had that night.

She wanted to be on the move by nine o'clock. Amy's house was well known to Maxwell, so Siobhan was going to avoid it, instead popping along to some shops to let Amy pick up some clothing. Kylie and Declan quickly packed from the small abode at the front. At nine o'clock, the four of them were sitting in the car as Declan drove off right towards Bangor.

The day was a bright but cold autumn day. Siobhan told her two younger colleagues to help Amy find some clothes quickly, while she looked for some accommodation. Siobhan took the car, leaving them in the clothing store, and drove to the nearest estate agents, asking what was available to rent, and fast.

She found a small house off the Gransha Road, not far out of Bangor, and was able to take the keys from the estate agent. Someone had moved out two days before, and Siobhan put down a deposit through a separate bank card she held. When you left the Service, you kept up certain identities, not as many as when you were in. Siobhan knew if she'd ever have to move or run, she'd always have funds and a name with which to travel.

Picking up the younger people at the clothing store, Siobhan took them to the supermarket and bought some food. She then had Declan drive them out to the new abode. From the road, there was a small driveway leading down to the house, which was surrounded by trees. You had to come right to the house to see it, suiting Siobhan down to the ground. The car would be hidden, although she'd change it anyway, for a different hire car.

That morning, she'd briefly watched the news, which had talked about a mishap at the hotel. The story was of a fire hose going off accidentally. There was no mention of anyone looking for them. The police hadn't come round, so the car they'd disappeared off in probably hadn't been spotted, at least not by anybody that was looking to report it. Maxwell would come after her on his own.

Once inside the house, Siobhan took the groceries and made some tea and coffee in the kitchen. Amy was sitting in the front room, and when Siobhan saw her, she realised that the woman needed something to do. She was thinking too much about what had happened. It was traumatic, absolutely, but she couldn't take her for any counselling over the trauma just yet.

Instead, as they did in the Service, Amy needed to push it to the back of her mind. A job easier said than done, for you had to function, and if they were going to catch Maxwell out, she thought Amy might get involved. In any case, she couldn't just mope around the house, because all she would think about was the incident at the hotel. She was a bereaved woman, after all, and a downward spiral would be too easy to sink into.

'You're going to be on lunch after this,' she said to Amy, 'because we have some planning to do.'

'In what way?' asked Declan.

'Well, the way I see it,' said Siobhan, 'is Maxwell has got to be in this for the money. I believe he's ex-Service, because I've seen him somewhere, but he may be quite high up. That would tie in with a lot of the Service closing doors, not looking at it too closely. They would need some ones at the top to order investigations. When you're lower down, you don't know why people are involved. Sometimes they're running covers. Sometimes they need to be at the heart of something bad to find out that it's wrong, to bring it down. In the Service, you don't ask. You're merely on a need-to-know basis, so we can't leak any information to other people.'

Siobhan sipped her tea and continued.

'Maxwell will receive a large payday from this. We know the Russians want this hotel on the Causeway coast. It's obviously going to make them a lot of money, but it's more than the hotel, probably. There'll be other deals tied into it. We need to infiltrate the Russians and see if we can set Maxwell up. If we make the ground too hot for the Russians, they'll clear off. I'm sorry, but bringing them to justice, as in putting them away in jail, that's tough. Maxwell, however, we can expose. Once exposed, the police can go after him. Those in the Service who don't know what's going on will see it, and may even go after him too. They'll want the Russians, too.'

'I don't see why we can't go to the police.'

'I've told you already, Kylie.'

'This seems dangerous. This seems like we're putting our necks out.'

'We are. We're too far in,' said Siobhan. 'If we try to just clam down, act as if we won't say anything, it won't work. There's three people dead, because they went to the newspaper.' Amy sniffed.

'Sorry,' said Siobhan. 'That was a bit too blunt, but it is true. We need to do a set-up. We need to manufacture a situation where Maxwell's exposed and the police can find out what he is. Give them a route in for investigation.'

'Are you saying that we won't be able to go back?' asked Amy.

'No, I think we can go back to our normal life. We'll need to expose things in such a way that the people who are currently trying to close us down do not need to do that, because it's all out in the open. They'll be too busy trying to look after themselves. They won't come after us. There'll also be a point when the Service gets involved, that they will struggle to come for us. The Service won't let Russians do such a killing. Not here in the UK.'

Amy stood up and walked down to the kitchen, her face angry.

Siobhan held up her hand, letting Kylie know not to follow her. 'You and Declan, see what you can come up with in here. We need to make a plan, even if it's a loose one.'

Siobhan turned and walked out to the kitchen, where she saw Amy beginning to chop up a pepper. Siobhan had never seen a pepper chopped like that, from top to bottom. Normally she'd cut the top off, then strip down the sides, picking out the seeds so you'd got strips. Amy had left the stalk intact. Now there were seeds everywhere.

'Are you sure you want me to cook?' Amy spat.

'What's up?' asked Siobhan. 'Apart from the obvious, you were nearly taken against your will, and also your man's dead. There's something more. What's up?'

'It's not justice, is it? It's not justice if we don't expose them.'

'You're welcome to go to the BBC, see if they'll run a feature on it, but I'll tell you now, they won't. We haven't got enough. I'm sorry,' said Siobhan. 'I'm sorry. I can't do some sort of documentary and highlight to the world how corrupt this has been, but I'm going to do my best to expose it.'

Amy grunted.

'This is life,' Siobhan said. 'That's why we have these secret Services, people working in the dark when you can't do what should be by the law, but you have to stop something. You need to expose it. Make sure it doesn't happen. This is the way we must do it.'

'But it's not fair,' said Amy. She slammed the knife down and Siobhan watched the tears falling down onto the pepper. 'They just bloody killed him. They just bloody well murdered him, and I'm meant to sit there and not acknowledge that.'

'You can acknowledge it,' said Siobhan. 'When it will come out, I don't know. When the police work through all this, they may find it, or they may not. The Service may find it out and tell them, or they may hold it because they see it not as in the best interest of the country to expose it. There is too much of this that goes beyond my control,' said Siobhan.

'By the way, I didn't choose to get dragged into this any more than you. My friend's dead. In fact, my old lover is dead. I shared moments with him every bit as close as you did with Simon. Yes, it would be great if everybody could be there as we tell them they murdered him, lock them away forever. But it will not happen that way. We need to expose what's going on and hope for the best.

'I need to get you back to a normal life. A life where you're not being pressured and hunted down for the things that you know. With what's happened, this is the only way I know how to do it, so I'm sorry. If I had a better way, we'd do it. That's the harsh truth of it, so please dry your eyes, focus, and make some lunch for everyone. Try to be a useful part of the team, and as much as you can be.'

Amy sniffed and nodded. 'Still not fair, though, is it?'

'Of course, it isn't.'

She turned and walked back towards the front living room of the new house. She tried not to say one more thing but Siobhan couldn't help herself.

'And another thing,' she said, stopping suddenly, 'you cut peppers at the top, then you lift out the seeds, then you cut them down the sides into strips. If you cut across the top, you can get a bit more of the pepper that you've lobbed off the top. Okay? If you don't know how to cut a pepper, just ask.'

'Simon didn't like peppers, really didn't like peppers.'

Amy burst into tears again, and Siobhan hugged her. She held the woman as she shook, and then she heard the sniffing. Amy backed up and handed Siobhan a knife. Siobhan showed her how to cut a pepper before walking back into the living room where Declan and Kylie were sitting together.

'Have you got any ideas,' asked Kylie, 'because we're not very good at this thing?'

'Just a moment,' said Siobhan. She walked out of the front door into the cold air, pacing over towards one tree. She could smell the damp wood, and it was a comfort, but she kept her back to the house.

Tears were streaming from her face. She felt her shoulders shudder. In her mind, she was in Russia, and she was on the banks of a river. Eamon was standing beside her. He was saying they were alone. He said that the day was warm and his hand was reaching for her. Her hand was reaching back for him, and she remembered laughing on those banks.

She remembered how they enjoyed each other on those banks. Remembered feeling alive. Siobhan had loved him, even if he didn't truly love her. She remembered how she cried when she was posted elsewhere, but also how she realised he hadn't loved back. She'd lost him because he had chosen a job over her and yet he'd always been there. Part of her, she knew, always hoped that in retirement, maybe he would come back, maybe they would find each other again.

Now he was dead. She stared and cried, her tears falling down onto the damp grass beneath her, her hand up against a tree to support her. For a whole five minutes, she just let it go.

'Lunch is ready,' said Amy, and Siobhan put her hand up to acknowledge what was being said. Amy must have been close to the front door because the voice came from a reasonable distance away. Siobhan took the corner of her jumper and wiped her eyes dry, and felt better for that. Her head was becoming clearer.

So far, this had been about seeking what was up with Eamon, seeking those who had killed him. Was it a bit of revenge? Revenge was never good. She had to make this about exposing the truth, about stopping those who were doing something wrong. Now she knew what it was, she needed to act properly like the professional she used to be.

Siobhan turned and walked back into the living room to

find several omelettes sitting on plates. Three of them were being tucked into by the trio there, and she picked up her own. It wasn't the greatest omelette she'd ever had. Probably slightly overdone. Halfway through her first mouthful, she stopped.

'Ernie,' she said, 'we get to Maxwell through Ernie. That's how we did it before. That's how we'll do it again.'

She then put her head down and ate the rest of her omelette. No one said anything, but she'd have to refine that, have to work out exactly how to do it. But he was the line in, and Maxwell didn't know he was compromised yet. Siobhan smiled and let her mind drift away again, back to that riverbank in Russia.

Good times, she thought. *Damn, good times.*

Chapter 31

Siobhan was in a brighter mood the next day. Maybe it had been acknowledging her past with Eamon, getting out the hurt that she felt at his passing. Maybe it was because she was operating again, away from the retirement she had planned and was back in the game. She had missed it. It had only been a brief while since she'd retired, but she'd been an analyst for too long. This was different.

She breakfasted that morning with a couple of croissants and her smoky tea. The only problem with breakfast had been Kylie's face. It was glued to Siobhan, constantly giving an air of doubt. Siobhan didn't know exactly what the plan would be, except that she was going to tail Ernie Savage. From him, she would try to understand the various processes that were going on around the hotel deal.

There was a lot of money to be made out of this hotel on the Causeway coast and whatever else was coming along with it. Siobhan didn't know exactly how it was working, but she could soon throw in that she was interested. No, her client was interested. Another Russian dealer. That would be it. Involve another Russian, but don't say who it is. Have the Russians panicking, scrambling, looking for links, but they wouldn't know who.

It would upset people back in Russia as well. It was the sort of mayhem she was looking to create. A frenzy to bring things to the surface, stir the pot, see what rises, what genuine agencies could get hold of, and then investigate properly.

But she couldn't tell Kylie that yet. That wouldn't work. Kylie wouldn't be satisfied, but that was because Kylie didn't know how things worked. Kylie was still of an age when everything was black and white. There was no grey and there was certainly no fumbling around in the dark to work out what on earth was happening.

Siobhan told the other three to remain at the house. She believed they would be safe there, or at least as safe as anywhere else. There were no indications that anyone was watching the house, but then again, they shouldn't have been able to be followed. No one had tailed them the day they arrived. She was now going to change the car so no one would identify them driving about. She would pick up wigs, makeup, make sure that they looked different if they went anywhere.

The first order of the day was to change the car and pick up a new one from the hire firm. Siobhan booked it in under her false name and using her false credit card. It was her runaway name, her name if everything went wrong, the one she would use to escape the country. It came from a backup plan she'd never had to use, but it was always good to have these things there.

Having picked that car up, she then bought various makeup items and wigs and several new outfits. It also included a long pair of black trousers for herself with black boots underneath. There was a black leather jacket to go over the top of it, and a floppy hat, broad-rimmed. She looked like someone from the seventies. Then again, weren't they back? She couldn't keep up with modern trends. Siobhan also bought a pair of glasses with clear lenses, hoping she looked distinctly different. Finally, she put on a jet-black wig underneath the hat; her disguise was complete.

Ernie Savage was at the hospital, which hadn't been a great deduction, considering he worked there most days of the week. Siobhan sat watching his car until six in the evening when he took off back to his house. Would he be disappearing out that evening looking for some female company? Siobhan didn't know and having had a long day, she couldn't be bothered waiting.

Instead, she approached his house, walked around to the rear, and sat in the darkness of his garden, watching the man in the kitchen. At one point, he opened the rear door, threw something into the bin, and went back inside. Clearly, he hadn't locked the door, so Siobhan approached when he was occupied at the stove.

He heard the door open, and Siobhan said in her best Russian accent, 'Don't. Don't turn round, Mr Savage. I just want another conversation. Keep stirring whatever's in your pot.'

Ernie did so and Siobhan walked up behind him, placing a gun into the back of his neck. 'I heard,' she said, using a deeper tone than she had previously, 'that some of my country folk are involved in buying a hotel on the coast. I think you call it the Causeway coast. My boss is an investor. He would like a chance to bid on this.'

'Whoa,' said Ernie. 'I don't have any say in that. I'm not taking the bids. I just was involved in making sure certain things were smoothed out.'

'But you know who is involved and you know who is controlling that because you were hired to smooth things out, no?'

'I have nothing to do with it. Sorry, you've got the wrong man.'

'I know you to be lying, Mr Savage, and I want in. My boss won't be too happy if I go back with nothing to say to him. No chance that the bid is put in because I was fobbed off by a mere pawn in the game. He'd tell me to find another pawn and get rid of the first. On the other hand, Mr Savage, if you do as we ask, there'll be some money in it for you whether or not your boss accepts the bid. I think we can put a small fee your way. Maybe ten or fifteen thousand...'

'Right,' said Ernie. 'And this just to . . .'

'This is just to pass the message on with no complications. Of course, I could double that if you actually make sure we get a meeting with whoever is running the process.'

Ernie moved his hand down and Siobhan smacked it with her free hand.

'Hey.' he said, 'I'm just turning the gas off, otherwise this will be ruined. Can I turn around?'

'No,' said Siobhan. 'For fifteen thousand pounds, you can let it ruin. You can tell whoever's in charge that we'll offer twice the amount the other bidder is offering.'

'But you don't know . . . you do not know what the other one is offering.'

'Exactly,' said Siobhan. 'Exactly.'

She could see sweat now pouring down Ernie Savage's neck. The kitchen was warm, and she was feeling the heat under her wig and hat, but Savage was sweating.

'I don't see you have a lot of choice, Mr Savage. You can either wind up dead or you can do what I ask. Just be aware that I know where you live and if you don't forward this message, you won't be living here for long.

'I found you once, and I walked in. You're not really cut out for this, are you? So probably best to pass the message on. Probably best not to take the risk that you anger someone. Your boss will not care, will he? Somebody came to you in the dark offering twice the amount and told you to pass a message on. Just do it. Nice and easy. Then Ernie earns a lot of money. Do we have a deal?'

'Okay,' said Ernie, 'but I'm just passing the message on. Okay? Hopefully, he'll meet, but he'll want to know about you. He'll want to . . .'

Ernie went to turn, and Siobhan shoved him up against the cooker. 'Don't,' she said. 'I'd hate to kill you, especially as we're now so close to getting an arrangement organised.'

'Do I get any money upfront?'

'No, you don't. When you make the deal, I will visit again and you'll tell me a bank account. The money will arrive. That's how we do it.'

'So, I'm just to trust you. Just trust you that you'll put the money in my account, and I have to risk myself by talking to my boss about people I don't even know.'

'I don't see that as the choice. I see the choice being to die or do that and don't mess this about. My boss is very good with people who do what they say they do. You put the bid over, he'll give you the money. Don't, he'll kill you. You tell your boss about the bid and he arranges a meeting. You'll get double. My boss doesn't mess people about, but he doesn't enjoy being messed about either.'

'Okay,' said Ernie, 'how do I tell you?'

Siobhan reached inside her pocket and pulled out a mobile phone she'd bought earlier on in the day. She'd entered one number into the address book of another phone that she'd bought along with it.

'The address book in there has a phone number. Text it with details of a town. I'll then scope that town and suggest where we meet. We communicate with these phones. We'll have the meeting sorted within a couple of hours of communication and we will dump the phones and then we will meet face to face. Simple as that.'

'Okay,' said Ernie, 'I won't look at the number. I'll just pass the phone over.'

'You're wise and learning quickly. You'll be worth your money if you come through.'

'Don't step back from the cooker for the next four minutes. After that, you can do what you want. Turn or twist, Ernie, and I'll kill you. It has been a pleasure doing business with you, Mr Savage. Goodbye.'

Siobhan backed out of the kitchen, the gun trained on Savage the whole time, but he didn't move. Instead, his eyes were peeled to a clock on the wall. Siobhan stood outside in the garden, hidden in the dark, and watched when Ernie Savage stepped back from the cooker after four minutes had passed.

He looked at the phone he'd been given and then pocketed it. Taking out his own phone, he dialled a number. Siobhan hoped it was the right call. When he disappeared out the front door two minutes later, she followed him, tailing him in the car to a car park at a DIY superstore.

Ernie sat in the car until another one pulled up alongside

him. Windows were rolled down and Siobhan got out of her own car trying to clock a better view of those inside. As she walked past the cars she saw inside. Maxwell was there. He was talking directly to Maxwell. She couldn't have hoped for better.

Without hesitation, Siobhan walked back to her own car, got in, and drove back to the new house. As she came through the front door, Kylie raced over, looking at her.

'You've been gone all day,' she said. 'Where were you?'

'Told you before, just setting things up. We should hear from Maxwell shortly. Get a lead-in.'

'What did you do?'

'I told Ernie Savage I'd double whatever anybody else was paying to get involved in this scheme. Told him I'd pay him a fortune just to get Maxwell involved. He's done so, told Maxwell, and pretty soon I think we'll be hearing from him. If we don't hear in the next two days, I'll be off to pay Mr Savage another visit.'

'How's this going to work? How are you going to expose things?'

'One step at a time,' said Siobhan. 'You've got to get involved. You've got to be able to play. Once you get a way in, then you make it work. There's a lot of terrain still to see.'

Kylie shook her head, and walked back inside, but Amy appeared at the door of the kitchen.

'You look tired. Do you want some food? Can I knock you something up?'

'Please. Where's Declan?'

'He's upstairs sleeping. He got little sleep last night. Apparently, he was thinking things through.'

'He does that, then gets really excited by them and doesn't

get any more sleep either. I'll see him,' said Siobhan.

She climbed the stairs and opened the door into a bedroom where Declan was asleep. When he heard her, he woke up sitting upright with a bare torso, undisturbed by it in the way only the young are.

'What's happening?' he yawned.

'Nothing as of yet. We'll see if they take the bait. I've told them we want in on the action.'

'Brilliant,' said Declan. 'This is proper spy stuff now.'

Siobhan nodded and closed the door. She'd have something to eat, get a shower, go to bed, but the mobile phone wouldn't leave her sight. This was proper spy stuff, she thought, and she'd missed it. She'd really missed it.

She'd played Ernie Savage correctly. A man chasing money, just the money. How much more could he need? He was on a consultant salary, for goodness' sake, or did his taste in younger women require a more lucrative feed of money into his bank account? She didn't know, and she didn't care. Things were about to step up.

She had a plan in place after spending so long trying to work out what was going on. She didn't know fully, but if she brought it into the light, someone would blow it apart. Someone would highlight it and she'd send the rats scurrying away, back off the ship.

Chapter 32

Siobhan had returned that evening, happy that her plans were going well. Kylie's face, however, said differently. Siobhan didn't know if it was because she was more out of the loop now, Siobhan choosing to do the last escapade on her own. Or whether it was because she didn't simply understand what Siobhan was trying to do.

People had a very narrow view of justice. Everything had to be brought into the light and the correct people punished by those in the judiciary. Over the years of her time in the Service, Siobhan saw many types of justice. Some better than others, inevitably. Some people didn't get what they deserved, whether that be punishment for things they'd done wrong or retribution for injury suffered. You could only ever do your best. That was the long and the short of it.

'I still don't see why you couldn't go to the police,' said Kylie, almost ambushing Siobhan. 'Just let them deal with it from here on.'

'Because they have nothing. It would end up going nowhere. We'd end up with someone with a gun coming after us to silence us, just in case it carried on in the future.'

'I understand,' said Kylie. But Siobhan doubted she really

did.

'We have to get them out in the open,' said Siobhan. 'We have to get everything put out there so others will take it on board. Others will go with it. At the moment, Ernie Savage has contacted Maxwell. He's going to contact me on this phone,' said Siobhan, taking it out of her pocket.

'From there, I'll arrange a meeting. He thinks I'm a Russian agent, or at least working for a Russian oligarch. I'm keen on putting in a rival bid. Double the money. I have no idea what money they're talking, but it's got his interest piqued. If I can get a meeting and if we can get them together, we might form some sort of trap, some sort of event, where we can bring them out into the open. Police can catch them red-handed. That would be the ideal situation, or something else we can manufacture with the press.'

'As long as you know what you're doing,' said Kylie.

'Of course, she does,' said Declan from behind. He had just exited from the living room to meet the two ladies in the hallway. 'It's all been quiet here, Mrs D. Very quiet. To be honest, I think we all could have done with catching our breath.'

'How's Amy?' asked Siobhan.

'I think it's taken a lot out of her,' said Declan. 'We've tried to keep her spirits up.'

Siobhan saw Declan had a very straight and simple view of life. Person down, pick them up. Person up, join in with them. Problem to be solved, go solve it. And all done with a rather cheery disposition.

That evening, Siobhan took a long soak in the bath upstairs. You never quite understood the tension that ran through your body when you're pretending to be someone else and when you could be caught out at any moment. She remembered it from the operative days, but it was more of a high then. She was younger, able to carry that strain. At her current age, she was wiser. Could play it cooler, but it took a lot more out of her.

She sat in the water, stretched out, and thought of what she really wanted. Part of Siobhan was enjoying this. Part of Siobhan was actually embracing it. But she couldn't be an operative again. She couldn't go back.

For a start, they wouldn't accept her. She was too old. Her face was probably too well-known in certain places. As an analyst, there were others coming up better than her. She could have stayed on for a while. The technology had changed as well, and she struggled with it. She had to fight hard to keep up. That was a sight she didn't want. But what would she do?

What would Siobhan do with her life, retired? Did she just want to go bowling? Did she just want to be in a needlecraft club? Would she spend her days walking around, use her National Trust membership, and keep looking at really delightful houses?

She needed a purpose. Siobhan was always a woman of purpose, and at the moment, she had purpose. She also had young people around her. She had learnt that as you grew older, they kept you fresh. Some older people just withered away. The spark of life that they had when they were teenagers disappeared some time ago. And yet there were older people in their eighties who hadn't realised they'd left their teenage years. She wanted to be one of them, not somebody who had died inside.

The tune the mobile phone was playing was one of the old

electronic ones, simple, and Siobhan jumped when it went off. The phone was sitting just out of reach of the bath. As she stepped out, the water dripping off her, she tried to compose herself. She saw the text. It simply said, 'Yes. Portrush.'

Siobhan thought about Portrush. Where could she meet in Portrush where it would be easiest? It needed to be somewhere that she could escape easily. Somewhere with a crowd of people, easy to disappear. You could see people from a distance. You could also set up lookouts of your own who'd go unnoticed. Or would she be better on her own?

This could be a trap, after all. There was one thing saying, 'Let's meet in such-and-such a place, you're going to get double the money,' but Maxwell may think that it wasn't worth it. A deal was done. Would he want to go against other Russians? He'd have to sell it as a competition after they'd done a lot of the work.

It was too risky, she thought. I need to be somewhere I can be on my own, somewhere I'm happy I can get out of. She knew also that at some point, she was going to have to bring the others in as part of the Russian group. She said she was the go-between. She was arranging something for her boss. Someone was going to have to play that boss, and probably Declan.

You didn't get that many female bosses, especially in the Russian underworld, and if so, well, they were usually known. Bringing in somebody new with money was easier if they were male. Kylie would have to play as his lady on his arm. *She'll love that,* thought Siobhan, and she gave a little laugh. *That was wicked of me.*

There was a fun park, mostly indoor, with an outdoor section at the rear. It had been the mainstay of Portrush for years. It had been taken over after having stayed in the hands of a family concern for a long time, but now there was a new one, Charlie's. In some ways, it was the same as the previous one.

Siobhan felt cold now as she was standing out of the bath, and she stepped back in, holding the mobile above the water. As usual, once you got out of a bath and got back in, it never felt quite the same, the water never as warm as when you first embraced it. Siobhan typed in Charlie's in Portrush, then a time of three o'clock, the middle of the day. She put in Saturday, thinking it would be open then because it didn't always open during the day at this time of year. Siobhan put down the phone at the side of the bath and lay back again in the water.

Her muscles felt rejuvenated, but her mind drifted. *Julian,* she thought. He just sort of arrived in her mind. Maybe it was because he was one good thing going on at the moment.

Going on,' she thought, *'he's not going on, I just met him again. He told me to be careful.' He also said he was available there if you needed him.*

She didn't want to need him; she didn't want to bring him in. He was still in the Service, and he may find his duties conflicting with helping her. She hoped not; she hoped this was not something gone awry in the Service, there was too much of that.

Siobhan nearly jumped again when the tune played on the mobile phone. She picked it up and simply got an, 'Agreed.' The tune started again a minute later. 'How will I know you?' said the message.

'I know you, Mr Maxwell,' she wrote, 'I shall see you at three.'

Siobhan switched off the phone and broke it, putting it down to one side. They would have a signal if they've contacted the phone company, they would know which mast the mobile was operating off. There would have been an amount of ground. She'd only switched the phone on a couple of minutes previous when she'd driven back in the car. She'd popped it on every ten to fifteen minutes. They would struggle to trace her. She was confident of that.

Siobhan allowed herself to soak for a while longer before stepping out and drying herself down. She thought about wrapping herself up in a dressing gown and then realised she didn't have one, so she popped on a pair of leggings, a T-shirt and her baggy jumper. When she reached the living room, there was a fire going, and three quiet younger people sitting around it.

'Can I get you anything?' asked Kylie.

'Do some toast for everyone and I'd like a cup of my usual.'

Kylie nodded and stood up, disappeared out. When she returned with the toast and the tea, Siobhan sat for a while eating it and drinking her fill. Only then did she turn to the rest of them.

'I've had contact back. I'm meeting them on Saturday, so two days' time in Portrush, we're going to lie low here until then.'

'Where do the rest of us go then when you're meeting them? Do you want us with you? Do you want us on the side looking in?' said Declan.

'I want you here,' said Siobhan.

Declan looked like he was being destroyed, like the child who was told they couldn't have the candy apple.

'How's that fair?' he said.

Siobhan nearly snapped, 'It's not about fairness, Declan. I know you're keen, but I have to keep you safe; you, Kylie, Amy. What I'm about to do on Saturday, it could be very dangerous. If I haven't played this right, they might decide that it's actually better to meet me and take me out. If that's the case, I'll have to be on top form and I can't hang about for you lot. You don't know how to disappear like I do. You don't know their techniques for finding us. I do. I know how to get away from them—you don't.'

'So what, we're sidelined until you get this done?'

'No, if this goes well and I get what I want, which will be a public meet, you'll be heavily involved. You'll be my gang lord.'

'Cool,' said Declan.

'Kylie will be the lady on your arm.' Declan smiled again, but Kylie scowled.

'It's a modern day. I could be the gang lord.'

'Not in Russia you can't,' said Siobhan. 'I've been this go between, so I'll need to stay at that. Besides, I'm the only one who can speak Russian. You need to stay quiet when we meet. Haven't got Russian accents. You won't sound it, but I can dress you up so you look the part.

'What I can't do is have you meeting them beforehand. I'll be disguised, but if they found out who you were because they saw your face, they'll know it's a hoax. Your face has already been put in front of them at the dinner, mine too, but I can be more disguised. If they don't make me at this one, they won't make us at the next one.'

'And what about me?' said Amy. 'Do you need my help?'

'I don't know, possibly, we'll see. But I think you've done enough. You put yourself in harm's way for us already.

'You need to understand something,' said Siobhan, standing up. She walked over to the fire and turned, warming her backside against it. It felt good. The days outside were getting colder. She was feeling them more than she ever did. She stared back at them all, her face serious.

'We're coming towards an endgame,' she said. 'There's going to be a lot of risk in what comes ahead. I'll minimise it as best I can, but we won't get away from it. If anybody wants to pull out, that's okay. I'll do it without you and I won't think anything less of you for it. You're not trained for this. Heck, I'm not trained anymore, been a long while since I did the field.'

Siobhan coughed for a moment. 'I'll make my meet with Maxwell, work out what he's going to do. From there, we'll plan it. But the meeting after that is the big one. The meeting after this one is where we'll do the exposé, however it comes about. You can't keep these things going too long. We'll get caught out and people will know we're missing. So, rest up these next couple of days because I think it's going to get frantic after that.'

Chapter 33

Siobhan was feeling anxious about the meeting in Portrush but dressed in her jeans, a large fleece, and a scarf around her neck. She wore a red wig and a pair of sunglasses, although the tint in them wasn't strong at all. To anyone looking at her though, all they saw was a reflective mirror. It was pretty crass, but it helped keep her disguised. Her aim was to get in, have the meeting, set up a new meeting, and get back out. She wouldn't be hanging around.

Siobhan recognised that she might have baited a bear on the other side. Maxwell might have told them there was another interested buyer and so they would scope her out. When a Russian gangster scoped you out, it wasn't always with the idea of just seeing what the opposition looked like. Some of them got rid of the opposition. It would be subtle, of course. This was Northern Ireland and not their territory. There were other factions abroad, local ones that would take issue with open murder such as that.

Charlie's funfair was in the middle of Portrush and as Siobhan walked past the train station, she came into a more open area. There was a path that led down to the full glass-fronted opening of Charlie's. There was a separate funfair off to the right, but Charlie's had always been the one to go to. Outside was a helter-skelter, something you rarely saw anymore, and inside, the rides began as soon as you got through the door.

It wasn't overly busy, but there were a good number of families running around. And in front of her, a large mechanical device with long arms and seats on the end spun round, bouncing people up and down. Siobhan wasn't a funfair person, but she was glad of the noise, for it'd give an excuse to come close to her contact.

She started scanning for Maxwell as she walked around the large spritzer, as it was called. They always had those weird names and yet some of them were very similar. You got the waltzers, the twisters, the dodgems, and to her right was the ghost train.

It had a single track at the front where the train cars were stacked up, waiting to enter. There was a door that would open to let you in and the other door further back down that let you back out. Beyond it were slightly more traditional games, shooting at targets, and basketball to win back cuddly items. They were probably more of Siobhan's thing. A game of skill if you could believe it to be true.

Something brushed her shoulder. Siobhan turned to see a man walking away. She checked her pockets. Nothing had been taken. And then saw Maxwell further into Charlie's, standing beside one of the tuppenny drop machines. You put two pence in the top, it slid down, and fell onto a bar that was moving backwards and forwards. As it moved back in, hopefully your tuppence moved other tuppences off the edge and down onto the next level. So, it continued until, hopefully, more coins would drop into your collection area at the bottom.

Maxwell was putting several two pences in, and Siobhan walked up and sat with her bottom against the glass, looking around her for anyone else.

'Hello, Mr Maxwell. It's good to do business with you,' said Siobhan in her best Russian accent.

'Good evening to you as well. Is your boss prepared to give his name?'

'No, but he is prepared to give his money. Double the amount, he said. How much, exactly, are you being offered at the moment?'

'Fifty million.'

Siobhan tried not to look shocked. 'And the best way to transfer that?'

'Oh, I'll take a small sum in cash, say two million. The rest can be transferred to this bank account after we've concluded.'

'Concluded?' queried Siobhan.

'Yes, I advised my other interested party whom I have conducted extensive negotiations with.' Maxwell smiled. 'It seems like they'd like to do an auction.'

'I can understand that,' said Siobhan. 'It's a good deal. We've invested a lot of time looking at it. Where would you like to do your auction?'

'I thought the Giant's Causeway,' said Maxwell. 'It's very— how shall I put it—appropriate, considering the hotel's going to be down that way. It's what's going to bring the business in. It's what's going to make you your money.'

'And you'll get rid of all planning restrictions, any issues?'

'Of course, for my fee. Two million will be brought on that night, and I'll take it from whoever wins the bid. That's a non-refundable amount of money. Of course, whoever wins will then transfer the full amount into the nominated Swiss bank account. Once it's in there, I'll make the full arrangements.

'You've done well to get your interest to me in time,' said Maxwell. 'I was just about to conclude the deal with the other party. They understand my position, of course, selling to the highest bidder. We had a previous bidder, but they dropped out. I don't really go into the affairs of others, but I said to my other party we can't bring attention to this. Any disputes will need to be dealt with quietly.'

'I'm sure you don't mean that they can't be managed with appropriate force.'

Maxwell dropped a couple more two pences into the machine. After a few moments, there was a clatter of two pennies in the cup below. He went over to Siobhan.

'I really couldn't give a damn what you do to each other,' he whispered. 'As long as you don't do it out in public. If you do and the police get onto us, I am gone and the deal's off. Oh, and I'm off with your two million.'

Siobhan nodded and looked beyond Maxwell. The same couple had just come past her three times. On the left-hand side, a man had been standing eating candyfloss that was down to the bare stick and was still watching her.

'When you said that you had somebody else looking,' asked Siobhan, 'did you tell the other interested party about it? The fact you were meeting me here?'

'I wouldn't be so bold, but knowing that someone else is involved, it stands to reason that they might tail me. They'll want to see who the opposition is, although they'll not see much with what you're wearing.'

Siobhan wrapped her scarf up and over her mouth. 'No, they won't,' she said. 'Giant's Causeway, when?'

'Two days, midnight. There'll be no one about. I'll take care of that. But I don't want just you. I want whoever I'm dealing with to be there. Once we've done the auction, I need to run through things. Make sure that we're all on the same page, so we don't cock this up. I've had it before with foreign types coming in. We have other interested parties here that might need a small amount paid to them, just to keep everyone happy.'

'We are aware of the history of your island.'

'Our wee country,' said Maxwell. 'Call it that, and it means one thing to one side and something to the other. Call us the island and it says one thing to one side and something to the other. Call us whatever, the province, the six counties. It all means something to each other. They read into it what they want. As long as they get the money, they'll keep off my back. I'm not inclined either way. As long as I get my money, this country can do whatever the damn hell it wants.

'So,' he said, 'two days, midnight, Giant's Causeway. Bring me two million. Be prepared to bid. I expect the money to be in the Swiss Bank account within another four days.

'I understand you fully, Mr Maxwell, and I will relay your instructions to my boss. Right now, I need to get out of here. I fear you have been tailed, and I fear they may try to prevent me from passing your instructions on. Good day to you, Mr Maxwell. Good doing business with you, as you say.'

Siobhan turned and walked away from the two-penny machine. She headed straight for the nearest exit, which was on side one, except she saw a group of men. They didn't look like they were here for a family day out, all large individuals. Siobhan returned and went to walk out towards the rear of Charlie's, but again she saw several people drifting towards her.

She turned and tried to take a route towards the exit at the front. Again, she could see herself being cordoned off. Before her was the large ride she'd seen on the way in, the ghost train on her left-hand side and those games of skill beside her. The only one to give her any cover would be the ghost train. She walked up to go on and a young lad turned to her.

'Yes, where's your ticket? You need tickets to go on here. This one's three for someone of your age.'

'Of course,' said Siobhan, and then she turned and pointed. 'What's that up there?'

The boy turned his head. Siobhan slipped past him and pushed open the door of the ghost train, stepping inside into the dark.

It wasn't completely dark; there was the occasional light. There were large boards and screens, skeletons hanging down, a vampire in the far distance. Siobhan pursued the track round before stepping off into the rear. She heard the front entrance open and saw the rear door do the same.

Siobhan could handle herself to a point. When she was at Dunluce, she was able to isolate one of her pursuers, prepare a plan, and execute it. She also managed to get past the man on the bridge. She needed the element of surprise, though. Here, there would be a lot of them, and she couldn't get into a fistfight. If she got stood up at all, she would be disposed of.

Also, the men that were pursuing her, they didn't seem like the half-amateurs that had picked her up at Dunseverick. These looked like people who were sent out to kill. Minimal engagement was the order of the day.

Siobhan crouched low, watching as the men spread out through the attraction. They were struggling to see as well, eyes adjusting to the dark. One man bumped his head on a low-hanging image of a malformed crow. Another one walked into a skeleton, grabbing it, and throwing it to the ground. Siobhan would have to be quick.

She counted three had come in from the front, three from the back. She leant up against the wall, sliding along it at the rear of the attraction. A car burst through the front door, suddenly making the men turn back. It was empty. Should Siobhan jump on it?

She thought not. Too many of them, too easy for them to grab her when it was going at such a slow speed. Instead, she made her way towards the rear entrance where the track came out. She saw a large man hoking around in the dark. Quickly, she walked up behind him and kicked him hard in the backside. He shouted, turned, but she was gone.

'She's over here,' the man shouted to the others in Russian. But Siobhan had jumped track and was moving up the other side of the ride. She saw four of them racing along in the dark. Three had come in at one end, three from the other. She'd met one of them, that accounted for five. It would be her best chance. Get to the front entrance. Get in there and go.

Where was the other man? Siobhan didn't hesitate. Instead, working her way through the dark, she pulled her glasses forward slightly, looking past the lenses. As she got to the front entrance, she thought she would make it. All she had to do was . . .

Somebody hit her in the back. Siobhan stumbled forward, and put her hands out, stopping herself from hitting the wall. She tripped over some tracks but maintained her footing. Her shoulder was turned, spun hard, and it hit the wall. She yelped in agony.

Before her was a man at least three to four inches bigger than her. His hand went straight to her throat, lifting her up as he carefully stepped over the first bit of track. The wall here was close to the track, and he wasn't able to step across the second rail, instead only getting his foot onto it. Siobhan reached up with her hands, grabbing his wrist, trying to wrench his hand off her throat. He was squeezing incredibly hard.

She tried to punch him in the side, but it was useless. She could not take on someone like this. His strength was far beyond hers. Siobhan wheezed, struggling for breath. She was running out of options. Carrying no knife, she had nothing to stab him with. She tried to kick out, but the man was immovable. So, this was it, years of working in Russia, years of escaping thugs like this, and yet he kills her in one of her favourite childhood haunts.

The doors burst open, and a train car barrelled through. It hit the man in the shins and must have been moving with quite a force because it made him tumble; the cab rode up onto his legs. His hand let go of Siobhan and she dropped to the floor, the car missing her by inches, but his legs were at least trapped under the wheels.

She didn't wait. Instead, she picked herself up and ran through the entrance. There were several shocked-looking people, but she had the sense to lift her scarf, wrapping it across, covering her nose and mouth. The glasses were pressed back up and she tore out of Charlie's as fast as she could.

Once outside, she cut through this street, that street, and disappeared into a shop, purchasing a different coloured jacket. She changed into a skirt she bought as well. She ditched the wig, too. As she headed out on the road, now clear of Portrush, Siobhan could feel her hands beginning to shake. She had trouble holding the wheel steady and had to pull over into some services. A cup of tea or something else was required.

Siobhan bought one and then stepped out to the rear of the building so no one could see her from the road. There was a light drizzle in the air. It was cold. Holding the cup in one hand, Siobhan raised her hand up and felt her neck. It was sore to the touch, deeply bruised. She felt like her knees were going to go weak.

'Come on,' she said, 'come on.' She drank her tea, in between breathing in huge lungfuls of cold air. When she got back in the car, she drove, gripping the wheel like it was about to roll away.

Chapter 34

When Siobhan had arrived back at their hideout, Declan asked if she was all right. Kylie didn't, and neither did Amy. They could tell she wasn't. But Siobhan had things to do, and whatever had happened needed to be pushed to one side.

'Two days,' she said to them. 'Two days and we've got to be ready to go. That's all I've got to make you a gangster,' she said to Declan. 'Two days to make you a bodyguard,' she told Kylie. 'Two days more for you to sit here, Amy. But you can help make some props.'

Siobhan hadn't been up for organising much that night. All she had said was that Declan should set up a meeting with his uncle because they would need Ken to blow this wide open.

Siobhan went to bed and was fitful during her sleep. She woke three times because she was dreaming about a face planted in front of her while she couldn't breathe. It had been too close, too damn close. She had thought that Charlie's would have had many escape routes. They'd come in such numbers. Daniil Baranov was clearly a bigger operator than she'd taken for granted. At breakfast the next morning, she sat silently in her jeans and T-shirt.

'You all right, Mrs D?' asked Declan.

Kylie slapped him on the wrist. 'Of course, she isn't.'

'Right,' said Siobhan, ignoring the comment, 'we've got to get shopping for Declan. I'm meeting Ken later on to set up his response. I've got to hire a decent car and we've got to teach you how to shoot, Kylie.'

Kylie looked rather perturbed at this prospect.

'Sorry, but we do. We need to give you a chance to protect yourself in case this goes wrong. Now I've seen who they are and what they do, I wouldn't want you involved in it, but this is the only chance we've got. And if we don't do this, Amy is compromised. Compromised to a point where they'll come for her. They know that she's more deeply involved. She's not just a widow now.'

'You're the boss, Mrs D,' said Declan. 'We'll just get on with it. I think we all trust you here.'

'I don't think trust is the issue, Declan,' said Kylie. 'I think it's the rather large and scary people we're working against.'

'Don't!' said Siobhan. 'Don't think of it like that. Think about what you must do.'

That day, Siobhan took five thousand pounds out of her bank account, bought a briefcase, and got Amy setting up fake notes in amongst the real ones. You only had to be convincing for a short period. Siobhan wouldn't let it get to a point where they'd count it. Besides, she was planning on coming back with the briefcase. Five thousand was a lot of money, although she could afford to lose it if she had to.

She met Ken, Declan's uncle, and briefed him on what was about to happen. He would need to contact the police. He would also need to operate from a long distance, so he needed someone who could work a proper telephoto lens.

'What about a drone?' Ken had said. He had a young lad who could get a drone in. They could be quite quiet, too. In fact, Ken and the lad could be over a mile away with certain drones. Siobhan liked the idea but told him that the police needed to be coming as soon as he got footage of the meeting, and Maxwell's face had to be front and centre. Also, Daniil Baranov. Those two faces would set the alarm bells ringing and start the investigations.

Later that afternoon, Siobhan practised on Declan, changing his appearance completely. She shaved his hair, giving him a bald look, cutting his hair low but not off completely. It wasn't easy to put the flesh-coloured cap on and make it look real, but Siobhan had skills from her days. She bought him a suit and tie. In truth, he looked rather fetching.

'Remember, you don't speak. I'll speak for you. You utter a word, they'll realise there's no Russian accent in there.'

Kylie was also dressed in a suit. She'd have her hair tied and down her back under her jacket. Siobhan thought it a bad idea to both be appearing as women. Originally, Siobhan was going to bring Kylie along as a status symbol on Declan's arm, but now she decided with what had happened, he would come in force.

It wasn't easy trying to make Kylie look less feminine. She had curves, but the jacket looked like it had a bulletproof vest underneath. Siobhan worked her makeup and packed Kylie's arms too, to make them look less feminine. Overall, she was happy.

That evening, she gave Kylie a crash course on how to fire a gun. They would have the next day to wait, but at least everything was ready. The hire car had been booked and Siobhan took a deep breath as she sent them all to bed that night.

On her own in the living room in front of the fire, she thought about Eamon; she was doing this for him. For him, she'd go through with this. She realised that outside of Amy, the other two were doing it for her. She'd have to correct them on that, but not till the job was done.

Siobhan thought about Julian. She really could do with his help, but with the way the Service was, she wasn't sure how much help he would be.

The next day was a quiet affair. The car was picked up, and the gang took it easy until teatime. Then they made sure that Declan was made up correctly, before Siobhan and Kylie, too.

Kylie drove the car all the way from just outside Bangor up to the Causeway coast. They arrived at half-past ten, and Siobhan got Kylie to drive around the area while she overlooked it. They parked up in the Causeway car park, waiting until close to twelve before driving through and down. The area should have been closed off, but for some reason it was open.

As they took the BMW down the road that only the bus normally travelled, Siobhan looked out, wondering where Ken was. He'd said a mile, and if he'd any wit, he would use that mile. Was there a drone already filming them? She hoped so.

When they arrived, she could see people out already on the Causeway. The night was windy, and Siobhan could see Maxwell standing aloof, well down on the stones.

Kylie parked the BMW up beside another car and together Kylie, Siobhan, and Declan stepped up the steep climb onto the Causeway. It was said to have been built by a giant. The tale seemed incredibly convincing as you watched it disappear out into the sea. Here and now, it looked quite fabulous. Although it was windy and cold, the moon was shining down and the waves, as they hit the edges of the Causeway, erupted into a fan of white.

Close to this visual delight stood Maxwell and a small party on the other side. They walked close to him, watching their footing across the causeway where it was anything but even. The hexagonal rocks at different heights caused you to pick your way through. The wind howled out on the edge, but Maxwell's voice came over the top of it.

'Hello, our mystery guests. Mr Baranov here was rather disappointed that he wasn't able to speak to you two days ago, but it honestly pleases me because it tells me you're a player. Let's get our auction underway, shall we? I'd rather not hang about.'

Declan stood looking around him, and Siobhan stepped forward in front of him. 'My boss won't speak. I'll speak for him. His English is non-existent.'

Daniil Baranov looked over and said something in Russian. It meant we might talk in the mother tongue, but Siobhan shook her head and replied in English.

'He won't do that, he won't speak to the likes of you,' and then she reiterated it in Russian just for good measure.

Daniil Baranov wasn't a tall man, around about five feet seven, but he had a scowl that drove a fear into you. He looked slightly deranged, and he certainly was angry at having to bid for this contract that no doubt he thought he had sewn up some time ago.

'Let's see your money,' said Maxwell. 'I don't want this turning ugly; I just want it settled.'

Siobhan turned and took a case off Kylie, opening it, and

Maxwell stared down at the money. He went to count it, but Baranov told him not to. 'It's cold here, we're not messing about, they have the money, let's get on to it.'

Maxwell nodded, and Kylie took the briefcase back.

'Fifty million is where we stand at the moment. It's against your boss,' said Maxwell to Siobhan.

'I said we would double it. One hundred,' said Siobhan. She could see that Baranov was already angry at this. 'One hundred and ten,' he said.

'One-twenty,' said Siobhan. Maxwell was smiling. 'One-thirty, one-forty.'

Baranov was about to say something else, but he halted. He looked up and Siobhan could see what he was looking at; it was the drone. It had come in low, maybe thirty feet high. Baranov went to pull a weapon, and the drone took off. As Baranov lifted the weapon up, Siobhan could hear something louder in the distance. It wasn't the quiet whirr of a drone; this was a helicopter. This was—

Over the top of the large rock formations that outlined the coast, a helicopter came sweeping in. Its searchlight raked across the Causeway before settling down on Maxwell and the two parties. Baranov screamed something in Russian that Siobhan couldn't quite make out, but he was definitely swearing at Maxwell. Some of his goons ran over, one pushing Siobhan to the ground, the other grabbing Kylie.

She took a punch to the mouth and fell. Siobhan rolled over towards her, kicking the man who was attacking her. Declan tried to step in and then he was dragged away. Siobhan pulled her gun, pointing it at the man holding Declan, but another gun was being held to Declan's head.

Kylie said nothing. She should have screamed, she should

have yelled out, she should have blurted something in English, but she didn't, holding to her part. Siobhan stood up, ran over to Maxwell, and shoved him to the ground.

'You will pay for this,' she said to him in her best Russian accent. She turned and indicated Kylie should follow her. Together, they remained at a distance as Declan was hauled off the Causeway, a slow manoeuvre given the rocks. The insistent beam of the helicopter's light made it even more difficult. Its speaker told them to wait, told them they were under arrest and to lay down their weapons.

Daniil Baranov, along with Declan, got to the car that was parked beside the BMW. It disappeared off. The helicopter followed it, and Siobhan shouted to Kylie for the keys. The two women got into the car, Siobhan driving, following the other one.

'What will they do to him?' blurted Kylie.

'They'll bloody kill him if they don't torture him first. Bollocks,' said Siobhan out loud. 'Bollocks.'

Above her, the police helicopter was passing back and forward, no doubt trying to trace them. What would Baranov do? Try to shake the helicopter? Where would he go? Would he hold Declan hostage in case the police got there? It had all gone wrong, too wrong. Until the point where they grabbed Declan, it was perfect. Everybody would have fled. Everybody would have gone their own separate ways, but Ken would have had the footage. Maxwell would have been lifted, things would have been investigated. It all would have come out in time. Baranov would have been implicated in a strange deal, a bidding contest out on the Causeway. Maxwell clearly had a flair for the dramatic, and it would cost him.

Siobhan tore out of the main Causeway car park and

onto the minor roads. She glanced at Kylie. The girl's face was white, paler than she'd ever seen. Siobhan's own heart thumped. She had to get Declan back. Whatever else happened, she needed to keep him safe, whatever the cost.

Chapter 35

Think Siobhan, think. Come on!

It was hard enough focusing on what the car ahead was doing, never mind thinking. At least the BMW she was in had power. They were tearing off along a small narrow road. Could she corner them? Get into a standoff at least? Could she throw them the money and take Declan?

Siobhan needed ideas. She needed to think about what to do. Ballintoy Harbour was just up ahead. If she could force them down the Ballintoy Road, if she could get them down to the harbour, it was more contained. There were fewer places to go. If the police were coming in cars now, for they would have launched the helicopter first, they would be here soon.

Down the Ballintoy Road, they could close everything off. If the police came and arrested everybody, so be it. She'd involve Julian, she'd make sure. Then in her stomach she thought about the fact that Julian said somebody in the Service was making money, but that person was Maxwell, wasn't it? If he was caught out, the others would throw him under a bus, wouldn't they? She didn't know; she didn't know how this would pan out, but she had to get Declan back.

As the road twisted along, Siobhan drove as hard as she

could, catching the other car. It turned a corner near the Ballintoy Road, and she drove hard, forcing the other car, hitting it along the side and turning it down the Ballintoy Road. It had to go that way. She had left them no other choice. If they turned back, the road would be blocked by Siobhan coming behind them.

The road down to Ballintoy Harbour was winding. There was one way down. It swung left and right, coming down the hillside, eventually into the harbour area. This was always a stunning place, with the tides running into the harbour and onto the rock formations. Now at night, the harbour was lit up.

As the car ahead reached the harbour, it drove off to one side and Siobhan stopped the car.

'Sit across the road here with it. Take the keys. I'm going in to get him.'

'Do you want me to help you?' said Kylie.

'Kylie, don't be stupid. You stay here. Anything goes wrong, just get out. If the police come, hands up, walk over to them. Just let them take you into custody, okay? Ditch the gun before you do it, though. Throw it away into the sea somewhere. Rub it with a cloth. Take the fingerprints off it. I'll explain everything if I'm still alive. If not, you're a nobody. You're not involved in this. Not to any degree. Tell the story as it is. You can take them to Amy. That'll help corroborate what's happened with you, okay?'

'What do you mean if you're not alive?'

Siobhan took the gun out of her jacket and opened the door. 'Kylie, it's the endgame. Your end is going to be an okay one. Do as I ask.'

The helicopter was up high, its beam searching around.

Siobhan ran off to the side. There was a building alongside the harbour. A small one, possibly where they would have kept the fishing gear. She saw the men run in there with Declan. He was kicking, but somebody slugged him across the jaw.

They left a man outside, so Siobhan climbed up onto the grass above the rocks, remaining low in a crouch. She hoped the helicopter wouldn't come down and spot her, but its beam was shining down on the shed the men had run into.

Siobhan came out above the shed from the high ground. The man in front couldn't see her above and behind him. She got close to the small building and could hear screaming. It was Declan. The Russians were shouting at him, demanding who he was. Declan wouldn't understand. Declan couldn't answer. He was now screaming in English, telling them to get off.

Don't, she thought, *don't!* If they think you're a British spy, they'll just finish you.

She had to be quick. The man at the front of the shed was looking up, watching the helicopter, then glancing over to where Kylie was in the car. He didn't see Siobhan running across the roof of the shed. She didn't want to shoot, alert those inside. Instead, she dropped behind the man, hitting him across the back of the head with her gun, but she hit him three times more, making sure he was knocked out.

Siobhan listened and heard Declan screaming inside again, but the Russian was saying something.

'When the boat gets here, we'll take you, we'll take you somewhere secure and we'll find out what you're really doing. Find out who you really are. It won't be nice. There won't have much left of you by the time we're finished.'

Siobhan flung open the door at the front of the shed. The Russians were looking at Declan and she walked in and announced herself, telling them not to move in Russian.

'Guns down,' she said. Her weapon was pointed at Daniil. 'You'll die first,' said Siobhan. 'Guns down now. I count to three. Three, two, one,' she said quickly. There was a nod from Danil and the guns went to the floor.

'Good,' said Siobhan. 'What's this about a boat?'

'A boat is coming,' said Danil. We could all get on it. We could all . . .'

'Where is it coming from?'

'The other side of the rocks. It won't come into the harbour,' said Danil. 'They'll see it. Instead, we'll make like we're going to get into the boat in the harbour. At least we were going to get you to do that. Then we could get away. It's good that you have turned up like this. Is the money you came with still in the car too? We'll bring that with us.'

'You forget,' said Siobhan. 'I'm holding the gun.'

She looked at Declan. Blood was pouring out of his mouth. He looked a mess. He was staring at her, but he didn't seem to understand what was going on.

'Change of plan,' said Siobhan. 'We'll be taking the boat. You're going to come out there with us and you're going to pretend to kill us. Then you're going to take this other boat. Maybe you've got enough clout behind you. Maybe you'll be able to chase the police off, but we'll be away because we need something to distract that helicopter.'

Inside, Siobhan's heart was thudding. She had Declan, a kid, and she needed to get him out. In the car was Kylie. They'd done nothing like this. Why had she brought them into it? Why had she? Well, because she had to, because things had run away from her. It was like she was back in Russia, back playing the games they played there.

Deadly ones, but ones everyone was trained for, ones everyone understood. *Idiot*, she thought to herself; *idiot*.

'When does the boat arrive?'

'Any second,' said Danil.

Siobhan walked closer, pointed a gun at Danil's head. 'Let him go, and then you come with me.'

'I think not,' said Danil. Siobhan felt metal at the back of her head. It was being pressed in firmly. *Bugger*, she thought. *I didn't check for more. I didn't check for the other person.*

She felt like an amateur. It was basic. Count the people, count who was around. One was missing. Siobhan slowly knelt and placed her gun on the ground.

'And who are you?' asked Danil in Russian. 'This one isn't Russian. You? Maybe. You've been to Russia. Your accent from St Petersburg. Very good. Nearly perfect, but I think you're not from there, are you?'

'And you're not from here,' said Siobhan. 'You shouldn't be here. You don't understand our authorities. I could get you away. I could get you clean out of here. If you let the both of us go afterwards, if we make a deal.'

'I don't need deals. I will be fine. Mr Maxwell may still have a deal after all. If we can put the blame on you. On the bodies I leave behind. It was nice having a brief acquaintance with you.'

Siobhan saw the man about to give a nod but then his eyes went wide.

There was a thud from behind her. Followed by another one. Then the words 'Bloody go down' before another thud. Then someone was kicking the man behind her. Stamping.

Siobhan grabbed her gun. Turning, she saw Kylie frustratedly kicking a man. He was holding his head. Siobhan held her weapon, covering Danil.

'Kylie, just point the gun at him,' said Siobhan. She was shaking, but not as much as Kylie's hands. If she fired, she could have hit anything in the room, the way her hands were bouncing about.

'You,' said Siobhan to the groaning man on the floor in Russian. 'Get over there.' She forced them all into the corner, told them to turn and put their hands on the wall. They did so, and Siobhan asked for the keys to their car.

Declan wandered over to her, groggily, and she gave him the keys and told him to get into the car. Slowly, she backed away, the gun still trained on Daniil. She opened the doors behind her, slipped out with Kylie and closed it, waving at Declan. He drove over in the car and Siobhan indicated for him to put it across the doors, preventing them from opening. She opened the passenger door after he parked the car, letting him climb across and come out. The searchlight from the helicopter above was on them. The police would be here soon. They couldn't hang about much longer. She could hear sirens in the distance.

'What do we do?' said Kylie, holding the gun.

'You run back to the car. Take out my money. Declan with me.'

Siobhan ran round the side of the concrete harbour jetties and over towards the rocks, disappearing out of the lights that lit up the harbour. From the other side, the helicopter would have difficulty trying to put its beam on them because of the high rock formation.

Siobhan listened. Amongst the crashing water and the

roaring wind, she could hear a voice. It was in Russian. She called to it in Russian, telling it to come over. The boat was ten metres away before she fully clocked the figure. It was an inflatable and black. The motor was small and the man inside it was wearing black.

Maybe he'd been at the causeway standing by in case they needed rescue. Whatever. He was now here, and Siobhan trained a gun on him.

'Bring that in or I shoot you dead,' she said in Russian. The man's face went white, but he brought the boat over and Declan wearily grabbed hold of it.

'Kylie' she shouted behind her and Kylie wandered through carrying the briefcase with the money. 'Get Declan into that boat with you.'

Siobhan turned round to the man. 'If you want to live, you will do this. I will fire shots into the air, at which time you will walk out to that harbour. You will try to open the shed door. If I see you fail to do this, I will fire from here and kill you.'

The man looked a little bemused, but he nodded.

'Good' said Siobhan. She turned, pointed the gun off into the water, and fired six times. However, she fired three all at once and then single shots with short bursts in between. *Execution*, she thought. *They'll have heard an execution.*

The man walked forward as Siobhan had told him, her gun trained. He made his way out onto the pier, round across the concrete and towards the shed. Once he'd arrived at that point, she jumped into the small boat, started the engine, and they tore off into the night. The helicopter was fascinated by the man at the shed, and Siobhan could see the long beam of light glaring down at him.

They went further up the coast until Ballintoy was out of sight. They continued on their way before Siobhan took out her mobile and called Amy back at their hideout just outside Bangor. She told her to get in the car and come up the coast. They'd keep going for the next hour to get in somewhere and get Amy to pick them up.

Having completed the call, Siobhan asked Kylie to take the rudder, telling her to keep whatever she could see of the shore in sight and keep going along beside it.

She looked at Declan. He was sore, but Siobhan couldn't find any broken bones. He was certainly bloody. There'd be bruising, at least, but that was okay because he could rest up. She hoped Ken had got enough. She prayed Ken had got the faces of Daniil Baranov and Maxwell on his drone. He would give it in to the police and make a great story out of it. Had they done it?

Siobhan didn't know, but as she looked in the boat, she at least knew she had two people, safe and well. It was about an hour later when they came ashore, and Siobhan rubbed down the boat before sending it back out into the sea. They made their way up towards a roadside and she texted where they were to Amy. They sat in the dark, cold and wet. Siobhan collected the guns, throwing them out into the sea as well.

'We did it,' said Kylie, a smile on her face. 'We damn well did it.'

But Siobhan's face showed a concern.

'We left the damn BMW at Ballintoy. It's a hire car. It can be traced back to me, eventually. Damn it,' she said. She slumped down, but looked up. They were alive. Whatever the consequences, they were alive.

Chapter 36

Siobhan sat in her living room in front of the large fire that Declan had built for her. The smell of the wood was good and was calming her nerves. In reality, she was nervous. It was the middle of the day following on from the previous night's excursions. Amy had brought them back to her own house, and Kylie and Declan had gone back with Amy, off to the rented safe house.

Siobhan reckoned they'd be music to face, and the last thing she wanted was the other two there. It was easier if she spun the story; easier to keep them out of it. Besides, Declan had a couple of welts on the side of his face. Kylie had cleaned the blood off him. Siobhan thought she saw a look in her eye of at least admiration, if not deep affection.

It was now late afternoon, and other than an unexpected visit from Declan to build a fire for her, Siobhan had otherwise been on her own, contemplating all that had gone on. She was berating herself, not factoring in the car, not factoring in getting away. But then again, Declan had been kidnapped. She had to get him back, and in that, she'd been successful.

She wondered who would come, and would the police drop by, or would it be a visit from the Service? The police she could handle. They'd ask questions. Was she here? Was she there? Why was her car at Ballintoy? I mean, they were bound to trace it, and it would come back to her. Other identities were good. They were useful, especially for the short term, but if something got left behind, it would come back to bite you.

If she had have been someone on the move, someone who could just pick up sticks and go elsewhere, it wouldn't have been a problem, but Siobhan was done with that. This was home, Northern Ireland was home. This coastline, these waters, it was all home, the place she wanted to be, and she wouldn't run from it.

Siobhan stood up, like she had done several times during the afternoon, and started walking round the living room. Maybe time passed quicker when she was on the move. She was wearing her favourite top, with the long roll neck, and her blue jeans. She imagined the conversation at the door, when the officer or the Service operative stood there as she opened it. Her husband, Andrew, had always said she had blue eyes that could dazzle anyone, but obviously, they hadn't had enough sparkle for him in the long run. Eamon had spoken about them before, too, but it was Julian who had mentioned them the most.

The doorbell chimed. Siobhan swallowed hard, turned and made her way to the front door. She was going to peek through the alcove door, but she decided against it, and simply opened the front door, but with a smile on her face.

In front of her was Julian Patterson. His face was smiling. And she looked down and saw a bottle of red wine in his hand.

'I hope you don't mind, Siobhan. Can I come in? I think there's plenty to discuss.'

Siobhan stepped to one side. It would be very like the Service, to send someone she trusted to give her bad news. She showed Julian into the front living room and to a seat beside the fire. Siobhan disappeared back out to the kitchen, and got two glasses for the wine. Back in the living room, Julian had already opened the bottle with a corkscrew of his own.

'I thought I'd pick a good one. Though you're not really into the wine, are you?'

'Not really, Julian,' she said. He tried to put on a faint smile, but her worry was obvious.

He poured the wine and handed a glass to Siobhan. As she went to drink it, he reached forward, tapped his glass onto hers and said, 'Cheers.' They both sipped slowly.

'You've been busy,' he said. 'First off, can I say I'm relieved to see you're okay?'

She smiled because she knew Julian was genuine in what he was saying. It sounded like a Service statement, but he cared.

'I hope your colleagues are okay, too. The man took quite a battering to the face, especially when they disappeared off with him.'

'How did you know it was us?'

'The car,' said Julian. 'There was a car left at Ballintoy. I was given the task of checking it out.'

'Okay,' said Siobhan. She took a gulp of the wine this time, and then sat with her hands fidgeting, wondering what was coming next.

'Maxwell, I believe, was his name. He was influential in setting up the Causeway Coast Hotel proposals, the whole grand scheme of it. Quite a complex it was going to be there, and profits from the business would have been at the extreme end. He wanted to take some of that profit for himself, but it took us a while to work out who he was.'

Siobhan cocked her head. 'It took you a while? I thought he was Service.'

'He is Service, and he's in the upper echelons, but very few people really know him. I didn't. I'd never come across him.'

'Really, because I did,' said Siobhan. 'Distant past, though. I never spoke to him. Just saw him in an office somewhere.'

Julian nodded. 'He was silent in the Service, but clearly he was looking to make as much money as possible. He was selling the idea and the venue, and it was all tied in with hedge funds, and ultimately to Russian businessmen, or gangsters, as you and I call them. How did you get this involved?'

'Eamon. Eamon left a mark for me.'

'Eamon's death was a shock to the Service. He obviously alerted you. He mustn't have had time to alert anyone else. The trouble with Maxwell, as I understand it, whose real name is Philip Lawrence, was he had many friends high in the Service. We're weeding them out as we speak. They were benefiting from the money too. That's why it wasn't dealt with. Eamon being Eamon, of course, had plenty of enemies. Most people thought that's what happened to him.'

'Did you get Maxwell?'

'No,' said Julian, 'but we got the Russians. The police found them stuck inside a shed, some nasty bangs to the back of the head. Trapped in by their own car too. Your accomplices have disappeared as well.'

'They were just doing as instructed. I shouldn't have brought them in.'

'Maybe not. The press, of course, will have a field day. I've held them off so far. I've been speaking to the man who contacted the police. Funny enough, he's the uncle of your gardener.'

Siobhan blushed. It was hard not to give things away to Julian. She watched as he stood, walked over to the window of the living room. He could see the sea from there.

'I've always wanted to settle down somewhere like this, too,' he said. 'A lovely house you've chosen. The Service wanted you to stay, but you needed out. With Andrew gone as well, you could go back to being your own woman here in the province.'

'I guess that's all over,' she said. 'Do you want to ask the questions here, take confessions, and then take me in, or should I come with you now?'

Julian turned round, something in his hand. He swung his hand carefully, letting the object go. Siobhan instinctively put her hands out and caught it. It was the keys to the hired BMW.

'It's in the drive,' he said. 'The police believe it was one of our people involved in capturing the Russians. Talking to some of the higher-up members of the Service, they agreed with my suggestion that it wouldn't look good for an ex-service person to have been involved in the exchange. Other Russian parties seem to have disappeared.'

Julian gave a faint smile. 'We've got the Russians. We'll get Maxwell. The Russians are going to clear off anyway, those we haven't got. The press coverage is coming out. We spoke to your pressman, told him how to report it, what way to do it. He was quite over the moon. Of course, the police will take a lot of credit as well, but that's all right. You don't join the Service for credit, you join it to get things done.'

He turned and sat down again, opposite Siobhan. He

reached forward and placed his hand on her knee.

'Siobhan, listen. I'm very fond of you. You know that. I have pulled every string I can to keep you clear of this. Ultimately, it was in their best interests. The Service didn't want the embarrassment of one of their own mopping up on home soil where they didn't, bringing in the newspaper. That was clever, the drone. The footage from it got to the police before it got to us. All good, and probably saved your backside.

'You can bring the others back here. There's just Maxwell left, and I don't think he's daft enough to come after you. If he even knows it is you. He'll be on his way elsewhere. Another country, trying to set up again. Trying to make a life for himself.'

Julian suddenly looked more serious. 'You're clear, but I was told to tell you this. You're not to interfere in Service matters again. Don't pretend to be us. You are to retire. Civilian life. I told them it was because of Eamon, and they believe that. I believe that. Settle down. And if you can't, make sure you get fingers into pies that don't belong to the Service.'

Siobhan stood up, stepped forward, reached down and kissed Julian on the forehead. He gave a smile and walked over to the window.

'Yes,' he said. 'I can see the attraction of here.' He turned round and looked at Siobhan. 'There's plenty to attract me here.' He turned back to the window, and without looking at her, he said, 'I'll be gone. Leave you in peace.'

She followed him towards the door. As he opened it, she pushed it shut again. Siobhan stepped up, put her arms around him, and kissed him. It was a deep kiss. When she stepped back from it, she looked up into his eyes.

'Thank you,' she said. 'Thank you for sorting it all out.

You're a good man. A wonderful man. Sometimes I feel quite tempted to . . .'

Julian put his finger up to her lips. 'Don't tell me what you feel tempted by. It's hard enough keeping a distance. Tell me when you don't want there to be one.' He opened the door and stepped out and began walking up the drive.

'You said you needed a lift,' said Siobhan.

'I did, but given the moment that's just passed, I thought maybe better to put some distance in.'

'It's just a lift,' said Siobhan. 'That's all I'm promising.'

'Greater things have happened from a lot less,' said Julian. He turned and walked up the drive.

As he reached the end, Siobhan shouted after him, 'Julian, I will see you.'

The smile on his lips made her heart jump just a little.

Epilogue

Siobhan dug down with the trowel, but it went only halfway through the weed, the top coming away, but the bottom remaining. She swore and Declan reached over with his own trowel.

'Got to get down underneath it, Mrs D,' he said.

Siobhan yawned and stretched. 'You're better at this than I am, Declan.'

'But it's your garden. I can do it if you want, everything. Just keep it nice and neat, but the joy of a garden's in what you do with it.'

'But it's cold, Declan. Half my fingers went into the soil there. My hand is frozen to the bone. I'm cold. How is that joy?'

'It's not cold yet. Not even hit December.'

'Whatever, Declan.'

Siobhan stood up, turned around, and saw Kylie hanging up the washing. There was a light breeze blowing. It was a wintry day and it would take most of it to dry the washing to any degree. Siobhan had said, 'We should just stuff it in the tumble dryer,' but Kylie liked to be environmentally friendly. Siobhan did too, but not to that degree. She liked her clothes dry. But that was up to Kylie, as long as she sorted it out.

Siobhan had kept a close eye on the pair. It wasn't difficult. Kylie was living in the small house at the front of the property. Declan was round most days. It was rather an indulgence, the amount of work he did in the garden, but Siobhan could afford it. It kept her feeling young.

She had tried to go out to different things. There was the art class she had joined, but she felt her drawing was at the level of a three-year-old. Then they talked about still life. There was the man who had come along to pose and Siobhan had sat beside the paper trying to draw him and thinking, *Why do I want to draw this?*

Drawing wasn't her thing. What was her thing? She had gone jogging. Not far, and it had been reasonably successful. It was just mile after mile. The most she did was five, and it kept her fit. Siobhan was hungering for something else to do.

'Shall I make the tea?' asked Kylie.

Siobhan nodded and made her way inside to wash her hands, clearing off the muck and swearing next time she'd be wearing gloves. Declan never wore gloves, unless he was picking up something that could sting you. The boy had a care for the environment, a real heart for flowers and an eye for what looked good.

Kylie had softened to him as well. Not to a point where she was ready to accept him in any romantic role, but she was becoming good friends with him. Siobhan had even seen her give him a hug on occasions. When he gave her one back, she didn't push him away. It was good they were getting on together.

Siobhan finished washing her hands, and made her way through to the kitchen, where Kylie was pouring from a hot kettle. The smoky, familiar waft of her tea told Siobhan which cup was hers. She hadn't convinced either of the other two to drink the same. Kylie just wanted that supermarket brand, ordinary tea, and not even good stuff at that. Declan would drink whatever you put in front of him. As he wandered in, with Kylie putting his cup down in front of him at the table, he threw the paper onto it.

'Remember, Mrs D, paper boy just flung it over. You should tell him to come in and put it through the door.'

'He only does it when it's dry and only if you're there in the garden. He's fine, Declan. Just let him be. You don't have to mollycoddle me. If I think it needs put in through the front door, I'll soon get hold of him.'

'Yes, Mrs D.'

Siobhan sat down, took a sip of her tea, and looked over at Declan. 'I think you've been coming here long enough. You can call me, Siobhan.'

Declan stopped, looked at her, and shook his head. 'Mrs D to me. I told my father Mrs D came and got me. Mrs D wouldn't let me get into trouble.

'You told your father?' blurted Siobhan. 'You told your father I took you in front of a group of Russian mobsters?'

'No. I told him I'd fallen over and that's what's wrong with my face. Tell my father, Russian mobsters? Just catch yourself on. He'd think I was away with the fairies.'

Siobhan smiled and unfolded the paper in front of her. There had been a death on the coast and a body recovered. It had been at sea for a couple of weeks, apparently. The paper linked it to the incident that night with the Russian mobsters. Siobhan contemplated it. It was about half an hour later when her phone buzzed, and she looked at the text message.

'Julian. It's over, Siobhan. Body found at the rough shore. Philip Lawrence aka Maxwell. The Russians are out of here, too. It's all done. You can relax now.'

Siobhan put her tea on the table and spread her hands out and looked over at the other two.

'What's happened?' asked Kylie. She was always more astute. Declan was blissfully unaware.

'Text message from my friend,' she said. 'Maxwell, the man that was doing the trade, the man who caused all this issue, they found him dead in the water. The Russians either got a hold of him later that night or shortly afterwards. Been dead for a few weeks. My contact from the Service says that the Russians are gone, too. We're in the clear.'

Kylie smiled, reached forward and took Siobhan's hand, holding it tight.

'That's good news, Mrs D,' said Declan. 'I guess you can now focus on your garden.'

Siobhan just stared at him. 'No, if it's that cold,' she said.

'Then what are you going to do?' asked Kylie. 'You're retired now. You've had your bit of excitement, but you're clear, aren't you?'

'My friend from the Service told me the Service doesn't want to see me again. Doesn't want me involved. It's part of the condition of wrapping it all up, though. They would have been embarrassed by what we did and them not getting to it first.'

'I thought we did a good job,' said Declan. 'Don't you?'

He reached down and took a large gulp of his tea. Siobhan stood up from the table and walked over to look out the window of the kitchen. The rest of her life was here. She would be best in this house, and yes, she loved it. She loved the coast, but she'd been so damn active, been so busy in the Service. Excitement, puzzles that had challenged her, opportunities that provoked terror, fear, as well as the adrenaline-kicking fuel that had kept her going. How could she retire?

Suddenly, there was a pair of arms around her waist, and Kylie was pulling her close.

'We're clear,' she said. 'We don't want to go back into that sort of thing, do we? But sometimes it was fun, wasn't it?'

She looked over her shoulder at where Kylie was looking up. Kylie only came up to the top of her shoulders, and Siobhan saw Declan stand up and come over. His right arm, he put around the shoulder of Siobhan, and his left arm went around the waist of Kylie.

'We made a good team,' he said. Siobhan thought about how, just a month ago, both women would have thrown him off.

'Yes, we did, Declan,' said Siobhan. Although she wasn't too sure how true that statement was.

'Your life ahead of you, though,' said Kylie. 'A new, quiet life.'

'Maybe we could still do some investigations. Just not like with Russian mobsters, but the local things,' said Declan. 'A bit of fun like that. What do you think, Mrs D?'

Siobhan looked first at Kylie. The girl shook her head at first, but seeing that Siobhan was still staring back at her, she murmured, 'It's your retirement; it is up to you.'

Siobhan lifted her head slightly, looking at the taller Declan.

'Are you wise?' he said. 'Really?'

She turned and looked out the window.

Deep inside, the itch was growing. *Investigations? Northern*

Ireland always had its problems, didn't it? Always had things to be looked into. Maybe, Declan, she thought. *Just maybe.*

She pulled the arms of her two young assistants, wrapping them up in a tight hug. Maybe retirement would be fun, after all.

The end.

Read on to discover the Patrick
Smythe series!

Patrick Smythe is a former Northern Irish policeman who after suffering an amputation after a bomb blast, takes to the sea between the west coast of Scotland and his homeland to ply his trade as a private investigator. Join Paddy as he tries to work to his own ethics while knowing how to bend the rules he once enforced. Working from his beloved motorboat 'Craigantlet', Paddy decides to rescue a drug mule in this short story from the pen of G R Jordan.

Join G R Jordan's monthly newsletter about forthcoming releases and special writings for his tribe of avid readers and then receive your free Patrick Smythe short story.

Go to https://bit.ly/PatrickSmythe for your Patrick Smythe journey to start!

About the Author

GR Jordan is a self-published author who finally decided at forty that in order to have an enjoyable lifestyle, his creative beast within would have to be unleashed. His books mirror that conflict in life where acts of decency contend with self-promotion, goodness stares in horror at evil, and kindness blindsides us when we at our worst. Corrupting our world with his parade of wondrous and horrific characters, he highlights everyday tensions with fresh eyes whilst taking his methodical, intelligent mainstays on a roller-coaster ride of dilemmas, all the while suffering the banter of their provocative sidekicks.

A graduate of Loughborough University where he masqueraded as a chemical engineer but ultimately played American football, Gary had worked at changing the shape of cereal flakes and pulled a pallet truck for a living. Watching vegetables freeze at -40'C was another career highlight and he was also one of the Scottish Highlands "blind" air traffic controllers. These days he has graduated to answering a telephone to people in trouble before telephoning other people to sort it out.

Having flirted with most places in the UK, he is now based in the Isle of Lewis in Scotland where his free time is spent between raising a young family with his wife, writing, figuring out how to work a loom and caring for a small flock of chickens. Luckily, his writing is influenced by his varied work and life experience as the chickens have not been the poetical inspiration he had hoped for!

You can connect with me on:
- https://grjordan.com
- https://facebook.com/carpetlessleprechaun

Subscribe to my newsletter:
- https://bit.ly/PatrickSmythe

Also by G R Jordan

G R Jordan writes across multiple genres including crime, dark and action adventure fantasy, feel good fantasy, mystery thriller and horror fantasy. Below is a selection of his work. Whilst all books are available across online stores, signed copies are available at his personal shop.

Death of the Witch
https://grjordan.com/product/death-of-the-witchwaters-edge
A woman found dead on a witch's pillory. A sister distraught and claiming multiple murders. Can Siobhan expose the secrets of a female society to the light in order to bring a killer to justice?

When a woman is found dead on an ancient witch's pillory in Carrickfergus, her sister petitions Siobhan to help bring the guilty to light. But when the dead woman is found to belong to an order long forgotten, she is forced to enlist to learn the secrets of the cult. Can Siobhan keep mind and soul together to bring home the first case of her fledgling detective enterprise?

Hubble, bubble, toil and so much trouble!

Highlands and Islands Detective Thriller Series https://grjordan.com/product/waters-edge Join stalwart DI Macleod and his burgeoning new DC McGrath as they look into the darker side of the stunningly scenic and wilder parts of the north of Scotland. From the Black Isle to Lewis, from Mull to Harris and across to the small Isles, the Uists and Barra, this mismatched pairing follow murders, thieves and vengeful victims in an effort to restore tranquillity to the remoter parts of the land.

Be part of this tale of a surprise partnership amidst the foulest deeds and darkest souls who stalk this peaceful and most beautiful of lands, and you'll never see the Highlands the same way again.

Kirsten Stewart Thrillers

https://grjordan.com/product/a-shot-at-democracy

Join Kirsten Stewart on a shadowy ride through the underbelly of the Highlands of Scotland where among the beauty and splendour of the majestic landscape lies corruption and intrigue to match any city. From murders to extortion, missing children to criminals operating above the law, the Highland former detective must learn a tougher edge to her work as she puts her own life on the line to protect those who cannot defend themselves.

Having left her beloved murder investigation team far behind, Kirsten has to battle personal tragedy and loss while adapting to a whole new way of executing her duties where your mistakes are your own. As Kirsten comes to terms with working with the new team, she often operates as the groups solo field agent, placing herself in danger and trouble to rescue those caught on the dark side of life. With action packed scenes and tense scenarios of murder and greed, the Kirsten Stewart thrillers will have you turning page after page to see your favourite Scottish lass home!

There's life after Macleod, but a whole new world of death!

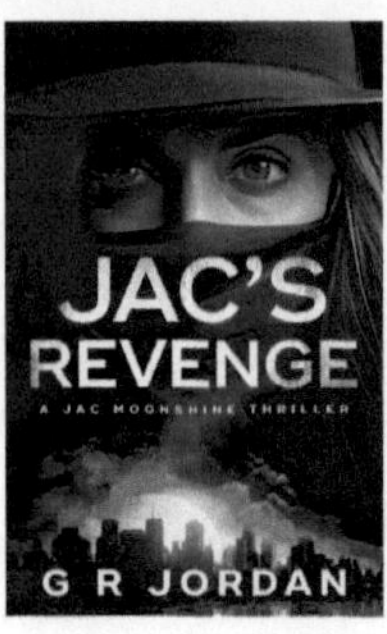

Jac's Revenge (A Jack Moonshine Thriller #1)

https://grjordan.com/product/jacs-revenge

An unexpected hit makes Debbie a widow. The attention of her man's killer spawns a brutal yet classy alter ego. But how far can you play the game before it takes over your life?

All her life, Debbie Parlor lived in her man's shadow, knowing his work was never truly honest. She turned her head from news stories and rumours. But when he was disposed of for his smile to placate a rival crime lord, Jac Moonshine was born. And when Debbie is paid compensation for her loss like her car was written off, Jac decides that enough is enough.

Get on board with this tongue-in-cheek revenge thriller that will make you question how far you would go to avenge a loved one, and how much you would enjoy it!